The Uncertainty
of Memory

A Novel by

C.M. Ruane

Foxford Press

The Uncertainty of Memory
Copyright © 2023 by C. M. Ruane

Grimm's Fairy Tales quote: Jacob and Wilhelm Grimm, *Household Tales*, translated by.Margaret Hunt, London: George Bell, 1884

Margaret Mead quoted from *Sex and Temperament in Three Primitive Societies*, Preface (p. ix), Routledge & Kegan Paul. London, England. 1977

Cover photograph by LumiNola via Getty Images

Foxford Press
Published by Foxford Press, Asheville, NC

Library of Congress Control Number: 2022924057

Paperback ISBN-978-1-948907-12-5

First American Edition, January 2023

Printed in the United States of America

Dedicated to Gita,
wherever she might be.

The Uncertainty of Memory

From that time forth, a change came over the child.
As long as the snake had eaten with her,
she had grown tall and strong, but now she lost her
pretty rosy cheeks and wasted away...

— Grimm's Fairy Tales

Chapter One

JAYA STOOD IN THE SHADOWS, watching an acrobat perform backflips. The girl bent backwards until her palms touched the ground, close to her heels. In the crowded marketplace, no one but Jaya was watching. It was getting toward dinnertime, people had shopping to do. A wooden bowl, set upon the ground, was empty.

The girl locked eyes with Jaya. She kicked off, thrusting her legs skyward, standing on her hands and balancing by scissoring her legs. The ragged top she wore fell away, revealing a skeletal rib cage.

That was the moment Jaya decided to invite the girl for a meal.

The girl ordered for both of them, in rapid-fire Hindi. The waiter grunted as he put two steel glasses and a water pitcher on the table. He'd clicked his teeth watching the girl enter the restaurant. Jaya wished then that she'd bought a samosa for the girl, from one of the street vendors. They might have sat together on the steps leading up to the shuttered cinema. But her *Lonely Planet* guide warned against eating street food. She laid the guidebook on her stomach, as if that would ward off germs.

Tossing a waist-length braid backwards, the girl said, '*Lonely

Planet saying, "The delicious jalebi and malpua with rabdi is a showstopper." '

'Is that what you just ordered - the showstopper?' asked Jaya.

'No. Showstopper meaning sweet.'

The space was illuminated by a low voltage bulb, casting everything in a jaundiced tinge and making it impossible to tell the color of the girl's eyes, even when she stared without blinking, just before saying, 'You are from America, I know.'

Jaya was reminded of her mother's friend, the tarot card reader, who managed to make an obvious statement sound like the voice of an oracle.

'Your slippers,' said the girl. 'American brand.'

Jaya flexed her toes in the Chaco sandals.

'How long in India?' asked the girl. 'Newly arrived?'

'I got in late last night.' Jaya looked at her bracelet, as if it were a watch.

The girl scrunched her face before saying, 'How do you like Delhi, *so far*?'

Not wanting to offend, Jaya answered by shrugging a shoulder. Before the girl could press for an answer, the waiter returned balancing thali platters on a tray. He let them clatter to the table, spilling lentil dal and rice. Jaya called to his retreating back; in the presence of food, she was suddenly famished. She asked for a fork, repeating the word while moving a hand to her mouth. Pointing to a glass-fronted refrigerator, she said, 'And I'll take a Coke, if it's cold that is.' The girl was wide-eyed, jittery with excitement. Jaya added, 'Two, please.'

The girl dipped a *chapatti* - a round, unleavened bread -

into a small bowl filled with lentil dal. After swallowing, she said, 'What brings you to India?'

Jaya suspected that the girl's vocabulary would be exhausted once they progressed beyond these introductory phrases. They were not going to have the heart-to-heart conversation she was longing for. When she spoke, it was more to herself than to the girl, 'My mother...well, she lived in India, once. But maybe *lived* isn't the right word. Traveled. She traveled for many—'

The waiter interrupted by flipping the caps on two glass bottles. Jaya thanked him and then turned her attention back to the girl, who said, 'You saying, "Once upon a time, my mother lived in India." My mother, also, she lives in India.'

Jaya sighed. 'So, you're not an orphan?'

'Pardon? This word is new to me.' The girl squinted her eyes. A moment later she said, 'Orphan, yes, I know! O-R-P-H-A-N. I learn this word from reading book called *Oliver Twist*. But, no, I am not orphan.' Using a straw, the girl drained the Coke bottle, sucking until the straw collapsed. Then she continued her inquiry, asking for Jaya's 'good name.'

'My *good* name? Oh, I see - it's Jaya.' *Jaya the Orphan*, she thought.

The girl's hand froze mid-air. 'This is Indian name. Are you Indian also?'

'As I said, my mother - well, she thought Jaya was a pretty name, I guess. It's Sanskrit for victory. I think at the time she hoped to learn the language, read the *Tibetan Book of the Dead* or something.' Jaya pictured the book laying upon the fireplace mantel, under a layer of dust and incense ash.

'Victory,' said the girl, as if this word were new to her.

'You see, she wanted a child for a long time, but for one reason or another—' Jaya glanced around the cramped space and decided against eating there. She pulled a 500-rupee note from a pouch hidden under her waistband. She called for the waiter, but saw he was busy at the cash register.

'Barren like Sarah, wife of Abraham,' said the girl. 'I learn with Miss Elizabeth from Manchester, England, UK, reading *Book of Genesis*. And this.' The girl reached into her bag and brought out a book wrapped in a tea-towel.

'*Grimm's Fairy Tales*,' said Jaya.

'This book was gift. I did not steal.' The girl returned the book to her bag.

'Of course not,' said Jaya, tugging at the bottom of her shirt until it covered her waistband where the money pouch was hidden. 'My mother wasn't barren. It's just that' - she paused, taking a deep breath - 'she hadn't met the right man. Not one she wanted to share a child with anyway. My mother was forty-one when she had me. With a sperm donor, purportedly a poli sci major at Reed College. A donor of Indian descent, she was told.' Jaya mopped her brow with a stiff paper napkin. 'Sorry. I don't know why I'm babbling away like this.'

She thought back to the months cooped up in the shingled geodesic dome, talking to herself mostly, as her mother slipped in and out of lucidity. On the flight over, she'd rattled on to a complete stranger until he excused himself by pulling on an eye mask.

'Is your mother here?' asked the girl, looking around the restaurant.

'No,' said Jaya, feeling more tired than she thought possible.

The cardboard box containing her mother's ashes was in a backpack, left at the guesthouse.

The girl patted her conclave chest. 'My esteemed mother is from America.'

And because Jaya didn't have the energy to correct the girl, she said, 'Your English is remarkably good. You must have a gift for languages. I studied French for two semesters but don't even remember how to conjugate *être*.'

The waiter was now standing beside the table, polishing a fork on his apron. The girl flinched when the fork hit the table. 'I go now,' she said.

'Sit!' said Jaya, even though she wanted to leave herself. Her mother would have gone ballistic on the waiter; at the very least, she would have denied the man a tip.

When he returned to the kitchen, the girl said, 'You don't like food? This is very clean food.' She poked around in the rice and then smiled. 'Everything is good, lady.'

But the fork, Jaya saw, had dried food webbed between the prongs. She set it aside and imitated the girl by dipping a flatbread into the dal. The dish wasn't as spicy as she feared. Her mother's Indian cooking had always required a dollop of yogurt.

Jaya noticed that a man seated at the booth behind theirs was looking on angrily, rocking his head. He bunched rice with his hand, shaping it into a fist-sized ball. For a moment, Jaya worried that he'd throw it at the girl. He mumbled under his breath, and the girl's head whipped backwards. After that, he stuffed the rice into his mouth.

'What did he just say?' Jaya asked the girl.

The girl laid a half-eaten chapatti beside the platter. Her

eyes darted nervously around the restaurant before settling on Jaya's half-finished Coke bottle.

'Go ahead and polish it off,' said Jaya, gesturing toward the bottle. 'I shouldn't be drinking caffeine. I'll never get to sleep, I'm so wired. It must be adrenaline or something.' She nibbled on the edge of a flatbread, watching as the girl sucked greedily at the straw. Her body was that of a child's; yet, when she sucked at the straw there were deep wrinkles around her mouth.

'*Achchha*,' said the girl, stopping to take a breath and wipe her nose.

'How old are you?' asked Jaya, watching as the girl wobbled her head left to right, keeping the straw in her mouth. Jaya repeated the question more slowly.

After emptying the bottle, the girl answered, 'Twelve years? Thirteen years.'

'You mean to tell me that you don't know?'

Jaya remembered her birthday parties. The cake was always carrot, her name written in pink frosting made with beet juice, topped with candles formed into numbers. Was this how she'd kept track of her age? She closed her eyes, listening for her mother's voice singing 'Happy Birthday to You.' She patted the girl's hand and said, 'You should eat more. You're skin and bones.' If there was one thing Jaya's mother had excelled at, it was proper nutrition: breast milk, followed by organic vegetables and free-range meat.

The girl pushed the platters aside, laying her elbows on the table and knotting her hands below her chin. 'May I ask, lady - do you have tattoo?'

Jaya laughed. 'You like tattoos, do you? Okay.' She lifted a foot to the seat, exposing her ankle, running a finger over a small pink ribbon. A memorial to her mother.

The girl stood from the table, bowing at the waist. 'Very nice to make your acquaintance, Jaya-*ji*.'

Jaya laughed again; the girl's gesture was so ridiculously formal. 'Nice to make your acquaintance, too. I apologize, but I should have asked your name earlier.'

'Aasi is my good name.'

The food, Jaya realized once the girl was gone, was barely touched. The waiter asked if she wanted to take what remained in a package. She considered this for a moment and agreed, expecting to be waylaid by a half-starved beggar as soon as she stepped back into the Main Bazaar.

Chapter Two

A STEPLADDER TEETERED UNDER the pharmacist's feet. He reached for the top shelf, balancing on one foot, his body stretched to its full length. Jaya removed the lid from a jar of throat lozenges. If she kept a supply in her bag, she would have something to offer street children. There were dozens of them begging in the Main Bazaar.

Tilting her head upwards, she said, 'My room faces onto the street. I tried stuffing tissue into my ears, but it didn't help.' A voice blared from a speaker outside the shop. To Jaya, it sounded like a political speech, although the cadence was closer to a radio preacher's. 'It's awfully loud here,' she shouted.

'A sale on mangos,' said the pharmacist, inclining his ear as he stepped down from the ladder. He raised an index finger, 'Very good prices, too. But you bring up a good point - an excellent point. Indeed, we have a noise pollution problem in Delhi.' He spread a variety of packages on the counter. 'Have your choice, madam,' he said.

Jaya examined each package before picking earplugs made of fluorescent orange foam. They would be easier to find with her glasses off; besides, she told herself, if she ever needed silence during a white-water rafting trip, they'd perfectly match a life vest. 'And I'd like some Valium,' she said. 'Or any tranquillizer that makes you so chill you can't help but nod off. Honestly, I don't have an issue with anxiety." The truth was, her room faced onto the Main Bazaar. Without air-conditioning, the windows had to be left opened. 'For sleep, in other words,' she explained.

The pharmacist placed the earplugs into a paper bag, closing it with transparent tape. 'Very well, madam, earplugs.' Then, tapping his lips, 'But you must bring a script for Diazepam tablets.'

'I was told that in India—' Jaya remembered the times when her mother needed painkillers but hadn't had a prescription. 'Now in India,' she'd say, always ready with a comparison.

The pharmacist lowered his eyelids, flickering the lashes until his eyes were closed. 'There was a time, madam, not long ago, when the government trusted my profession to make these judgment calls.' He inhaled deeply and held his breath.

Jaya wondered if the pharmacist was meditating. This was India, after all, and her impression had always been of massive yoga classes, everyone twisted like pretzels and chanting secret mantras. But surely that couldn't be true, she thought. In the awkward silence that followed, she said, 'Maybe you have Benadryl? That sometimes works for insomnia.'

The pharmacist opened his eyes and smiled serenely, as if a crisis had passed. After examining Jaya from head to toe, he said, 'There are those who came into my shop asking for the entire supply of tranquilizers. To resell to unsavory characters in their home countries. Russians mostly. But you, I see, are not one of them.' He paused, then added, 'You need the tablets for sleep, do you? In that case, I might be able to make an exception for a respectable young lady like yourself.'

'Thank you,' she said. (Jaya wondered why it was they were whispering.) 'A couple of pills would be plenty, just to get me over the hump.'

'Ten or five milligram tablets? With your body weight I recommend ten.'

Jaya hunched her shoulders, trying to make herself smaller. 'It's just that I'm so tired, but my mind is running a million miles an hour. I missed two days of sleep flying here. And then with the time change...'

'No need to explain. I can see simply by looking at you. Come a long way, have you? Bloodshot eyes - for this I recommend Ciplox.'

'From San Francisco. With an eight-hour layover in Qatar.' Jaya couldn't believe she'd been to such an exotic place. In truth, she hadn't ventured from the terminal. But she'd eaten a pistachio baklava and a tiny cup of Arabian coffee, seated in a food court filled with sheiks and their burka clad wives.

'A great distance,' said the pharmacist. 'Then perhaps I can supply you with twenty tablets.' He surveyed the shop. 'But you must promise not to mention this to anyone, madam.'

Jaya ran a finger across her lips.

'Allow me a minute to prepare the order,' he said.

As she waited, Jaya scanned the Main Bazaar. From her vantage point a few steps above street level she looked upon a sea of heads, some covered in silk or cotton and others bare. Aasi stood across the way, staring at Jaya with those clairvoyant, limpid eyes. Jaya raised a hand, just as an auto-rickshaw filled the space that separated them. She watched a woman usher three children into the rickshaw, placing shopping bags on their laps before squeezing herself in. When the rickshaw moved on, Aasi was gone.

Jaya stepped aside as someone entered the pharmacy. His face was backlit, and it wasn't until he stood inside that Jaya realized that he was a foreigner, too. His clothes were anything but. In response to a nod, Jaya said, 'Oh, hey, hi,' thinking how lame she sounded.

The man kicked off his flip-flops using his big toes. Jaya hid one sandaled foot behind the other, realizing that she'd violated a cultural norm. So, this was where her mother's practice originated: a basket of slippers in the geodesic dome's vestibule, next to a rack for shoes and gardening boots. When she noticed the man's blackened and callused soles, she was glad to have made the mistake.

'Anybody home?' asked the barefoot man.

'He's' - Jaya pointed to the back - 'getting my prescription ready.'

The man flapped the hem of his shirt. Sweat beaded on his stomach, which was several shades lighter than his arms and face. His nipples showed through the cheesecloth fabric. Jaya felt herself blushing, which was ridiculous considering that she'd grown up near a nudist beach.

'You don't want the seat?' he said, gesturing toward a bench.

'I'm fine standing,' said Jaya, even though she was feeling a bit weak-kneed.

The man sat in the center of the bench, stretching both hands to its width. Jaya wished she'd taken the seat so as to not be standing under his gaze.

He said, 'New to India I see. Let me guess. Delhi belly? Best thing for that is white rice and bananas and plenty of clean water. You definitely don't want to plug yourself up with Imodium like all the other idiot tourists. Now me, I'm immune. I can drink water straight from the tap. Whereas you shouldn't even brush your teeth with it.'

'My stomach is fine, thank you,' said Jaya.

'Give it a day or two.'

Sweat dripped from Jaya's underwire bra, making crescent shaped stains on her shirt. She crossed her arms over her chest to hide them.

He looked toward her hand. 'For starters, the guidebook is a dead giveaway. Carry that around and you'll be a target for every shyster in Paharganj.' He reached into his pant pocket and removed a pouch containing rolling papers and loose-leaf tobacco. From the other pocket he produced an antique cigarette case with intertwined initials engraved into the silver. Keeping his eyes on the task in front of him, he said, 'Don't tell me they've already hit you up for powdered milk? Those girls carrying around sickly babies. *Waah, waah.* Five-hundred rupees a box and then mamma sells it back to the shopkeeper for twenty.'

'Really, I'm not *that* gullible,' said Jaya, fearing that maybe she was.

She watched as his tongue ran across the edge of the tissue-thin paper. He placed the newly rolled cheroot in the cigarette case, next to others of identical size and shape, then rolled another and tucked it above his ear.

The pharmacist appeared, holding another paper bag. 'Mr. Rodgers,' he said, drawing out the name. 'I see that you've returned.'

'Your loyal customer. I wouldn't frequent any other chemist.'

'Your prescription, madam,' said the pharmacist, handing the package to Jaya.

'See you around,' said Rodgers, as Jaya stepped down to street level. 'And watch out for counterfeit notes.'

Jaya caught the sound of his laugh, and his verdict: 'Newbie.' She got her revenge by comparing Rodgers with one of her mother's boyfriends, an acupuncturist and traditional Chinese medicine practitioner who came at her with needles and nasty tasting teas. She wished now that she had chosen a different hotel, in another part of New Delhi. Somewhere with less hippie travelers.

She dropped the guidebook into her bag.

A group passed in the opposite direction. They were loaded down with backpacks, fresh off the train, no doubt. That was why Jaya had booked a room in Paharganj: the neighborhood was near the New Delhi railway station where she needed to get the train for Varanasi. As their paths crossed, she saw that one of the travelers had a guidebook in his hand. Jaya found him particularly attractive: tall and fit with a buzz cut. '*Tout droit!*' she heard him say to his friends, pointing from the guidebook to an alleyway.

'*Fabuleux!*' said a willow-thin woman, looking at her compatriot as if he were a rock star.

Another Frenchman clapped.

Jaya walked on, with her back a little straighter.

Chapter Three

AASI SAT ON A CINDERBLOCK, wrapping a bracelet around her ankle. She'd grown. This time last year it had been too big. 'Stupid clasp! Why are you broken?' she said. The silver was tarnished black. Hoping to bring up a memory, she rattled the tiny bells that dangled from the chain. A few were missing and others had lost their ringers.

'Wake up, girl!' said Mr. Aggarwal, the jhajariya sweet seller. 'Don't you hear me calling for you?'

'Don't waste on that one,' said his wife, pursing her lips.

Mr. Aggarwal delivered broken pieces of sweet to Aasi's hands, still warm from the oil. Another girl, with clothing even more ragged, appeared with an open palm.

'Move on,' said the wife. 'And stop blocking the way for paying customers.'

'Have more compassion,' said Mr. Aggarwal, pleading with his wife.

Aasi motioned toward the girl. 'More for her,' she said, knowing that the girl couldn't speak for herself.

'Move on,' said the wife again. 'Or I'll call the police!'

Aasi gave half of her syrupy pieces to the girl. 'Nothing is free, Kamika,' she said, explaining that she would be requiring the girl's help. Kamika licked her lips. Aasi put another piece of broken sweet into the girl's dirty hand. She was shorter than Aasi by at least two heads. A real asset when searching people's legs.

'Delicious, *na*?' said Aasi when Kamika finished the last piece. She swatted the younger girl's arm before running to catch up with a Westerner she'd seen pass by. The Westerner had dreadlocks falling below the knee. The long strands swung back and forth as she walked. Aasi's toes kept bumping the heels of the woman's hiking boots.

'Stop following me,' said the woman, speeding up.

'*Vieni*,' said a man, taking the woman's elbow as if to protect her.

'My mistake,' said Aasi. 'So sorry. I see now you are not my mother.'

'A beggar's trick,' said the man.

Aasi began to tremble. She rubbed the ankle bracelet between her fingers, hoping it would give her courage. They wanted her to go away, but she wouldn't go empty-handed. Pointing to pink packets strung above juice cartons, she said, 'Please, sir. You buy me shampoo. Two packets are nothing for you.'

But the couple's attention was drawn to a cake, displayed in a shop window. As they mounted the shop's steps, Aasi shouted the curse of Bhrigu at them, so that they would suffer the pain of birth and death many times over.

'Off with you!' said the moneychanger, waving a dark blue passport at Aasi. He would not tolerate beggars loitering in front of his business. The competition was three stalls down and had recently applied a fresh coat of paint. Since the day

Axis Bank installed an ATM machine in the Main Bazaar, five moneychangers had gone out of business. Hardly anyone carried foreign currencies or traveler's checks anymore.

Aasi hissed at the moneychanger and then hid in an alleyway, where she had a view of his shop. She'd seen the eagle on the passport, under the words *United States of America.* A few minutes later a familiar American exited, counting rupee notes before shoving them into his shoulder bag. Aasi got to him just as he was about to step into the coffee shop.

'Mr. Edward Rodgers, sir!' she shouted, hop-skipping until she was exactly six footsteps from the entrance, as close as she dared. 'Good day, friend.'

Rodgers steadied himself by holding onto the doorframe. He turned his head toward Aasi and smiled weakly.

'*Namaste*,' he said. 'You caught me at the wrong time.'

Was there ever a good time for Edward Rodgers? There were the telltale bruises under his eyes, matching the color of his unshaven face. Once again, he had forgotten to pull a comb through his hair. Aasi thought, Too many *Boom Boom Shivas,* the salutation he recited before taking a hit from his chillum. It sat in an embroidered pouch, strung around his neck. Aasi knew its shape because he'd sometimes let her clean the chillum using a stick, in exchange for ten rupees. Good practice for picking wax from ear channels, which would earn as much as two hundred rupees per ear.

Rodgers came from Colorado, USA, only a day's journey to Arizona by *Greyhound*, which Aasi had been told was a type of dog. Surely he'd met her mother.

Once, when she described the rattlesnake tattoo on her

mother's leg, he'd said, 'Stranger things have happened,' blowing smoke into her face. If she wanted him to remember correctly, it was best to make her inquires after his espresso one-shot, when he was most alert. After smoking ganja, he sat in the sun until his nose needed aloe lotion from the chemist. Or he might take an auto-rickshaw to Connaught Place, where he liked to go for a McDonald's Maharishi burger and a hot fudge sundae.

Today she rubbed her chin and said, 'I am happy to run errands. May I fetch razor from chemist? Your beard is making the face itchy.'

'I'm good,' he said.

She began the next sentence with one of Miss Elizabeth's expressions, because it was impossible to disagree with whatever followed. 'Wouldn't you agree - Delhi is too hot?'

Rodgers nodded his head languidly.

Aasi began her pitch: 'Everyone is going north to the mountains, even birds are flying north. The result is frightfully long lines at the New Delhi railway station. People waiting in lines many days. Some dying from heat, as a matter of fact. But I, sir, will go to the station in your place. For a small fee only. So small you will not notice it missing.'

'Actually, that's not a bad idea...maybe.'

To Aasi, his hand signal looked like a flapping bird wing, but she knew that it meant she must wait patiently. She scanned the Main Bazaar, looking for a better prospect, but found none.

Rodgers stepped into the coffee house and ordered an espresso. Aasi stood in the street, watching as he greeted a woman seated at the corner table. She heard him say, 'How's it going?' in the American way, with his body swaying loosely.

'Figured you were long gone by now. With that friend of yours, the one with the gapped teeth.'

The woman had red curly hair, tied back with a scrunchie. Sweat poured from her face and down her neck, wetting the front of her T-shirt. Aasi detected an Australian accent, which held no interest to her. The woman pointed a battery-operated fan at her sunburnt nose. After making room for Rodgers, she turned the fan on his face.

Aasi knew that the Australian woman was new in India: the newest edition *Lonely Planet* guide was in full view for all to see. Scam artists would target her with gold-plated necklaces and plastic bangles. Kashmiri men would fool her with photographs of pristine houseboats floating on mountain lakes, in what was now a war zone.

Aasi hoped so, anyway. She didn't like the way the woman occupied Edward Rodgers's attention. The way she leaned in to touch his knee. Positively scandalous.

The guidebook slipped to the floor and Aasi tried to figure out a way to get to it. By memorizing the guidebook, she hoped one day to become a bona fide tour guide. She owned a 10th edition *Lonely Planet* guide which someone had left behind at the railway station, but it was proving to be useless. Already she'd made the mistake of suggesting a hotel closed more than two years. Then there was the travel agent, commended in the 10th edition for his 'indispensable advice,' replaced by his son, a cheat who ran a credit card scam. And this new coffee shop wasn't in the old guidebook, even though it was already 'world-famous' for its lemon poppy seed cake. A sign in the window said as much.

Rodgers picked up the *Lonely Planet,* blowing dirt from the cover. The waiter brought over a tiny cup, splashing espresso onto the saucer. Rodgers reached into his bag, tossing rupees to the table without taking his eyes from the guidebook. The waiter pocketed the change. Never mind, Aasi thought. The change only came to her if Rodgers drank the espresso one-shot at the counter. In one gulp.

An hour later, he left the coffee house. Aasi drew attention to herself by jumping up and down and waving her arms above her head.

'You're still here?' he said. "I hate when you stalk me."

'You hired me to buy train ticket, remember?'

'Train ticket, right.' He knit his eyebrows.

'You made promise.'

He snickered. 'I never make promises. It's one of my cardinal rules. Keep your options open, that's my motto. And how many times do I have to tell you that maybe isn't a promise. It means I'm weighing my options, getting a feel for something, scoping out the terrain.' He used his hands like a scale. 'But check back with me tomorrow, kid. Maybe I'll have something for you.'

Aasi kicked the ground, sending up a cloud of dust. 'Tomorrow, my friend,' she said, 'please don't be forgetting.'

Chapter Four

JAYA WOKE TO FIND THE SUN illuminating the curtains. The bedsheet was wrapped around her legs and she kicked it off, feeling the ground for her sandals. She avoided looking toward the corner of the room where she'd placed the cardboard box.

Her throat was parched and she reached for her water bottle. The room was worse than she remembered. Paint chips fell from a moldy ceiling, scattering on the bed like confetti. She undressed and stepped into the bathroom. It was so cramped she had to shower with her knees wrapped around the toilet bowl. The drain was stuffed with hair and, before long, murky water lapped against the pink ribbon tattooed on her ankle. She winced before extracting a slimy clump from the drain.

After shutting off the water, she heard a knock on the door. 'Give me a sec,' she said, grabbing her glasses and throwing on the same clothes she'd been wearing.

A young man stood outside the door holding a tray with a tea pot and packages of Nescafé and granulated sugar. 'You requested coffee?' he said, checking the room number against a slip of paper.

A door opened across the interior space. Enough light filtered through a skylight for Jaya to see a man wrapped in a towel and nothing else. 'Over here, *Ji*,' said the man, directing the way by waving a hand toward a nightstand, topped with an overflowing ashtray.

The room service waiter apologized to Jaya. She was closing her door when the towel-clad man shouted, 'You try to steal my coffee?,' tempering the accusation with a chuckle. But before Jaya could respond, he retreated into his room with the tray. The waiter knocked and said, 'My friend, must pay now!'

Jaya closed her door quietly, hoping not to draw attention.

A few minutes later, she entered the lobby café. It was lit with fluorescents and she switched to sunglasses. A migraine throbbed at her temples.

A waiter said, 'Take any seat, *Didi*. As you like.'

She picked one far from the pool table, where a group of foreigners alternated between billiard sticks and cigarettes. Jaya began fanning herself with the guidebook, which she'd meant to keep hidden. The waiter responded by rolling over a gigantic fan.

'Please?' she said, motioning for him to back the fan up.

'Too cold, *Didi*?'

Jaya wondered if he was confusing her with someone else or if *didi* was a salutation. The guidebook included a glossary of terms, but she decided to wait until she was alone in her room to look for the word. Adding *ji* to the end of a name appeared to be a sign of respect, she realized, the way Americans began letters with *dear*. Although these days, emails often opened with *hey*, which wasn't quite the same.

The waiter brought over a menu with the lamination peeling from the corners. The offering was a mishmash of international dishes: pizza and egg rolls, French fries and curries. What you'd find at a Long Island Greek diner, thought Jaya, thinking back to a time when she'd shared a piece of Boston cream pie with her mother. 'Why is it called Boston, if this is New York?' she'd asked. This was before they'd moved west.

The menu was full of spelling errors. There was an item called banana filters, which Jaya guessed meant banana fritters. She stifled a laugh, saying, 'I'll have to try the cheese sand*bitch*.'

The waiter apologized, explaining that the dish was no longer available. 'You order grilled cheese sand*wich* instead. This is top favorite.'

Jaya ran her hand down the menu until she came to a list of beverages. 'I'll start with coffee. Do you have fresh brewed?'

'Very fresh, *Didi*. Brewing right at table.'

'Nescafé, you mean.' She pressed her temples.

'And something more?' He thrust both hands toward a display cabinet filled with cakes, pastries, and donuts.

She ordered a cinnamon donut, thinking it would mask the taste of instant coffee.

A few minutes later, the man last seen wearing a towel passed en route to the pool table. He wasn't bad looking, Jaya thought, in a disco dancer sort of way. She licked sugary cinnamon from her fingers and let her eyes wander around the room. There was a Scandinavian looking man reading a Henning Mankell novel. An Asian man - Japanese, maybe? - working on his Sony laptop. Two blonds chatted away in some version of Slavic.

A bent-over Indian woman approached. Drums of various sizes hung from her shoulders. She tapped one or the other as she went. After sizing up Jaya, she chose the largest drum.

'No rhythm, I'm afraid,' said Jaya.

The woman moved on to the pool table. One of the foreigners was wearing a bikini top and a multi-compartment belt slung low on her hips. She examined the drums and said, 'Junk,' curling a lip. The waiter delivered a plate to the group and Disco Dancer shouted, '*Lama kacha? Ji*, I ordered fried eggs not scramble!'

Jaya still hadn't placed his accent. Spanish, probably.

The donut was stale and the coffee still hadn't arrive, so there was no chance of dunking. Jaya stopped the waiter as he made his way back to the kitchen carrying the rejected plate on the palm of his hand.

'I'll take that,' she said, just as her stomach churned.

On the plate were fried potatoes and white toast cut into triangles, already buttered. They looked like eggs she'd eaten a thousand times before. The guidebook warned against eating raw vegetables, but the tomatoes on the plate were cooked to oblivion. Jaya shoveled them into her mouth. Disco Dancer was watching, gyrating his hips to the beat of trance music piped from a mini speaker. Jaya angled her shoulders away as she scarfed down the buttered toast.

The waiter rushed past carrying a plate of fried eggs. He swung back to lay a cup of hot water and a packet of instant coffee on Jaya's table. As she tried to get the waiter's attention, Disco Dancer placed the plate of fried eggs on the table and took the opposite seat.

'Oh, hi,' she said, 'It's you again.'

'First my coffee and then my eggs. How were they?'

'They were overcooked.'

He leaned back until the chair was half airborne, wrapping his feet around the legs and folding his arms smugly. Showoff, thought Jaya, reaching for the salt shaker. Using salt crystals for buttress, she balanced the shaker until it was leaning like the Tower of Pisa.

'Why!' he said.

'Because I can?'

'No, no. *Why* in Hebrew means *wow* in yours.'

Jaya hummed the only Hebrew song she knew, 'Hava Nag-ila.' One of her mother's friends, a Cabalist, used it for a ring-tone. Jaya was usually the one to dial his number while they listened for the song coming from between sofa cushions; or, more likely, his back pocket.

'You are Jewish?' asked Disco Dancer.

'No, but my mother went through a Jewish phase. That was after she'd blazed through Catholicism and Presbyterianism, be-fore she gave up on Western religion to delve into Buddhism.' Jaya closed one eye, hoping to remember the order of events. 'Next was her Jain phase, I think. That was when we had to be careful not to step on ants. After that she ricocheted back to Hinduism via the Hari Krishnas. Bought a harmonium and lots of carnations. Sufism was the closest she got to Islam. That's when she became especially adept at whirling in circles. We had to rearrange the furniture to give her enough space. To be honest, I was into that myself. Because what five-year-old doesn't mind a good spin? We listened to roots reggae during her Rastafarian phase. She had me in Hebrew school for a nanosecond, studying for a Bar Mitzvah that never happened.'

'*Bat* Mitzvah. *Bar* means boy, *bat* means girl.'

'Well, you see what I mean?'

She slid the last triangle into her mouth and called for the waiter: 'When you get a chance,' she shouted, standing abruptly and bumping the table. The salt shaker teetered and crashed, raining salt and white rice on the floor. Not exactly the graceful exit she'd hoped for.

'*Beseder*. My name is Yoel. Maybe I'll see you around.'

Jaya removed her sunglasses. 'Yoel. That's Hebrew for Joel?'

He winked and then strolled back to his friends.

Chapter Five

THERE WAS TIME BEFORE THE Jaipur train arrived. Aasi walked slowly, stopping whenever she passed a café. Although it was late afternoon, many of the Westerners were eating breakfast. She knew that the word *breakfast* meant muesli with curd and fruit topping, sometimes banana, sometimes apple. Westerners ate this from bowls, using spoons. Only pizza, butter toast, and finger-chips were eaten using the fingers, and she was yet to figure out why this was. She stopped to watch as a couple ordered, first taking a yellow pencil and slip of paper from a cup. They consulted the menu, then wrote their selections on the slip, passing it back and forth until they were satisfied.

Aasi knew that the waiters had trouble reading these chits. This was the moment when they were most inattentive, when it was possible to dig leftover oats and nuts from abandoned bowls.

A man seated near the couple tore the crusts off the edges of his toast, leaving them beside his plate. 'So wasteful,' Aasi whispered.

She stepped close enough to hear the couple speaking Russian. She should have known sooner: a steel water bottle sat on the table. It lacked the three letters found on most American water bottles.

✳

For a time, Aasi possessed a water bottle marked with the letters *REI.*

The bottle was clipped to an Osprey backpack, another American brand. Which was why she had followed the backpack all the way from the Sujay guesthouse to track #4 at the New Delhi railway station, where there waited an overnight train to Pathankot. The backpacker's blue hair showed brown near the roots. A skirt covered her legs, so that Aasi couldn't tell if they were tattooed or not. The woman carried the heavy backpack, with hiking boots tied to the loops, swinging by the shoelaces. She was searching for her assigned car. 'Get lost!' she said, when Aasi tried to help.

Aasi knew that the woman was on the wrong end of the platform, where the first-class car was boarding. Only businessmen, carrying attaché cases and tiffin prepared by their wives, bought first-class tickets. Or rich Westerners with rolling bags and trousers that unzipped at the knees. The woman with blue hair belonged in a 2 class/three-tier car with the other backpack-carrying budget travelers.

All the rushing had made the woman thirsty. She reached for the water bottle, which was stuffed into the backpack's side pocket.

'Stuck - oh no!' cried Aasi, before the woman slapped her hand away. The bottle slipped, ringing against concrete, bumping feet and rolling across the platform. Bent over, the woman's skirt lifted above her calf.

And Aasi realized that the woman was not her mother.

Aasi kicked the bottle under a cart selling *India Today*, she was so mad. The woman swatted at Aasi's head, as if she were a malaria-carrying mosquito.

By then, everyone was moving in fast motion. Porters carried luggage on top of their heads, searching franticly for chalk markings on the side of the railcars. The woman ran for the moving train. She stretched out a hand and was hoisted up, then pushed into a knot of passengers bunched near the door. Aasi ran alongside the train, watching as a thief unzipped the Osprey backpack. He reached in and found a flashlight, the kind that strapped to the head.

This made Aasi remember the water bottle.

By the time she had circled back, the magazine wallah was reaching for the bottle. But he was fat and slow and no match for Aasi. She made herself like a jellyfish: invisible, slippery, and prepared to sting when challenged.

Water put into this bottle magically healed Aasi's stomach, or so she thought. Everything came out firm, like paneer instead of watered-down lassi. On January nights, when no one wanted chai, the tea cart wallah would fill the REI bottle with boiling water. Stuffed under Aasi's clothing, it warmed as well as a pashmina shawl.

Then one day she made the mistake of showing the bottle to a Banjara boy. He worked the waiting trains at the New Delhi railway station, snatching from passengers who had neglected to chain their bags. She showed him the letters, explaining that they stood for *Recovering Energy Insides*, for this is what she had decided after pondering over the letters. She offered the boy a taste of the healing water, first demonstrating how to drip water into the mouth without touching the rim to the lips.

The boy was long gone, off to drink from the headwaters of

Mother Ganges, clear and icy-cold. Using the REI water bottle, no doubt. The boy would pass through Delhi when snow fell again, when the Westerners he stole from grew tired of mountain views and wanted beaches instead.

Aasi would make her move then.

Chapter Six

JAYA HAD NEVER LIKED CITIES. Bolinas, where she'd spent most of her life, was a sleepy coastal community with crosswalks at every intersection and drivers who stopped to let pedestrians pass.

'I'll be back there before long,' she told herself.

It had been easy enough to find the railway station - a straight shot from the guesthouse - but crossing the road to the station was another matter. She saw a break in traffic and dodged across unmarked lanes, one hand pinching an ear closed and the other covering her nose and mouth. She wasn't sure which was worse, noise pollution or diesel fumes. Once on the other side of the road, she promised herself that after this trip she would never leave Northern California again. 'That's where I'll have my ashes scattered,' she said aloud, imagining the sagebrush covered cliffs and how the wind would sweep the ashes out to sea.

The station lobby was packed with people, some curled up asleep on the floor beside piles of luggage. Others carried suitcases on their heads, zigzagging around obstacles. Jaya looked for a path that might lead her to the ticket windows.

There didn't seem to be a semblance of a line and she had never been the pushy type. She began biting the cuticles on her thumb, wondering if it would be best to try the travel agent again. It was possible to fly to Varanasi but flying didn't seem right for this trip. This pilgrimage, if that's what it was. Jaya imagined herself walking to Varanasi, carrying the cardboard box while throwing dust over her shoulders. Or whatever it was mourners did in India: weep and wail and prostrate themselves?

'Excuse me,' she said, tapping a shoulder. 'Is this where you buy a train ticket?'

The shoulder was draped in taffeta, dotted with tiny mirrors. For a moment Jaya caught a glimpse of her face in one of them.

'Infuriating,' said the woman. The accent surprised Jaya, even though she'd heard there was a large Indian community in the U.K. 'We would do well to form a queue. The ticket seller is threatening to close his window and one cannot blame him.'

'Hardly,' said Jaya.

'Hold onto me,' said the woman, as if to say, *I've seen your helplessness and have come to your rescue!* Jaya was perfectly willing to be rescued. 'I'm going to force my way to the front. If you stay in my wake, there might be a chance for you, too. When does your train depart?'

'Well, I'm not sure. I wanted to ask for a timetable.'

The woman's head movement signaled disapproval. 'That won't do. Better to make up your mind now. Otherwise, you'll be sent away empty-handed.'

Jaya began saying she could leave as early as tomorrow morning or even that very night, although she'd already paid for her room. But then the crowd shifted forward, nearing toppling her before she had finished the sentence.

'Here we go. Stay close,' said the woman.

'Don't people die like this - I mean at soccer games and rock concerts?'

A chubby hand clasped Jaya's. The red dot on the woman's forehead moved up and down as she searched for a gap in the crowd. 'Don't lose my grip, that's a girl,' she said, using her body like a ramrod and pushing aside men by applying pressure to their foreheads. 'I'm a pensioner!' she shouted. 'Have respect for your elders!'

Jaya's stomach crushed against the woman's bare back and she felt a swish of silk against her legs. There was something comforting in the touch.

'Almost there!' said the woman, triumphantly.

Jaya knew that there were people who actually liked this kind of thing. Her mother, for one. They demanded the best cut of beef or the plumpest piece of dim sum. Didn't matter if someone else was waiting for a parking space, these were the people who stepped on the gas pedal first.

What was the Hebrew word for it? *Hutzpah*, that was it. If Jaya saw Yoel again, she'd be sure to use the word.

It described the times her mother bullied a teacher, demanding that Jaya be given the lead part in a school play, a better grade on an essay, or a seat at the front of the class. It didn't matter that Jaya was the beneficiary, it had never failed to mortify her.

Now she smiled: the first in a while that hadn't been forced. Trying to make sense of her mother's behavior, while being crushed by a mob...well, it was ridiculous.

The British woman swung her head around, making sure that Jaya was still in tow. She laughed joyfully and then continued the siege. Soon they were standing side-by-side at the ticket counter.

'Help this girl first,' said the woman, speaking into a hole in the Plexiglas.

'Foreigners upstairs,' said ticket seller, jabbing an ink-stained finger toward the ceiling.

Not a single tear in weeks, and suddenly Jaya wanted to cry an ocean.

'That's okay,' she said, wiping her eyes. 'Upstairs you say?' She began to turn away, hoping the crowd would take pity and offer a way of escape.

Then she felt fingers wrapping her arm. The woman was refusing to give up. 'Can't you see how upset the girl is, you stupid man! Sell the poor dear a ticket.'

Jaya found herself laughing. Maybe it was because the woman kept referring to her as a girl when she was nearly twenty-two. I'm a hot mess, she thought, not sure what would come next. As it turned out, hiccups.

In a tirade of Hindi, the woman continued to beleaguer the ticket seller, refusing to let go of Jaya's arm, as hard as she pulled in the opposite direction. Jaya closed her eyes and hiccupped again, hearing her mother's voice this time: 'Look up and take deep, slow breaths.' She raised her eyes to the vaulted ceiling. Tears streamed down her cheeks and filled the cups of her ears.

And for the first time since landing in Delhi, Jaya heard nothing but silence.

After purchasing tickets for Mumbai, the British woman joined her family. They'd been waiting at a tea stall, together with their matching luggage, drinking chai from small glasses. Jaya hoped for an invitation to join, but none had been offered and she walked away feeling lonelier than ever.

Following a sign that read: *International Tourist Bureau,* she mounted a staircase making sure not to touch the banister. She was dreading another crowd. At the landing, she was able to see into the waiting area. Unhooking a thumb from his belt, a security guard motioned for her to enter. Chairs had been placed in serpentine rows. Tourists - all foreigners but some of Indian extraction - sat quietly, reading books and smartphones. Others spoke in whispers. An acoustic tile ceiling defused the noise, although Jaya could hear the clicking of computer keyboards where a bank of ticket agents sat.

She watched as a woman held a rail ticket in the air, for all to see. People began standing to their feet. Jaya wondered what was happening, if maybe they would begin clapping. She had her hands poised, but saw that people were lifting their backpacks or using their feet to slide bags a few inches over. Taking one unified sidestep, they each took a seat nearer the bank of agents. Jaya was standing in front of a ticket dispenser, the kind found at Safeway deli counters. It seemed superfluous, but she ripped off a ticket anyway.

She found her way to the last empty seat, getting comfortable just as the reshuffling began again. Once reseated, she noticed that there were travel magazines and brochures laid out on side tables. The woman beside her took a magazine and proceeded to leaf through it after a bored sigh. Jaya pulled the guidebook from her bag.

She located Varanasi in the index and scanned a column of subpoints until she found the page for budget hotels. The page was marked with a boarding pass, wedged into the binding. It had been issued to her mother: Pan Am Airways, Flight 234, SFO-BOM. The guidebook margins were filled with notations, penned with pink and green ink. She turned forward a page and saw purple marks.

'Blue and black,' Jaya said. 'Never your style.'

The word *bedbugs,* in green, was penned next to a listing for a budget hotel. Jaya pictured her mother, younger and slimmer and covered with bedbug bites. She blinked back tears and wiped the page with the side of a hand. That's when she noticed a tiny star beside the listing for another guesthouse. She found a pen at the bottom of her bag and made a similar star beside it.

A knee bumped hers as a man spread his legs into her space.

'Banares, eh?' he said.

She felt her heart race when she realized that it was Rodgers, the man she'd met yesterday in the pharmacy. He'd spoken only two words, if even that, but Jaya was grateful for the recognition it brought. She lifted the guidebook, realizing that he'd seen it in her hands. 'Figured I was safe from scam artists here. I'm sure that's what the security guard is for.'

'One would hope,' he said.

'Banares - that's the original name, right? The way Bombay is now called Mumbai and Calcutta is Kolkata. I suppose it's important to know these things when making a train reservation.'

'Not really. But you won't seem like such a newbie using the old names.' He reached into his pocket for the silver cigarette case, moving it between his fingers.

Jaya didn't want the conversation to end. 'I'm from San Francisco. An hour north, anyway. So how crazy is it that they named the city after a man who'd never been there?'

'That's imperialism for you,' he said, rolling his eyes. 'Are you off to Banares to study sitar or something?'

'I'm not musical' - Jaya made an exaggerated frown - 'I failed at piano, then tap dance. I have no rhythm, whatsoever. How about you, are you musical?'

Rodgers pulled a wooden flute from its cloth sheath. 'It's perfectly pitched, not that *you'd* be able to tell. I can recommend a teacher in Banares if you want to give music another shot. He's very good, played with Ravi Shankar and Nora Jones once.'

'I love Nora Jones.' She began humming.

'Hey, you're not bad. I recognize the song. *Come Away With Me*. Great album.'

Jaya whistled the same tune. 'How about that?'

His tanned face stretched into a smile. 'I think you had a lousy teacher when you were a kid. I bet you're good at yodeling, too.'

They both laughed and then rose in unison. Jaya said, 'Getting closer,' as Rodgers sat in the chair she had last occupied.

Rodgers used a travel magazine to fan himself. 'What is it? Like 42 degrees?'

A beat later Jaya said, 'You mean Celsius. I get it, sarcasm. I'm a little slow on the uptake today. Jetlag. I slept for hours but I'm still exhausted.'

'They say it takes one day for each time zone.'

'Then I'll never adjust. I'm here for only ten days.'

Rodgers moved the cigarette case from hand to hand. 'I hope they have seats left. I hear there might be a two-week wait for any train going north. Not a problem for you. But who the hell goes to Banares at this time of year?'

'You think it could be any hotter than this?'

'I was there last week and barely made it out alive. If the planet warms even one degree the city will be uninhabitable. There's constant power cuts, what with everyone wanting to run fans and air-conditioners all at the same time. You have to keep a flashlight or an oil lamp handy in case it happens at night. Stayed in a place because they claimed to have a generator but then they ran short of petrol. I had an interior room. When the fan went off, this chick I was with started bawling. We ended up dragging our mattress to the roof. Look—' He pulled at an elasticized hem until his pant leg was stretched over his calf.

'You must have sweet blood,' said Jaya. 'That's what my mother used to say whenever I got bit by mosquitos. At least it wasn't bedbugs, *that's* the worst.' Jaya thought for a minute and added, 'Maybe you can mark that guesthouse in my guidebook so that I know to avoid it.'

He balanced the guidebook on a knee. 'No, no, no, no,' he said, scanning the page. 'It's not here, but I'll write the name. Give me your pen.' He scribbled *Happy Stay Guesthouse* in the margin, drawing a circle around the letters and finishing with a diagonal dash. 'It's cheap enough, that's one thing. And the manager was apologetic.'

'Not much help if you die from heat stroke,' said Jaya. 'Or get eaten alive. Or worse yet, contract malaria.'

The guidebook snapped shut. 'Better hide that away,' said Rodgers.

They sat silently for a moment, watching as a tourist tried to cut right to a ticket agent and the room erupted in protest.

'Hey,' said Rodgers when the room quieted again. 'I know Banares is iconoclastically Indian and all, with the Ganges and what-have-you, but you'd be better off going to Dharamshala. It's in the mountains. That's where I'm headed. We could book sleepers in the same compartment if you want. It's a good idea to travel in pairs on an overnight train. For one thing, you want someone to look out for your backpack when you use the toilet. That is if you have anything valuable in it.'

Jaya pictured the contents of her luggage. She imagined a thief gleefully sneaking away with the cardboard box. 'I brought those cables that wrap around your luggage,' she told Rodgers, roping her fingers around an imaginary backpack. 'And a combo Master Lock. So I'm not too worried about theft.' She went to touch Rodgers's knee. 'Thanks, I mean that, but I'll stick with Varanasi. I'm on a mission.'

Rodgers jerked his knee away. 'You're a missionary? *Geez!* These people have their own religion a lot more ancient than your Western version. Wrecking indigenous culture, I hate that shit.'

'Jesus was from Asia, technically,' said Jaya, trying to keep from smiling.

'Okay, whatever.' Rodgers rolled his eyes. Jaya noticed that they were bloodshot.

'Besides, I didn't say I was a missionary. I said I was "on a mission." As in: a noun that can be applied to numerous secular activities. As in, "Honey, I'm going on a mission to buy milk." '

'Or *Mission Impossible* and spy shit.'

'Exactly. And anyway, don't you realize that by coming to India we've impacted the culture? They serve pizza at my guesthouse. How indigenous is pizza exactly? Or donuts.'

'I had parathas for breakfast,' he said.

Jaya placed a hand on her stomach. 'I had scrambled eggs. And I don't think they agree with me.'

'White rice and banana, like I said.'

The conversation began lagging and Jaya rushed in with, 'I studied anthropology in college. I remember reading about an anthropologist who went to a tribe in Ecuador, or maybe it was Papua New Guinea. This was in the 50s. At first the anthropologist lived in a hut, same as the tribe: a platform and grass roof, but without walls. The tribe kept their history alive by singing songs to each other at night, everyone snug in a hammock. The anthropologist had a hammock too. She would listen to the stories and take notes on index cards. Then came the rainy season. Torrential rain for months on end.'

'Like the Indian monsoon,' said Rodgers.

'I wouldn't know. Anyway, everything got soaked. The index cards were ruined and with them a year's work. So, the anthropologist thought, For the sake of my project, I need walls.'

Rodgers began scratching his ankles franticly. 'Don't mind me. Go on with the story.'

'Well, the tribe got one look at the enclosed hut and everyone wanted one. As a result, the storytelling died out. The anthropologist was forced to abandon the project. My point is, whenever two cultures meet they are bound to change each other.'

'Did the anthropologist become a cannibal?'

'I - I hope not,' said Jaya.

'Okay, you win. But don't go Bible thumping me.'

'I had religion shoved down my throat.' Jaya stood to her feet and shook a foot that had fallen asleep. 'And I mean *dozens* of religions.' She threw her weight into the seat next to hers. 'Ever hear of Tenriism?'

'I have, actually. See, I grew up in Japan.' He looked sheepishly at Jaya. 'My parents were Baptist missionaries.'

'I see. Care for a cough drop?' She pulled one from her pocket and pointed out the brand name. 'Himalaya. Says here they're made in India. Indigenous cough drops.'

'I'm down with the Himalaya brand. I use their toothpaste. Looks and taste like mud but it gets the job done.' He smiled, showing off his teeth.

Jaya unwrapped a lozenge, licking it first. It tasted of masala chai. 'Spicy,' she said. 'So do you want one, Baptist Boy?'

'Ed. Call me Ed.'

A woman was finishing up at the ticket counter. She parted with the ticket agent by waving her hand in concentric circles. The ticket agent mimicked gesture. 'See what I mean?' said Jaya. 'She should have salaamed, but no.'

Rodgers agreed. 'Do you work as an anthropologist?' he asked.

'No one works as an anthropologist. Or very few who majored in anthropology, anyway.' Jaya clutched her bag, getting ready to spring at a ticket agent. 'I've done copyediting, mostly. For a small Buddhist press in Berkeley. My mother knew the publisher and she kept raving to him about my typo-free anthropology papers. Copyediting was something I could do from home.' A tear rolled down her cheek. She inhaled before adding, 'After my mother got sick.'

It seemed as if Rodgers hadn't caught the last part. He shoved Jaya's arm and shouted, 'It's your turn!' Pointing to an unoccupied agent.

Chapter Seven

HALFWAY TO THE STATION, Aasi sensed that she was being followed. The rag-clad girl with a dirt-smudged face was three steps behind.

Kamika was quiet, never interrupting Aasi's thoughts. The girl spoke by changing the shape of her eyes, nodding her head. Sometimes her face signaled awed devotion. It happened whenever Aasi succeeded in filling Kamika's stomach. For this reaction alone, she put up with the girl.

Aasi's ears were attuned to opportunity when it presented itself. Now, over a profusion of sounds, she picked out the voice of a Westerner. He was bargaining for a cotton gauze shirt. Before he had agreed to a price, the shopkeeper's mobile rang. Aasi shimmied up alongside the Westerner and said, 'Not here,' hoping that the shopkeeper hadn't overheard. What she really said was, '*Nicht hier,*' because she could tell that the Westerner was from Germany. She motioned for him to follow her to a better shop.

'Three for a thousand rupees,' she told the German once they arrived.

Mr. Wadhwa, the shopkeeper, and she exchanged a nod.

'Finest cotton. 100% real. Touching is free,' said Mr. Wadhwa.

The German ran his fingers over the cotton. He seemed pleased and asked if there was a place he might try the shirt on. Mr. Wadhwa gestured toward a curtain at the back of the shop and the German chose one shirt the color of pomegranates and another of night-sky blue.

He would be better off choosing a white shirt, thought Aasi. The dyes would run, turning everything purple: briefs, T-shirts, socks, and hankies. Dye would stain his skin at the armpits, around the neckband, down his back, wherever he sweat. But Aasi wouldn't share this wisdom until after the exchange of rupees, after the shirts were secure in a plastic sack. Best, in fact, to find the German later. After she had received the one-percent commission from Mr. Wadhwa. Only then would she say, 'Might I suggest soaking your fine new shirts in half a cup of salt to secure the dyes?' The German would thank her profusely. Aasi hoped for a little baksheesh as a reward.

'You will greatly enjoy the shirts, sir,' said Mr. Wadhwa. 'The stitching is very good, not like cheap imitations.' He turned the shirt inside-out. 'Observe the serged seams. And the double stitched hems. You can do no better. These shirts will last through many years. Into your retirement, I shouldn't wonder!'

The German tucked the paper sack under his arm, reaching for a change purse. Aasi saw that it was thick with rupee notes. He shook the purse until everything was scattered on a stack of shawls. There were euro coins amongst the rupees.

'It's not possible to exchange these coins,' said Aasi. 'Wouldn't you agree? Better that you add to my collection.' To prove its existence, she removed a shekel and a yen from her bag. This was part of a business scheme which involved intercepting Westerners as they boarded minivans headed to the airport. A van left at midnight when the moneychangers were tucked into their beds. Surely these travelers did not want to land in their home countries with only rupees in their pockets? They would be grateful to Aasi for providing a valuable service. But first she needed to increase her supply of foreign coins. So far, she had only succeeded in collecting these two.

The German stuffed the money back into his change purse, but not before handing a 10-rupee note to Kamika.

'She thanks you,' said Aasi, snatching the note from Kamika's hand.

They stayed close to the German's heels, Aasi asking questions the whole time.

'Berlin,' he said in answer to one question. 'Yes, I've heard of Arizona,' in answer to another. And when Aasi suggested that he partake in another of her services, he said, 'My ears are fine, thank you,' jiggling a finger into his left ear.

Aasi gave the evil eye to anyone poised to steal the German from her. Only a skinny cow was able to part them, as it made its way down the middle of the street eating trash. It was never good to argue with a cow, she knew, especially those with horns. If not for Kamika, Aasi would have lost sight of the German. But the girl was shorter, able to see below the cow's belly. They reunited with him in front of the chemist.

'Might I suggest the purchase of a bar of Lifebuoy soap?' said Aasi. 'It prevents heat rashes afflicting those with fair skin.' She pulled up a sleeve and held her arm against his milky complexion. 'Maybe you buy me whitening cream? Fair & Lovely Multivitamin Fairness Cream is best,' she said. 'It saying so on billboards.'

The German shook his head. 'So that you'll be inflicted with heat rashes like me?'

'May I help you?' asked the chemist, stepping to the doorway. He wore a white coat with a name embroidered on the pocket, and a black bow tie. Aasi tried to enter the shop, but the chemist stamped his foot. He yelled, '*Chalo!*' when he saw that she was holding her ground. 'Little thieves,' he said to the German, shaking a finger at the girls. 'Watch your purse, sir.'

Kamika hurried across the street. Aasi stepped backwards, out of reach but close enough to defend her position. The German leaned his belly against the counter and the chemist took his place behind it. The German removed his sunglasses, folding them away into his shirt pocket.

Aasi yelled, 'I'm still here!' in her sweetest voice. 'Don't forget me!'

The German smiled and then turned back to the chemist. 'A pack of razorblades, please,' he said, rubbing his chin.

'Gillette Wilkinson Sword double-edge,' said the chemist, sliding a package across the counter.

'That will work.' The German nodded at Aasi, who was jumping up and down while clapping her hands. Kamika was now pulling on Aasi's *kameez*, the knee-length top worn over a pair of pajama bottoms. They watched as the German examined a shelf of soap bars.

'*Dhanyavaad* - thank you,' he said once he received his package of Lifebuoy. He hesitated at the doorframe, making sure his sunglasses were balanced on his nose.

Aasi pulled Kamika to the front. 'This girl is hungry, look

here at her stomach.' Kamika sucked her stomach in. 'I knowing good thali shop, sir. But yens and shekel, these are no good. Perhaps they will take euro coins. We can ask.'

The German bent a finger and said, '*Komm die Mädchen*.'

Aasi led him to the thali shop serving dishes from Rajasthan. Curries simmered in oversized pots on the propane stove. 'Always hot and free of germs,' said Aasi, glad to see that Mr. Chandratreya was back. He allowed the girls to sit in a booth. Yesterday the waiter had almost refused service.

'Very good, very good. Welcome,' said Mr. Chandratreya.

Aasi said, '*Shubh Dhin* - good afternoon. I have brought you a new patron.' To the German, she said, 'The delicious jalebi and malpua with rabdi is a showstopper,' reciting a passage from the out-of-date *Lonely Planet* guide. At the mention of the old review, Mr. Chandratreya rocked his head sadly. His restaurant wasn't in the latest edition. It was rumored that someone had complained about a gecko turd in the rice.

Kamika slid into the booth first, placing her elbows on the table. Aasi reached over and slapped her head, but the awed expression remained on the smaller girl's face. In order for the German to fit beside her, Aasi crammed against the wall.

'May I please see your passport?' she said. 'To pass the time until the food arrives.'

The German unbuckled his belt, tugging at a pouch hidden below his waistband. His passport was red, but with an eagle similar to the one on American passports. Aasi was allowed to hold the passport and flip through the pages. She examined every stamp.

A young man came to the table bearing steel glasses filled

with tap water. Aasi rebuked him and he took the glasses away. While he went to fetch a sealed bottle of mineral water, she said to the German, 'I see that you traveled to America in 2006.'

'For business. In Silicon Valley.'

'Silicon Valley,' she repeated slowly, drawing out each syllable. 'This is near Arizona?'

Mr. Chandratreya stepped to the table, pad and pen ready. The German held the menu, running his finger down the column of appetizers.

'May I be so bold,' said Aasi, another of Miss Elizabeth's favorite expressions, 'to suggest aalo-pyaaz-paneer, along with dal baati and roti?'

'A very good choice,' said Mr. Chandratreya, as he collected the menus. He already knew what the girls wanted: dal and plenty of chapatti.

'How old are you?' asked the German. 'Aren't you in school?'

'How old do you think?' asked Aasi.

'Twelve? Fourteen? It's hard to tell.'

'Yes,' she said, not that she knew her age. She lacked a passport to show the exact date of her birth. She could only guess.

'And your friend?' He nodded his head at Kamika.

'Four,' said Aasi. Kamika raised a hand, spreading out the four fingers as she had been taught to do. Aasi had decided to celebrate their birthdays during Diwali, when everyone lit lamps, candles, and firecrackers. They celebrated Aasi's birthday on the first day of the festival and Kamika's on the last.

Aasi opened the passport to the page where a name was printed: PAUL FØNSS. She managed to read the first name but had trouble with the last. Thinking that the O was crossed out, she said: Paul Fa-noss.'

'It's a Norwegian name,' he said. 'My grandfather was from Oslo.'

'In America?' asked Aasi.

'No, in Norway.'

'I was meaning Ossning, which sounds the same. I once knew a man from Ossning, New York. He left for Sri Lanka when his visa expired and has yet to return. His profession is advertising. What is your profession?'

'High-Tech.'

'Then you will be visiting Bangalore.'

'No, this is a holiday.'

The dishes arrived at the table. Mr. Chandratreya made the girls go to a sink and wash their hands with soap. Paul Fønss was brought a fork and spoon. Aasi dipped a chapatti into the dal. The German looked nervously at his three dishes.

She chewed everything in her mouth before saying, 'No worries. Very clean food, vegetarian, too,' while examining the rice bowl for turds.

Kamika was eating shyly, as she always did in the presence of a stranger. When Aasi saw the chapatti droop in Kamika's hand, she signaled disapproval with a flick of her head. Kamika pressed her lips shut and Aasi crammed a chapatti into the girl's mouth. Kamika was about to cry. If that happened, the German would leave and they would miss out on Mr. Chandratreya's delicious jalebi and malpua with rabdi: The Showstopper.

Aasi kicked Kamika under the table and the younger girl

began scooping dal with a pained face. The plan was to meet the train from Jaipur and Aasi didn't want to be begging for food the whole while. She needed Kamika to pay attention to women's legs. The girl's short stature was an advantage there.

The German let his eyes rest on a portrait of Sai Baba of Shirdia, hanging above the table, then on a glass-fronted refrigerator. He called for Mr. Chandratreya to bring a Fanta. 'Sorry, but I should go soon,' he told the girls.

'Best to drink with a straw,' said Aasi, asking if he was still hungry. He patted his stomach and began tidying the table, stacking bowls and utensils and wiping the tabletop with a napkin dipped in mineral water. He threw the napkin onto the dishes and pushed the whole thing away from him. Aasi sighed. Good food would be thrown to the dogs when they might have requested a parcel.

Mr. Chandratreya hesitated with the bill, clearing his throat. Aasi said quickly, 'I suggest we sample showstopper jalebi and malpua with rabdi.'

'Pretty please,' said Kamika on queue, at the same time making her sad-sack eyes. These were practically the only words that ever passed her lips.

'Sit, sit,' said Mr. Chandratreya, bringing over a washing bowl. A slice of lemon floated on top of the warm water.

'Am I expected to drink that?' asked the German.

An hour later, a train pulled to a halt at track five and a boy held up bruised bananas. His mother stood beside him, waving flies off of a pile of samosas she hoped to sell. Porters rolled trolley carts to the platform edge; those lucky enough to have arrived first were already positioned where the first-class car was coming to a gradual halt. Behind scratched windows, passengers could be seen jostling for a place at the exit.

At a 2nd class sleeper car, Aasi waited for the doors to open. When they did, hundreds of voices rose in crescendo. An elderly woman stood in the train vestibule, clutching the doorframe and dabbing her mouth with the edge of her saree.

'What's the hold up?' came a voice from within.

'The drop is too great,' said the woman. She was about four-feet tall and the drop nearly half that. Passengers surged forward, threatening to topple the woman. She cried out when a slipper fell from her foot to the track below.

A porter came to the rescue, parting the crowd with his trolley cart. Even though he wore the obligatory red jacket and black cap, he identified himself by lifting an identity card clipped to his jacket pocket. He tugged at the woman's suitcase until it dropped to his cart. She handed him a satchel, indicating that she'd agreed to the hire. By now a crowd of spectators looked on, clicking their teeth as the porter thrust his hands under the woman's armpits, lowering her to the ground. She hobbled sideways, bracing herself against the cart. The next passenger stood perched at the door: a Westerner dressed as a Tibetan nun, with a shiny shaved head.

Aasi yelled: 'Here! Here! Take my hand!'

Kamika positioned herself flat against the train, rubbing against soot and engine oil. It was a game she had played many times before, and one she loved. Better than tossing stones at a wall.

'I'm fine,' said the nun. 'Step aside, please.' She carried

a four-foot-long horn in one hand and a plastic bag in the other. As she jumped from the train, both knees bent under the weight of a backpack. Aasi rushed forward, hoping to catch the horn.

'*Thuk jay chey*,' said the nun, by way of a thank you. 'But I've got it.' She repositioned the backpack straps and said, 'Heave-Ho,' before stretching her body to its full height.

'I never!' she said, seeing Kamika lift the hem of her maroon robe.

'I will carry your backpack,' said Aasi. 'The staircase is very steep.'

'You? You're too frail.'

'Music instrument, maybe?'

'I'll let you carry this,' she said, handing over the plastic bag. 'I'll give you ten rupees to bring it to the trash, fifteen if you bring it to recycling.'

Aasi jumped up and down. 'I know the place, exactly!' she said, taking the plastic bag. It contained nothing but empty water bottles. 'Before tomorrow this plastic will be an attaché case sold in Paris.'

'Paris...Incredible.' The nun didn't believe a word of it.

If only Aasi had time to explain.

About the Indian lady who fed Aasi dry chapatti and the scrapings from plates with three sections: a little rice filled one part with two empty spaces left. She had a mole on her cheek and every day the mole grew more pronounced. She was missing the middle right finger, too. Only a stub remained.

The woman's husband drank until he fell over. Aasi held her breath whenever he came close, afraid that he'd try to embrace her with that horrible taste in his mouth. She was glad that he was away most of the time. Once he was gone for so long, the mole-lady went around with an alms bowl telling people that she was a widow. But the husband returned after many months, carrying a bottle of Port Number 7, wrapped in newspaper. The mole-lady was so happy, she drank half the bottle herself.

They lived in a shack beside a muddy river, in a city constructed of trash. Mumbai, Aasi remembered, was the name of the city. She was made to scavenge things from the municipality dump. Broken umbrellas, pieced together, made one as good as new. Tires, seat belts, and plastic bags: everything had value. A businesswoman turned them into fashion bags she sold in Paris. She ran a small factory where plastic bags were melted into sheets of colorful material, then turned into wallets and carrying cases called *attachés*. This was the first French word Aasi learned.

Westerners are such fools, she told herself then - handbags from trash instead of buffalo leather, imagine that!

In the end, the mole-lady spent all day laying on a grass mat. By then Aasi was old enough to prepare the rice, if any remained in the tin. She knew how to light the kerosene stove with a match and how to boil water with a lid on the pot so that the steam wouldn't escape. Gradually the mole-lady stopped eating, until she took only a grain of rice a day.

Now Aasi jiggled the plastic bag. It was white: not as desirable as pink or blue. And besides, Mumbai was a day's train ride away.

'Promise me,' said the nun, holding rupee notes close to

her chest.

Kamika stood behind, pointing to the nun's calf and rocking her head mournfully.

'Promise,' said Aasi, cupping her hands before extending the open palms.

The nun climbed the staircase, her bald head bobbing above the crowd. Once she was out of view, Aasi threw the trash bag under the train.

Chapter Eight

BACK AT THE SUJAY, JAYA KNELT in front of the toilet with her head hanging over the bowl. She closed her eyes, conjuring an image of the womb-like bathroom in Bolinas, California. The floor and walls turned from cement to handmade tile, hexagons of cobalt and aquamarine. To her left was a tub carved from a single piece of cedar. Above her head hung a handblown glass lamp, made by a local man who also blew pipes. Jaya tilted her head, hoping to breathe fresher air, imagining a bay window with a glimpse of the ocean beyond a row of wavering eucalyptus. The image was so clear she expected to find a hand on the small of her back. She retched several times before the contents of her stomach poured into the toilet. Opening her eyes, Jaya let her back rest against the concrete wall. Then she began to weep.

'Mommy,' she said, over and over.

Jaya was a clinger. Her mother attributed the dependency to breastfeeding: Jaya was breastfed until three years old. 'Maybe I should have had another, to keep you company,' her mother would say whenever she wanted a little personal space.

When Jaya was five, a pregnant cat made its home under the geodesic dome. There were three in the litter: two healthy kittens and a runt. Before long, the healthy ones were bouncing after flies and caterpillars. The mother cat nosed at the runt, hoping to push it into the world, but the kitten tagged after, poking around for an extended tit. The kitten shied away whenever Jaya tried to hold it, until one day she caught it by the scruff of its neck. On the day she and her mother drove the litter to the Humane Society, Jaya still had scabs on her face and arms where she had been clawed. Not that it mattered. As they placed the litter into a cage, she felt her heart breaking. It was as if she were losing a soulmate.

When she was six years old, Jaya learned that her mother was pregnant again, a baby conceived with a man who led fermentation courses at the local food-coop. There was talk of him moving in with them but Jaya had nothing to fear. Like all her mother's relationships, that one lasted no longer than it took to make kombucha. When the baby miscarried, Jaya was secretly glad.

'It's you and me kid, and that's the way it will always be,' her mother said afterwards. Jaya responded with a toothless grin.

Then there was Girl Scout summer camp. After a four-hour drive with a busload of hyped-up prepubescent girls, the frazzled driver inadvertently left several suitcases in an undercarriage compartment. Several girls had only the clothes they'd traveled in. Jaya was in green shorts with matching socks. During the three days it took to locate the lost luggage, she managed to get twenty letters into the mail, each one shriller than the last: 'If you don't come get me, I'll die!' she wrote, dramatically. 'All the kids make fun of me!!! They call me Pigpen!!!!' The exclamation points got longer and longer until they filled whole paragraphs. She started underlining words. After the fifth letter was delivered, Jaya's mother drove to Camprocks. By then Jaya was wearing a clean T-shirt, cut-offs, and white socks. 'Hey, Mommy. They found my suitcase,' she said, 'but I wanna go home anyway.' After signing the necessary release forms, that's what they did.

In high school, Jaya dreamed about foreign exchange programs but only got as far as an attempt at reading *Les Miserable* in the original language. She was accepted to five colleges but chose one within commuting distance. An application for the Peace Corp remained half completed.

After the cancer diagnosis Jaya's mother said, 'Now it's your turn.' Which Jaya knew meant, *Your turn to take care of me*.

Terror turned to exhilaration as Jaya took charge of the household. For a girl who had always been told what to do, it felt like bungee jumping. Even if she did nothing more than switch from skim milk to whole, or decide to wash the kitchen floor *every single* week. These were steps toward independence. Or so she told herself.

She began filling the gas tank at Exxon, knowing her mother still blamed the company for the Valdez disaster. Pints of Häagen-Dazs were hidden behind frozen tofu burgers. Then came the day she tossed a subscription renewal for *Mother Earth*, throwing it into the garbage can instead of recycling. It was only ever little rebellions, things she could hide.

But as her mother's health deteriorated, Jaya began to panic. It was one thing to be left with responsibility for the household and her mother's care, another to be abandoned.

She found herself spending hours on the Internet searching for a miracle cure. For the first time she began putting hope in herbal medicine and vegan diets. She figured out how to operate the juicer and made tinctures using raw liver juice. Jaya said, 'I thought you were into all of this?' after her mother took one sip and refused the rest.

It was then she knew that her mother had given up.

The gas tank was filled at Arco again, and Jaya stopped eating ice cream all together.

Chapter Nine

THE SUJAY GUESTHOUSE WAS ON a narrow lane off the Main Bazaar, number 21 on the *Lonely Planet* map. Aasi knew that Europeans and Americans favored the Sujay. Across the passage was the Hare Krishna guesthouse, number 22, and full of Israeli backpackers. Both had spacious lobbies, lined with travel agents, tour guides, Internet cafés, bookstores, and clothing shops. But only the Sujay had a billiard table, a lobby café, and a bakery. Hare Krishna guests had to climb five flights to access a rooftop restaurant.

Israeli travelers didn't seem to mind. Most had only recently finished serving in the army and were the most fit of all Westerners. Aasi had once watched an Israeli do a thousand sit-ups followed by jumping jacks.

Sujay guests, on the other hand, were lazy. They sat around all day, eating and talking. A case displayed cinnamon buns and fudge cakes, both replenished hourly. Individually portioned pizzas needed replenishing every fifteen minutes. Kamika and Aasi were happy to share one between them.

Joe was the hotel manager. His name wasn't really Joe, but something with multi-syllables which Europeans had trouble pronouncing. He allowed the two girls to sweep the floor and empty ashtrays in exchange for the privilege of sleeping under the billiard table. They had to arrive at midnight and rise by six, although no one ever played billiards until after noon. If the floors were sparkling clean, Joe would give each girl a leftover bun. He would ask Shankar, who served behind the bakery counter, to warm the bun in the microwave.

The Sujay guesthouse was highly recommended by *Lonely Planet* for its budget prices and 'relatively' clean rooms. Aasi had already memorized the listing, which included a tele-phone number and a web address. Joe earned this praise for the guesthouse by instructing the housekeeping staff to wash their hands before changing sheets and pillowcases, to remove their slippers before entering a guest's room, and to always be courteous. This last rule applied to anyone Joe allowed to enter the guesthouse, which included Aasi and Kamika. Oth-erwise, he said, the houseboys might become confused and insult a guest. And that guest would surely lodge a complaint with *Lonely Planet*.

Joe's children lived in a South Delhi duplex: two boys and a girl. Aasi had yet to meet them. 'They have no interest in the hospitality business,' said Joe. His sons studied engineering at Delhi Technological University. His daughter was waiting until a suitable husband was found and in the meantime was taking a course in cosmetology.

But Aasi had met Joe's wife.

She was shaped like a *rasgulla* - a perfectly round sweet. Kamika and Aasi had to stay half-awake listening for her high-pitched voice, then run for the squat toilet used by the kitchen staff. Joe's wife never went there. She insisted upon using a Western style toilet. Aasi suspected that it was because her knees were too fat to bend. Air-con rooms had *en suite*, according to *Lonely Planet*. The wife would wait until a room became vacant, making the staff clean the toilet a second time. If the guesthouse was fully occupied, the wife would hold herself until she was back at the South Delhi duplex.

The clock above the reception desk could be read while standing in the alleyway. Aasi and Kamika kept their eyes on the hands as they jolted to the top. Kamika couldn't stop yawning, which Aasi thought a bad habit. They removed their slippers, stowing them behind a potted fern.

Joe sat perched upon a stool behind the front desk. The girls waited quietly while he finished checking in a new guest. This one had shaggy hair, needing a trim. At the first opportunity, Aasi would suggest a reputable barber. The buttons on his shirt were broken, meaning they'd been laundered in India, where garments were often beat against rocks. Aasi hoped to direct him to a laundry service using Maytag washing machines.

Joe opened a ledger book. 'Look up,' he said, pointing to a camera mounted near the ceiling. The shutter clicked before the Westerner knew to smile. 'Required by the police,' said Joe. 'In case you are lost. Not to worry.'

'Okay, huh,' said the man, irritated. He scribbled his information across the ledger's two pages. 'My girlfriend is flying in tonight. She'll arrive in a few hours. You'll be sure to show her to my room?'

His voice was American, but Joe said, 'Your girlfriend is from Canada, too? I'll leave a note for the front desk.' He looked at the clock. 'We change shifts, but I'll let the night manager know to expect your girlfriend. You may rest assured.'

All Aasi could do was rock her head. She wasn't allowed to speak to a guest. Not in front of Joe, that is. She knew that the girlfriend would get lost looking for the room. The numbers on quite a few doors had gone missing.

The Canadian took his key. Aasi helped him lift a backpack, hoping for a tip. But before she could put a palm out, the Canadian had mounted the stairs.

The girls stood with their backs to a giant fan. Their braids blew forward. 'Like sitting backwards on a speeding train,' said Aasi, and Kamika giggled. Aasi's top lifted to reveal her belly-button. She stuck a finger into her navel, thinking how she had once been attached to her mother. If only the doctor had not cut the cord, she thought.

It was impossible to hear Joe's voice over the roar of the fan. He used a broom to indicate the place where he wanted them to start sweeping. Someone, Aasi saw, had spilled salt and rice on the floor.

Later, the Sujay was quiet except for the humming of a refrigerator, working extra hard in the heat. They were tired after sweeping, and Kamika's eyelashes fluttered sleepily. Even so, she needed a bedtime story or she'd keep Aasi awake until she got one.

They cuddled below the billiard table and Aasi took *Grimm's* from her bag. The pages had cracked again, so that pieces of flaked paper lined the bottom of her bag. Aasi was afraid to open the book, afraid that the binding would break in two. She folded a rag around the book and slid it back into the bag.

The book had been a parting gift from Miss Elizabeth, an

English missionary who came to Paharganj to teach street children how to read and write. They met in a building behind the cinema. The alphabet was painted on the wall, both in Hindi and English. Although Miss Elizabeth was fluent in Hindi, she spoke to the children in English and they had to pay close attention or miss the lesson. They read old and musty books. If the children were especially good, they got to watch an English film. Aasi's favorite was *Miss Potter*, about the author and illustrator Beatrix Potter. Miss Elizabeth said the actress was an American pretending to be English. 'And not doing a good job of it. What dreadful vowels!' She wanted the children to pay attention to the other actors. Aasi ignored this advice.

Miss Elizabeth had white hair. For this reason the children were afraid, worried that she was a *bhoot*, the ghost of a dead person transformed into an animal. They claimed to have seen Miss Elizabeth in the shape of a rat and an elephant. Because of this, Aasi ended up being the only child in the class. She was desperate to learn English, she didn't care if a *bhoot* taught her. How else would she speak to her mother when they were finally reunited?

Aasi never saw Miss Elizabeth turn into an animal, although the teacher had other strange habits. For one thing, she prayed using a string of beads. Aasi had seen Tibetan monks praying with beads, but Miss Elizabeth wasn't Tibetan and her string had a little man hanging from the end. She ate thin slices of bread, toasted on the gas stove, impaling the toast with a fork and twisting and turning until it was burnt on both sides. At first Aasi thought this was another religious ritual, but the teacher corrected her. Miss Elizabeth ate her toast with a cup of milk chai. If Aasi was there at the right time, the teacher brought out a tin filled with Oreos.

Aasi was sad when she learned that the school was closing. She would miss the Oreo cookies and the way Miss Elizabeth listened patiently as Aasi stumbled over words. *Grimm's Fairy Tales* was a parting gift from Miss Elizabeth, who explained that it was too heavy to ship home.

Later, Aasi tried to sell *Grimm's* to a used book dealer. That was after she had two stomachs to fill instead of one. The book dealer examined the cracked spine and noted the warped cover and wavy pages. 'Water damage.' He clicked his teeth. 'In any case, my customers want Harry Potter and *Twilight*, and *Shanteram*. Bring me those and I'll give you good money.'

That's why she still had *Grimm's*.

'Here's a story I wrote myself,' she told Kamika now. Unfolding a stack of lined notebook paper, she added, 'Miss Elizabeth helped with spelling and grammar and with the order of words. English is a difficult language. Ten times she made me rewrite each story.' She shuffled the pages until she'd found a red mark. 'See the letter? Miss Elizabeth, she wrote this.'

'A,' said Kamika.

'Very good. 'A' meaning *almost* perfect. The story is about my esteemed mother.'

Kamika quivered all over.

The Girl and the Snake

THERE ONCE WAS A GIRL WHO lived in a sandstone castle more beautiful than the Red Fort. She had smooth hair reaching to her knees, and eyes the color of gold. Upon first seeing the girl, everyone was terrified.

You see, she wore a jewel in her hair. Whether topaz or yellow-diamond, I cannot say, only that it matched the girl's eyes. The jewel hung from a pendent, resting at the center of her forehead.

People thought that it was a third eye.

The girl's father never allowed his daughter to leave the palace grounds unless accompanied by a eunuch, lest the jewel be stolen and the girl violated. Because the eunuchs were busy singing, the girl rarely left the palace grounds.

She was terribly lonely.

So when a snake appeared in her chamber one night, the girl was glad for the company, having never met a snake before. The snake was frightened of the third eye, worried that the girl might be craftier than a serpent. Better make friends before playing tricks, it thought, saying, 'Your three eyes are lovely.'

Being modest, the girl confessed that only two of the eyes were her own. She told the snake that the color, as well as the jewel, had been inherited from her mother. Then the girl fainted, weak with sorrow for her departed parent.

The snake looked around the dark, shuttered room. 'Lack of light and air is your problem,' it said, promising that an outing would restore the girl's health.

The girl dried her two eyes as she explained her father's rule.

'I would be happy to offer my protection,' said the snake. 'No one dare bother a girl guarded by a rattlesnake.' Before the girl had time to consider, the snake jumped up, balancing on its tail. 'Come along then! If I could offer you a hand, I would.'

They traveled many months. The snake crawled on its belly, the girl walked. Sometimes they swam. As the snake promised, fresh air and sunlight gave the girl energy. By the time they reached India, she was strong. They arrived at a marketplace filled with sweet shops, and stalls selling carpets and silk sarees.

'You'd best exchange your palace robes for something less conspicuous,' said the snake. 'Might I suggest that you clothe yourself like a hippie?'

The girl was unhappy, preferring to dress like an Indian princess, in a gold-threaded saree with slippers to match.

'That's exactly how everyone expects you to dress,' said the snake. 'Do you want to be dragged back to that dark and lonely palace?' A forked tongue darted toward a pair of spandex trousers and a gauze shirt. 'Now, there's the perfect disguise!'

The girl was shocked. 'But my legs will show!' she said, blushing. For she had heard that in India only shameless girls showed their legs.

'I have a solution,' said the snake, leading the girl to a tattooist.

The tattooist suggested his most popular design: the Om symbol. The girl protested once again, saying, 'My father is Moslem. He will disown me if I put that symbol on my body.'

The tattooist made eye contact with the snake, who nodded its consent. Removing a silver encased binder from a cabinet, he said, 'My masterpieces,' and flipped through the pages, each one covered in rare butterflies. The girl picked a green winged butterfly, spotted with blue.

'Will it hurt?' she asked.

'Painless,' said the snake.

A lie, of course.

When the pain became unbearable, the girl passed out. She awakened with her clothes in tatters, her lovely hair in knots, and the precious jewel stolen.

'At least the devious snake is gone,' she thought.

Until one day she saw a reflection in a shop window and knew that the snake was still following her. In the form of a tattoo that crawled up her left calf.

Chapter Ten

JAYA ATE FROM A PLATE OF WHITE RICE and bananas. The restaurant manager watched, his head teetering left to right. He launched into a defense of the kitchen staff, as surely Jaya's stomach complaints did not originated there. The vegetables, Jaya learned, were rinsed in water coming direct from an Aquaguard Water Filter, *India's leading and most esteemed water purifier brand*. 'The cooks, madam, are required to wash their hands according to the Worldwide Health Organization, *WHO* for short.' A chart was posted behind the kitchen door if Jaya cared to inspect it. The manager demonstrated by kneading his hands together, this way and that, briskly rubbing his fingernails against each other before wiping his already dry hands on the front of his shirt and saying, 'Can we bring nothing else? Fried eggs and butter toast?'

Jaya placed both hands on her stomach and groaned.

'Very good, as you wish.' The manager tilted an empty tray defensively and backed away.

She watched as Yoel leapt down the stairs, taking two at a time and jumping to the landing. He approached Jaya at a dizzying speed, like a marathon runner about to thrash the finish-line ribbon. 'Don't make any fast movements,' she said.

'And kindly speak in a hush.' She wore sunglasses and they slipped to the bridge of her nose. She pushed them back into place and straightened her back, taking a deep breath.

Yoel threw himself into a chair. 'Tell Yoel - is it the tummy?' He pounded his abs.

Jaya blinked a reply.

'You made the mistake of eating at a dirty thali stall. I saw you there with that beggar girl. A big *ta-ut* - mistake in my language.'

'Why didn't you stop me?'

'This was before we met, is why. But Yoel noticed your... breasts. Very large they are. Impossible not to notice.'

'You're making my head spin.'

'Jaya, my queen. What can I do to help?'

It felt as if a poisoned arrow had pierced Jaya's large intestine. She gasped and panted before saying, 'When I was a child, my mother would rub spearmint and chamomile leaves on my stomach. Okay, laugh, but it worked. And she gave me ginger tea. Real ginger root, sliced thin, and not from a tea bag.'

'This I can do.' He pushed back from the table and returned a minute later passing a steaming glass from hand to hand. Slices of ginger floated near the brim. 'I brought you honey and lemon, too'

'I like you more and more,' said Jaya.

'This is my object.' Yoel lifted an eyebrow.

Jaya doubled over. Yoel knelt beside her with his hand on her back.

'Yoel, I have a ticket for the overnight train to Varanasi. At best, I'll eat this rice and banana and then plant myself in front of a bucket. You're sweet, really, and I'm flattered.' She took a deep breath. 'But, you see, I'm not in India to start a relationship.'

'No?' said Yoel, frowning.

'I guess I'm here to end one.' She considered this for a moment, thinking, That might be the most profound thing I've ever said. But then she spoiled it by burping.

'What can I do?' said Yoel, gently lifting Jaya's hand to his lips.

'You can help me back to my room. I don't think I can manage on my own. It feels as if I've been sucker-punched.' When she looked at the plate of rice and banana vomit rose in her throat. 'You might want to take your hand away from my mouth,' she said.

Yoel lifted the glass to her lips. 'Drink something, my queen. Finish your lemon ginger honey tea before it gets cold.'

'You're right, I should stay hydrated.' She took a sip.

They made the climb to Jaya's room, taking breaks at the landings. Once they arrived, Yoel said, 'You go another night to Varanasi.' By then he was sitting on the floor outside Jaya's bathroom door. She knelt in front of the toilet and their eyes met.

'I have to go tonight. I already have a ticket.'

'The toilet on an Indian train' - he dropped his jaw and made a sound approximating a death knell - 'will be a hole in the floor, last cleaned when who knows when. It will make you wish for this bathroom.' Using a pinky finger, he lowered the toilet seat. 'You want to be leaning out the side of a moving train?'

'I wish now I'd bought a first-class ticket.'

'First and second share the same toilets.'

She was glad for Yoel. Not that he would have been her first choice of a companion. Jaya's friends, the few she had, were usually the nerdy types. Yoel wore a dozen multi-colored wristbands, all for some music festival. It reminded Jaya of ski bums who kept old lift passes attached to their zipper pulls.

Jaya was accustomed to getting advice from her mother, whether she wanted it or not. Now she craved it. Better yet, she wanted someone to rub spearmint oil on her tummy. Her return flight was non-refundable and non-changeable, and departed in one week. She'd be able to rebook the train to Varanasi, but trains returning to Delhi were full and she'd been lucky to get a sleeper berth. As it was, she'd have only two free days at the end of the trip. She wanted to visit the Taj Mahal.

She looked at Yoel affectionately. 'You really think I should put off going to Varanasi?'

Yoel nodded.

'What if I can't get a train coming back?'

'Then you fly. Spice Jet, Indigo, there are a hundred airlines.'

'That's true... I could fly. Should I maybe move to a nicer guesthouse meantime? It's hard to be sick here. It's like a double whammy.'

'Only you can say.' Yoel lifted Jaya by her elbow. He took a quick look around the bathroom. 'If you want my opinion, I say *yes*. I say, get out of this shithole. You deserve the best, my queen.'

'It helps to hear you say that, Yoel. I'm having a hard time making decisions right now and if you could do it for me it would be great. My brain is all muddled. I think I have a fever. Maybe malaria. I've got mosquito bites on my back. And one on my face - see? Or is that a pimple? My mother's friend, Stephan, told me not to take anti-malarial pills because of the side effects. Do you think I should have listened to him, Yoel? He's a masseuse, not a doctor.'

Yoel snapped his fingers. 'I know the place for you, Jaya! Very *shanti*. This means *ma mash sāhaba*.'

'Well, in that case—'

He described the guesthouse where he'd once stayed with his mother. 'She flew from Israel to check up on me. No way she stay here. My *ema* say, 'Over my dead body,' so she look on the Internet and, *chick-chock*, we switch to a fantastic guesthouse, a real Maharajah palace, Jaya. It's behind the cinema.'

'Chick-chock?'

'Fast like lightening, Jaya. My mother paid for everything. Then she flew back to Tel Aviv and I return to this dump very sad. Not because I miss my mother, but I miss the Jyoti Palace like a pain in my heart. So clean' - he let his hands drift in the air - 'nice music in the background. Fantastic food. Oh, sorry - you okay, my queen? You don't look right. Your skin is green.'

Jaya bolted for the bathroom. Through the thin plastic door she heard Yoel say something. 'What was that?' she shouted, hoping to mask the sounds that were coming from her body.

'I miss my mother, I say. Her credit card mostly. You want I should see about a room? The staff, they' - Yoel smacked his lips - 'kiss your feet. They'll treat you like a princess.'

'If you could ask for a clean toilet,' said Jaya. She came out for air, fanning herself with the train ticket. 'And air-conditioning, because I feel like I'm burning up.' Then in a whimper, lifting her eyes, 'Would you mind feeling?' Yoel reached to Jaya's forehead. 'That's nice,' she said, closing her eyes.

'Fever, definitely.' He leaned in to kiss her brow.

'Don't take advantage,' she said.

'Wait here and I go see about a room.'

Once he'd gone, Jaya tore the train ticket in two. She was glad for a legitimate reason to put off the trip. She wasn't ready for Varanasi, for the never-ending processions of mourners carrying the bodies of loved ones to the river's edge. *Burning ghats*: hundreds of fiery funeral pyres, reducing bone to ash. It sounded awful, especially in this heat. And with a fever on top of it.

And besides, she wanted to write a eulogy, maybe use a verse or two from a poetry anthology packed away in her carry-on. She had a copy of *The Prophet* by Kahlil Gibran, one of her mother's favorite books. Before leaving Bolinas, she'd skimmed it looking for dog-eared pages. Funny, because the only place marked was the section *On Marriage*. But there was also one titled *On Joy & Sorrow* and another *On Death*. What could be more perfect?

Yes, she was glad for the delay.

Chapter Eleven

AFTER A MICROWAVED BUN, AASI and Kamika went scavenger hunting. Kamika hummed a song. Trash burning hadn't started yet and the air was cool and translucent. They walked to a dumping spot - an empty lot, really - hoping to find something to sell. Kamika spotted a rope and wrapped both ends around her wrists, swinging the rope and jumping at the same time. She kept missing, tripping as the rope hit her feet.

'Silly girl,' said Aasi.

Aasi found a broken fan that could be brought to a scrap metal dealer, but it was too heavy to lift by herself. They had to hurry before people woke to claim the fan belonged to them.

'*Pyaari beti*, sweet girl,' she said, 'come and help.'

Kamika tied the rope around her waist a few times, but needed Aasi to make a knot. With both girls pulling, they still couldn't move the fan more than a couple of inches. 'This is fortuitous!' said Aasi, who had seen the word used on a broadside advertising bank loans. The heavier the fan, the more valuable: scrap metal was redeemed by the kilo.

After combing the lot, they found a wood palette. Kamika spun as Aasi unwound the rope. They dragged the palette over to the fan and managed to tip the fan onto it. Aasi attached the rope. With both the girls straining and their hands burning, the crate slid along the ground.

By the time they reached the scrap metal dealer, the girls were exhausted. He had only just arrived and made them wait until the garage doors were open and he'd gotten his scale in order. It turned out that the fan was made of aluminum and they collected only twenty rupees.

'If only it was steel,' said Aasi.

'Better yet, gold,' said the scrap metal dealer.

'Better yet, tandoori chicken,' said Aasi, who was especially hungry after the exertion.

Twenty rupees bought each of the girls a cup of milk chai. Kamika was sleepy, yawning every two minutes.

'Time for washing,' said Aasi. They went to a lorry, mounted with a water tank. Aasi washed the sleepers from the corner of Kamika's eyes, cleaning her armpits as well. 'Stop your complaining,' she said. 'This is what it is like to have a mother.' She waited until Kamika composed her expression into something resembling gratitude. 'Today we will ask for shampoo packets again,' she said, combing Kamika's greasy hair with her fingers.

Kamika howled and a pack of dogs howled back. Aasi's body tensed, but none of the dogs acted rabid and she kept her place, continuing to untangle Kamika's hair. Nits clung near the neckline and Aasi picked them off one by one.

Once their hair was neatly plaited, Aasi led Kamika to a shop window which served as a mirror. The shopkeeper was placing watches on satin-lined shelves. He smiled at the two girls.

'Today I will remember to recommend this shop,' said Aasi,

even though she knew that hippies didn't wear watches. Only rich people wore watches. They stayed at the Taj Palace in Delhi Cantt, and not in Paharganj. The hotel was surrounded by high walls, topped with electrified wire. Security guards carried rifles and patrolled the grounds at all hours. Hotel guests rarely walked from the hotel. Instead, they traveled in air-conditioned cars with the windows rolled up. They bought from government-sponsored shops with grossly inflated prices.

Edward Rodgers called these people *The One Percent*. He explained this to Aasi, telling her that he was part of *The Ninety-Nine Percent*.

Any time now and Rodgers would be getting his espresso one-shot. The girls ran back to the Main Bazaar, hoping to catch him. They found him inside an ATM booth, pressing numbers into the keypad. A security guard sat outside the booth in a plastic chair. Through the glass door, Aasi heard the machine sounding with the flow of money.

'Edward Rodgers!' she said when he opened the door. He came alongside and pulled on the end of her braid.

He was in a good mood, so Aasi said, 'Maybe today I fetch train ticket?'

'Done deal,' said Rodgers.

'You promised,' said Aasi, pouting.

Rodgers reached into his sack, removing a tiny glass vial. 'A gift,' he said. The vial was filled with liquid the color of amber oil, but when Aasi pull the stopper she knew that the scent was a mixture of sandalwood and clove bud. She allowed Kamika to take two whiffs before pulling the bottle way.

'Thank you,' said Aasi, raising the bottle toward Rodgers's nose.

'I'm down-sizing,' he said, 'so I might as well give stuff away.' He knotted his arms petulantly. 'So, am I back in your good graces?'

'I think not,' said Aasi. 'Why do you make promises and not keep?'

She tilted the bottle and dabbed oil at the back of each ear. Kamika pulled at the soft ends of an earlobe and Aasi touched an oily finger to the place where she could feel Kamika's heart beating.

'Don't be like that,' said Rodgers, 'you're making me feel bad. I don't like guilt trips.'

Aasi tilted her head. 'Is this where you are going - on a *guilt trip*?'

He stroked Aasi's head, saying, 'I'll miss you, kid.' They walked on and he added, 'I'm off to Dharamshala actually, then overland to Nepal. I might even get myself an Atlas bike, put a big gear on it and cycle to Nepal. It'll be the kick in the butt I need. See, I've been letting myself go. Not eating enough and no exercise. By the time I get to Kathmandu I'll have calf muscles like Lance Armstrong's.'

'All that way to Nepal?'

'It's not very far. The next country over. The only problem is the kick-ass mountain range in between.'

They were almost to the coffee shop. Rodgers stopped to rest on a low wall, first finding a package of rolling papers in his trouser pocket. From a hemp pouch he pinched a clump of dry leaves, sprinkling them on the translucent paper.

'Ganja?' asked Aasi.

'Not this time.'

'I can do.'

'I've got it.' He licked the edges of the paper and rolled the cheroot in his fingers until it was shaped like a pencil. Then he twisted the ends to prevent the tobacco from escaping. Aasi watched carefully.

'Why you leave?' she said. 'Delhi is too hot?'

'That, and I need to get my head clear. The mountains will be a tonic. If I'm feeling up for it, I'll hike the Annapurna Circuit. Heck, yeah.' He spit on the ground. 'Delhi is a black hole. A black f - ing hole.'

'Yes, black f - ing hole,' said Aasi, pretending to understand what he was talking about.

'There's a lot of bad energy here,' he said, striking a match. 'I'll probably have to give up smoking if I want to make the summit. It's something like 15,000 feet altitude at the pass. But can you imagine the views? A person can black out at those elevations if they're not careful. Any higher and you need an oxygen tank. Not much air up there.'

'Best to stay here. Here is air.'

His laugh brought on a coughing fit. Rodgers hacked up phlegm before saying, 'This place is killing me.' He held the cheroot between two fingers, sucking smoke and then tossing the stub.

'Why you say I go to station, then changing mind?' She let her shoulders slouch. 'Bad karma for you, Edward Rodgers.'

Rodgers didn't respond right away, but finally he said, 'Look - I'm in a magnanimous mood, how about that? New leaf and all. What do you say I set you up with a supply of incense sticks? You can sell them to the tourists. Or maybe some of those cards with the Hindu gods on them. I'll even get you a bag like this one, too. To carry everything. I've got an extra one floating around.' He lifted a sack that hung from a shoulder. 'It will help my karma, like you say. But we better buy wholesale or you won't make diddly-squat.'

'Wholesale?'

'You know, cut out the middleman. Meaning the shop. Buy direct from the manufacturer.'

Aasi tried to make sense of the proposal. *Buy direct:* she pictured a man carrying a cardboard box into Mr. Wadhwa's shop, a Sai Baba devotee. The incense sticks came from Bangalore, she knew. Nag Champa was a favorite with hippies. But she worried that Mr. Wadhwa would be angry when he learned that he had been cut out.

'It's a dog-eat-dog world,' said Rodgers.

This is true, thought Aasi. A few meters away two dogs growled at each other, fighting over a discarded clay curd bowl.

'When is your train?' she asked.

Rodgers found the ticket in his wallet and read off the time of departure. 'I'd like to get there early. No stress. So, you snooze, you lose.'

'Maybe you give me the money. Easier for me, easier for you.'

'Maybe *not*.'

This was the problem, Aasi thought. Ever since the film *Slumdog Millionaire*, no one would give large sums of money directly into her hands, worried that it would end up in the pocket of a slave master. Aasi hated the film, even though she'd yet to see it.

'Where you be?' she asked. 'I bring incense wallah to you.'

'I'll be in my guesthouse packing. You know the one, room 203. I might run an errand or two, but I'll be there most of the day. Probably eat lunch at the Everest.'

'No problem absolutely! You will see me before long.'

Rodgers entered the coffee shop and ordered his espresso. The redheaded Australian woman was there again and they greeted each other by pecking cheeks.

Aasi leapt up the steps and into the coffee shop. The waiter swung a newspaper, which narrowly missed her head. Rodgers was sprawled out on a floor pillow, rolling another cheroot. As Aasi prostrated herself before him, the corner of his mouth lifted imperceptibly.

'I am in your debt,' she said.

'Nice to hear it,' he replied. 'Now scram.'

Aasi grabbed Kamika's hand, pulling her behind a parked rick-shaw. 'Hurry,' she said.

Mr. Aggarwal, the jhajariya sweet seller, had a crowd at his stall. His towers of jhajariya were quickly diminishing. The wife, Aasi saw, was away. So, while Kamika did her business, she went to speak with Mr. Aggarwal.

'I recommend your jhajariya to everyone!' she said. 'I say, "Oil is changed daily, never rancid," like you taught me. Already I have translated the word sweet into five languages. I know how to say "world's best" in all of these languages, plus Polish. Want to hear me say "world's best sweet" in Gujarati?'

'I trust you. Come back tonight at closing and you will have your reward.'

'At which time exactly?'

'Come back an hour or so after sunset. *Cake Boss* is on television tonight. It's my favorite program. If I have gone home early, I'll leave something for you on the ledge under the table. Keep promoting my jhajariya! I have a daughter needing fillings and another needing dowry jewelry. And now with the world gold price so high. I warned her yesterday - she might be thirty before she marries. I'm not Mukesh Ambani, after all!'

A customer wrinkled her mouth and said, 'Give me fresh, not from the bottom of the stack.'

A Westerner stepped up and asked, 'Are they gluten free?'

But Mr. Aggarwal was still on the subject of his daughter. 'She has made a love match. Must I still provide a dowry, I ask you?'

'May the gods bless you, Mr. Aggarwal,' said Aasi. 'And your daughters too.' Under her breath she whispered, 'Not your wife.' The woman would rather throw leftover pieces into a trash heap then give them away. She spoke a curse over Mr. Aggarwal's wife, one she used against heartlessness: 'May you live restless for eternity, for you killed an unsuspecting bird in love.'

Then she went to check on Kamika.

'*Accha*, Kamika,' she said. 'Now we find the incense wallah. You know what incense is?' She pulled Kamika to a shop where the red, white, and blue boxes were piled in a basket. Kamika touched her left calf. 'No,' said Aasi. 'We're not looking for my mother today. How can I make you understand?'

The shopkeeper worked at a sewing machine, with his foot pressed to the pedal and his attention diverted on stitching something made of stretchy nylon. The sewing machine was pushed up against the wall and his sweat-stained back faced Aasi. She crawled below the display table, reaching up from the other side. As her hand clutched the Nag Champa, she made a vow to return the box. 'I am not a thief,' she whispered.

The two girls ran around the corner, where Aasi held the box in front of Kamika's eyes. 'See - red, white, and blue. Same as the American flag.'

Kamika licked her lips, thinking there were sweets in the box.

'Not sweets, silly girl. This is incense for chasing away flies. Satya Sai Baba Nag Champa Agarbatti.' She showed Kamika the writing on the front of the box. Careful not to tear the cardboard, she slid a stick out of the box and let Kamika smell it.

'Ahh,' said Kamika. The girl enjoyed nice smells more than anything. Aasi thought that it might be because her voice was yet to work, that her nose and eyes were growing disproportionately strong. It's why they stopped to smell frangipani trees and flowering bushes, why they walked slowly when nearing spice shops, and why they avoided walking behind cows. Kamika wanted to hold the incense stick but Aasi replaced it, making sure that the box looked as if it had never been opened.

'*Mata-ji*,' said Kamika. Honored mother.

Aasi was so surprised, she dropped the box in the dirt. Then she realized her mistake. Kamika was still expecting to search for Aasi's mother.

'Today we look for a father,' said Aasi. 'A father wearing a white lungi tucked between his boney legs. A local man, not a foreigner. With a bald head, I think.' To be honest, she'd never looked closely at the man. 'He carries a cardboard box on his shoulder, his left shoulder.'

'*Mata-ji,*' said Kamika, this time looking directly into Aasi's face.

Aasi's eyes began to water. But she had no time for sentimentality, she had to concentrate on the task in front of her. 'Good girl,' she said, squeezing Kamika's hand. Their fingers remained intertwined.

She managed to return the box without being seen. They raced past shops, checking each for a photograph of Guru Sai Baba. Aasi was hoping to find the incense wallah doing puja below an altar. They made it to the Sujay, where the clerk at the reception desk said, '*Rukēṁ!*' Stop!

'Please!' said Aasi, with her palms pressed respectfully. 'We must give honor to Sai Baba-ji. The nearest shrine is inside Jet Travel Shop.'

A guest, needing directions to Humayun's Tomb, distracted the reception clerk long enough for them to pass. A moment later they stood outside the travel agency. The owner sat behind a desk topped with a computer and a credit card reader. He held his chin high, to show off his beautifully twisted beard. Aasi knew that he kept a photograph of his son in his wallet. The agent was proud of his son; only recently had he began putting photographs on his mobile.

A Westerner sat on the other side of his desk. The travel agent sipped tea from a small glass before moving his fingers above the keyboard. The Westerner was texting on her smartphone, chewing gum and not paying attention.

The travel agent said, 'Yes - it's possible to push back your travel date, but Swiss Air will charge a significant fee.'

The Westerner said, 'How much?'

'Oh, no,' said Aasi, realizing her mistake, 'this is the wrong shop!' Except for travel posters, the walls were decorated with pictures of the Golden Temple in Amritsar and Guru Nanak, the Sikh guru.

Aasi dove below the billiard table, pulling Kamika along. The floor was covered with cigarette stubs and wadded up tissues. Blue chalk covered the palms of Aasi's hands and knees. Billiard balls clicked together and rolled above their heads in all directions, aiming for the four corners. Four feet danced around the table. One man was barefoot, the other wore hiking boots with the shoelaces untied. The barefoot man won the game and walked away. Aasi laughed: the souls of his feet were blue like Krishna's.

Kamika had fallen asleep. Aasi was forced to drag the sleeping girl's body toward the Internet café. Every cubbyhole was occupied. Skype was open on most of the computer screens. People shouted in languages Aasi had yet to learn. One traveller said to a screen, 'The damn Wi-Fi never works in this country or I'd Skype from my phone.' On the back wall was a glass ledge, topped with a framed portrait of Guru Sai Baba. Aasi was disappointed to see that the incense wallah wasn't worshipping under the altar.

The attendant said, 'No computers free, come back in ten minutes,' then narrowed his eyes.

'See?' Aasi whispered in Kamika's ear while indicating the

portrait. 'That's the guru. He's expired, I think. It's his devotee we need to find. He wears white robes, not orange. And his hair is straight, not bushy. Thinner too. Taller maybe. Eyes the same color though.' If anything, she had only confused Kamika.

'Out, I said!' yelled the attendant. 'This business is for paying customers only.'

Aasi spoke her favorite of all curses, although its meaning remained a mystery: 'If you ever approach a woman with the thought of sex, you shall die then and there!'

The attendant's eyes opened wide with fear; the whites showed around his irises. He reached for a letter opener. Aasi worried that she had gone too far. Why had she spoken the curse aloud instead of in a whisper? She was not someone who could wield her lips like a sword and get away with it. 'Mistake!' she said quickly. 'Curse was not for you - for you I have a blessing! "May you have many sons... May your business prosper... May you, may you...win at Powerball!" '

At the mention of Powerball, he dropped the letter opener and sat again in his chair, rocking his head with satisfaction.

The sun was directly overhead, stealing what shade remained. Kamika whined and Aasi slapped her ear. 'Your noises make the air hotter,' she said.

Kamika dragged her feet and let both shoulders droop. Aasi pulled the girl along until they reached the traffic-jammed road separating the New Delhi railway station from the Main Bazaar. Vegetable sellers sat on the side of the road, their backs leaning against concrete traffic barriers. They cried out, desperate to save their produce from the rotting heat. Only the saffron seller smiled; what she didn't sell today would keep for tomorrow. Aasi asked if they'd seen a man draped in a white lungi, but the saffron seller raised her palms.

'Come,' said Aasi. 'We will take our rest.'

A pile of bricks provided room for one, and Aasi pulled Kamika to her lap. Before long she felt sleeping breath against her neck. She leaned her head against Kamika's. Too much responsibility, she thought, knowing that the girl would wake hungry.

She found the ankle bracelet in the bottom of her bag and began using it like prayer beads, pushing each bell against her fingers until she had reached the broken clasp. The motion had always helped to clear her mind.

After turning over every possibility, she realized that there was really only one. She hated to split profits, but with Mr. Wadhwa's help there might be a chance of finding the incense wallah before Edward Rodgers left New Delhi.

She shook Kamika awake.

Mr. Wadhwa was standing outside his shop, trying in vain to attract the attention of passersby. Seeing the girls he clapped his hands, but realizing that they had failed to bring business he let his arms fall to his side. Aasi offered her apologies and he reached below his sewing table for a four-tier tiffin carrier.

'My wife prepares too much food,' he said, twisting a hand. 'She prefers me to be fat.' He poked at his stomach making it shake below his shirt. 'Do me the favor of finishing so that I will avoid trouble later. The woman is easily insulted.'

Aasi unlocked the catch and a mix of spices - cardamom

and cinnamon, turmeric and mustard seed - reached her nostrils, causing her mouth to salivate. This was home cooked food, she knew, not hotel food. She dug her fingers into the gravy, licking three and leaving one for Kamika. In the middle compartments she found vangi bhaat with cashew nuts planted in the rice. She moaned so that Mr. Wadhwa would understand the full measure of her gratitude.

'Rice is there also... in the bottom tier,' he said.

Aasi had to make the proposal as fragrant as Mrs. Wadhwa's curry.

'Dear Mr. Wadhwa, as you are the most honorable merchant in the Main Bazaar, perhaps in all of India, I have chosen you for my business partner.'

He chuckled. 'Is this so?'

She explained her plan in detail. While he thought this over, she balled rice, dipping it into the gravy and filling her mouth. Kamika grabbed a tiffin box from Aasi's hand and managed to feed herself.

'What I am thinking, Uncle, is this: That since you are the expert, I will be your apprentice.' Before continuing, she knelt and touched his feet. He was wearing flip-flops and her fingers landed on the tips of his twisted toenails. Looking upward, she said: 'You have only to contact the incense wallah, the one supplying Nag Champa, and arrange for a delivery of one carton. This will be your only task: a phone call.'

Mr. Wadhwa stepped into his shop but Aasi knew that she had his attention.

'One phone call on your mobile.'

'Go on.'

'The American will pay for the merchandise and fly off to Nepal for trekking, first stopping in Dharamshala to pay his respects to the Dalai Lama. Now is the time to act, as he might later die in an avalanche. Or he might expire while attempting to summit Mount Everest on a bicycle.' She let the edges of her mouth drop. However sympathetic she might be to Edward Rodgers's fate, there was no time for elaboration. She pictured the American buried under snow and then forced the image from her mind. Mr. Wadhwa signaled for Aasi to get to the point.

She said, 'I will give you one percent of whatever I earn. We can use your calculator.'

'One percent, you say?'

'One percent of everything, of the whole-sale.'

'Seventy,' he said, beginning the negotiation. 'Of the retail price.'

They settled on fifty percent. Mr. Wadhwa went to his sewing table and shifted through a stack of business cards.

'He must come quickly,' said Aasi. 'Instruct him to meet us at the Hotel Jyoti Palace!' She was shaking as she spoke the words, and Kamika took hold of her hand, afraid that Aasi might be ill.

After making the call, Mr. Wadhwa slipped the mobile back into his shirt pocket. 'He is on his way directly.' With a flourish of his hand they became business partners.

'You will not regret your decision,' said Aasi, asking how much she should charge for each box of incense.

'Start at one-hundred rupees, go no lower than fifty. Try to sell to the Russians, as they rarely negotiate. Americans are even better. I suggest you stay away from the Israelis.' He began adding in his head. 'One hundred times one hundred is ten hazer. Fifty percent is, let's see, is 5000 rupee. Your profit will be the same, a fortune.'

'A fortune,' she repeated.

Despite the heat, Mr. Wadhwa pulled on an overcoat. The shop assistant swept dust from his shoulders using a whisk brush.

'Mind the shop,' said Mr. Wadhwa, mounting a scooter and indicating the seat behind him. 'Come along little ones. Why do you stand like mannequins?'

Aasi sat sidesaddle, with her legs dangling over the side and Kamika balanced on her lap. Mr. Wadhwa instructed Aasi to hold onto a sidebar.

After a bumpy ride, they parked in front of the Jyoti Palace. The owner was lounging on a couch, fanning himself with a magazine. Aasi let Mr. Wadhwa do the talking, as the hotel owner would only shoo her away.

'Business with a guest in room 203,' said Mr. Wadhwa, buttoning his overcoat. The owner waved his hand lazily, inviting Mr. Wadhwa to step inside. Mr. Wadhwa spoke in a raised voice, making sure that his instructions were overheard. 'I will bring the American down. You wait here for Ramakrishna's arrival!'

'I will wait faithfully,' said Aasi.

The owner shook his head, displeased with the arrangement. 'With which guest is your business?' he said, addressing Mr. Wadhwa.

'The American,' said Mr. Wadhwa.

'There is more than one.' The owner twisted the end of his

beard.

'A gentleman.'

The owner jabbed a finger toward the elevator. 'The guest has a train to catch. He must leave in ten minutes time. Remind him to not be late.'

'May I have a drink of water, please?' said Aasi.

The owner shut his eyes against the sun, leaning back into his chair. Aasi wanted to shout a curse at him but she knew better this time.

Soon afterwards, she heard the sound of a motorbike. Spinning around, she stared directly at the front tire as it skidded to a stop. Bungee cords attached a carton to the back rack. Stenciled on the side of the box were the words *Satya Sai Baba Nag Champa Agarbatti*.

'Here, Uncle! Here! I am Mr. Wadhwa's apprentice waiting for your imminent arrival.'

Ramakrishna swung his leg over the motorbike seat and lowered a kickstand. The lungi was tied up between his boney legs - checkered blue, not white - no wonder they hadn't found him earlier. After arranging the lungi so that it hung to his knees, Ramakrishna took the key from the ignition and placed his helmet between the handlebars. His eyes squinted as if he suspected a trick.

Aasi looked nervously at the elevator. Perhaps Edward Rodgers was delayed with last-minute packing. Thankfully she had a knowledgeable partner for this enterprise, one who would arrange everything, maybe even staple the rupee notes together into uniform stacks. Her heart beat as if she were running. She took Kamika's hand and squeezed. Kamika whimpered.

'Shush,' said Aasi, 'you ungrateful girl.'

'Where is the shop owner?' asked Ramakrishna. 'I only do business with him.'

He freed the carton from the motorbike and joined Aasi at the entrance. Five minutes passed and there still was no sign of Mr. Wadhwa and Rodgers... Seven minutes... Ten. The train would be boarding. It was never good, thought Aasi, to arrive late.

Finally, the elevator doors opened. Mr. Wadhwa stood there alone.

He held the door open, causing a bell to buzz incessantly. He shouted for the owner: 'Come quickly, sir! There is no time to lose.'

The hotel owner pulled up from the chair. He shuffled to the elevator while Mr. Wadhwa urged him to move faster. The doors closed again and they were gone.

The incense wallah stepped into the lobby, with Aasi's future balanced on his head. A sweeper appeared, swatting the floor and gathering dirt into a tidy pile. She stopped the wallah with the tip of her broom but then decided to let him pass. When Aasi tried to follow, the sweeper hit her shin. Kamika started wailing. Aasi ran back to the street, yelling curses at the sweeper.

That was when Jaya approached the hotel. Yoel was right behind, dragging a black suitcase. Its wheels kicked up dust, but a blue whirling light could be seen hovering behind their heads. A siren blasted. As Jaya cleared the way for the ambulance, she tripped over a pile of construction material: sand, bricks, and metal rebar. Aasi watched helplessly as Jaya's hands flailed at the air.

But, oddly enough, it was Aasi who fell.

Chapter Twelve

ACCORDING TO JAYA'S iPHONE, now equipped with an Indian SIM card, the temperature had reached 43 degrees Celsius. She was using the phone to fan a heatstroke victim. First chance she got, she would download a conversion app.

Aasi came to life when the cold back of the phone touched her forehead. She stared at a water bottle wedged into the side pocket of Jaya's carry-on.

'REI,' she said, and fainted again.

What next? thought Jaya, struck by the idea that this new chain of events might be the result of bad karma - a bad daughter who should be heading for Varanasi instead of checking into a luxury guesthouse. But she didn't believe that mumbo-jumbo, she reminded herself, no more than Ouija boards, astral projection, star-alignment, or the healing power of crystals. Life in the geodesic dome had turned Jaya into a skeptic.

She shouted to the paramedics but they rushed past, following the directions of the hotel owner. Jaya had trained in CPR, but she was quick with an excuse: It wouldn't be right to do mouth-to-mouth when she was sick with something herself.

Yoel took charge. 'Part of my army training,' he said, kneeling beside Aasi. He lifted both eyelids. 'Amber eyes. *Me'anyen may-od.*'

'Is she alive?' asked Jaya.

'Her pulse is weak. And she needs a bath, for sure.'

Jaya poked the girl's shoulder with the blunt edge of the water bottle, unscrewed the lid, and poured water onto Aasi's face. When Aasi opened her eyes, Jaya allowed the girl to sip what remained in the bottle. For a second there, Jaya was looking at her younger self. The clothes were all wrong...but the face in close-up. Eyes and skin in shades of molasses and wildflower honey.

Then she recalled having met the girl before.

'Mommy,' said Aasi, leaning on one elbow and staring into Jaya's eyes.

'It's the heat. Here, drink more water,' said Jaya, handing over the water bottle. If she didn't get out of the sun, she would faint herself.

Yoel, she saw, was talking with the hotel owner. He called to Jaya, 'Everything is set,' then hoisted her suitcase onto his head - even though it clearly had wheels - and set it beside the reception desk. 'They will help you from here, my queen. I have a WhatsApp call with my girlfriend in Israel, but I will return *chic-chock.*'

Jaya watched as he walked away. Girlfriend in Israel? she thought, surprised by her disappointment.

Meanwhile, Aasi was fixating on the water bottle. 'Sigg?' she said.

Jaya was surprised that the girl could read. 'It's Swiss, actually.'

'But, lady, you saying you are American.'

'Drink up and let's be done with this.' Jaya brushed dust

from her jeans. Standing too quickly made her head spin. She felt a faint breeze near her ankle and turned around to see a small child trying to push her pant leg up.

'*Saanp*,' said Kamika, staring longingly at Jaya's calf. The jeans were skintight and the girl couldn't get the fabric any higher than the anklebone.

A man stood in the lobby, shouting in a language Jaya couldn't understand. Aasi jumped up and pulled Kamika away. Only the Sigg bottle remained.

'We have been expecting you!' said the man. 'Take up your water container, madam. We will have it sanitized by our kitchen staff. You should not have let that beggar drink from it!'

Jaya followed him into the lobby. The guesthouse was featured in her guidebook. 'Zen-like ambiance,' it said. But the lobby resembled a Russian Orthodox church more than anything else, with gold gilded moldings and silk baroque everywhere. The only thing Zen-like was a water fountain bubbling into a pool of plastic lotus flowers.

The man gestured toward a loveseat. 'Sit, madam. Your friend has given us the details of your health crisis.' He took his place behind the reception desk. 'Give me your passport and I will record the pertinent information into the ledger. It is customary for the guest to do this themselves, but I will perform the task for you. More than happy to do it - delighted!'

Jaya fumbled through her bag, beginning to panic. Was the fainting episode part of a ruse? Only once before had she been robbed - by a knife-wielding crackhead at Opera Plaza in San Francisco. As she feared, the wallet was gone: passport, rupees, hundred dollar bills. All gone.

But an instant later she was clutching the passport, which had been hidden along with the credit cards under her waistband. Her mother would have called this feeling *Māyā*. She laughed.

'Something humorous?' asked the owner.

'Not really.'

He laughed along anyway. 'A good joke, yes. Very good for one's health.'

'You *do* have an air-conditioned room, right?'

He examined the key rack. 'I can give you a room with an air-cooler.'

'A what? Is that an air-conditioner?'

'An air-cooler uses water.'

'How cool does it get the room?'

'Not quite as cool as an air-conditioner, perhaps, but cooler than a fan. The room has a ceiling fan also.' His eyes swiveled toward the elevator doors.

Out stepped the two ambulance drivers, bearing a stretcher. Jaya recognized the sick man. His unbound hair swept the floor as the stretcher was carried across the lobby and down the front steps. 'I know that man,' she said, both hands rushing to her mouth. 'Oh, God, how awful.'

Mr. Wadhwa exited the elevator. Behind him a man boomed: 'East Meets West Clinic!' He took a seat beside Jaya. 'Sit, madam. There is nothing we can do. Drugs. A problem of epidemic proportion.' He rolled his lower lip downward.

'Good news, madam,' said the man holding Jaya's passport. 'An air-con room has become available if you are willing to be patient.' He barked out a command, 'Clean sheets for room 203!' A hunched-back woman materialized, carrying a mop and bucket.

Jaya bit the wick of a fingernail. 'Ed...he isn't...dead?'

'A mild overdose, madam. The man is an opium user, apparently. The patient will make a full recovery, you may be sure. His heartbeat is erratic but he is breathing. I made certain of this myself.' He placed a finger on his jugular vein. 'Terrible omen for a guest to expire in one's establishment, terrible blow to business. The patient will live, madam, you need not fear. Myself and my eldest brother here' - he made eye contact with the man holding Jaya's passport - 'are the proprietors of this fine establishment. As such, we make certain our guests are respectable. Even so, bad ones manage to slip in on occasion.'

The other man rushed in with an example. 'Why, last year, I traveled with my family to Lisbon. And what do you think happened? We were robbed! And yet the thief was disguised as a respectable businessman. He entered the hotel lobby as if he belonged. Only a minute before the theft I had been admiring the cut of his jacket. It transpired that as my wife and I discussed dinner plans, the thief had inched her bag away using his foot. A three-star hotel too! I let the proprietor know that we did not hold him responsible in *any way*. He was so relieved he insisted we help ourselves to beverages from the mini-fridge at no charge. The whole incident was recorded on security cameras. The thief was clever: the entire time he kept his back to the camera.'

'Our father first opened this hotel,' said the brother.

'There is his photograph, hanging in the place of honor,' said the other, pointing to the image of a dour man wearing bottle-thick, black-rimmed eyeglasses. If she hadn't been told, Jaya might have taken him for the triplet. 'Expired this past year,' he added.

'Not in the hotel, I hope,' said Jaya.

As she waited, Jaya thought about Ed Rodgers. She hadn't taken him for a drug addict, not that she was an expert. She remembered the time her mother allowed a junkie to crash on the sleeper sofa in the living room. 'He's detoxing,' her mother said.

Jaya was sixteen at the time. Her mother worked night-shifts, leaving Jaya alone with the man. Whenever she needed to use the bathroom, she tip-toed back and forth across the living room.

Three days into his recovery, the junkie stopped Jaya en route. He began waxing on about a plant that grew in the deserts of South Africa. It could change brain chemistry, he said. The herbs Jaya's mother fed him, stuffed into plastic capsules, had failed to take away his craving for heroin. He asked Jaya to lend him money for a flight to Johannesburg. At the time, Jaya worked part-time at the Safeway deli counter. She gave him forty-two dollars, all she had. He was gone by morning.

'I suspected as much,' said the one brother, and Jaya realized they'd returned to the topic of Ed Rodgers. 'One tries to give the benefit of doubt.'

'He seemed like a nice guy,' she said.

'Regrettably he missed his train. And his trip to Nepal will be delayed as well, which is a great regret.'

'I'm glad to hear that he'll recover,' said Jaya, not sure if it would have been a good idea to take the room otherwise.

'Only five minutes more and the room will be prepared. Take up a magazine in the meantime. We have the current issues.'

'Do you think I might get some bottled water?' she said.

'How remiss! We should have offered.'

'Really, no need to apologize. I'm a little dehydrated or I wouldn't bother you.'

'Ask up at the rooftop restaurant for the salt and sugar. There will be no charge. A pinch of salt and sugar in your water will help,' said one brother.

'Plenty of fluids,' said the other.

The one brother stood, reaching into his pocket for a stack of bills. He hurried from the lobby to a shop next-door. Jaya watched as he purchased a liter bottle, first checking to see that the cap was sealed. 'Allow me,' he said, when he returned to the lobby. Using his teeth, he removed the plastic wrap from the cap before twisting it open.

Jaya sucked down half the bottle before speaking. 'Thank you. It's been a challenging day.'

He directed her attention to a gilt-framed poster. It showed an idyllic Swiss chalet with an Alpine background. The caption read: *Lifes Challenge Make for Strong Spirits.*

'They've forgotten the apostrophe in life's,' she said weakly, to which the owner explained that the absence of the apostrophe was intentional, as we each have many lives.

Jaya took another sip. 'Then it ought to say, *Challenging Lives Make for Strong Spirits.* This happens to be my profession.'

He stepped closer to the poster, with his head cocked toward his left shoulder.

The cleaning lady returned, appearing even more diminutive as she hefted an enormous garbage bag. Spoiled sheets were tucked under each of her thin arms. Her face, Jaya thought sadly, showed years of drudge work.

'And now your air-con room is ready!' said one of the brothers.

'Enjoy your stay,' said the other.

Chapter Thirteen

THE AMBULANCE WAS AT A STANDSTILL. With one hand tightened around the door handle, Aasi lifted Kamika by her arms and onto the back bumper.

'Hold tight and don't be a coward,' she said, as a siren pierced their ears.

A wedding procession passed by, accompanied by a twelve-piece orchestra. The bridegroom rode a white horse and kept a mournful face below his red turban. Kamika's face lit up when the tuba player passed near.

People looked at the ambulance and rocked their heads.

Aasi jumped from the bumper and yelled at the crowd, 'Move over! Make way!' The ambulance driver tapped the horn. Finally, a path cleared and Aasi ran back to the bumper, only to find that Kamika had slipped away. When she located the disobedient child, she'd box her ears until they bled.

She found Kamika huddled behind a dustbin. Forgetting her anger, Aasi stroked the girl's head, drying Kamika's tears with the end of a braid. Wagging a finger, she said, 'You silly girl. Now what will we do? Do you have the money for a rickshaw?'

'*Maafi*,' said Kamika. Sorry.

Aasi searched her vocabulary for an appropriate expression. 'This is what Miss Elizabeth calls a pickle,' she said. 'Like when her visa ran out, it was a pickle. And when there was a power cut and it rained for twenty straight days and the roof began to leak, and the time bookworms ate Charles Dickens. It's the English word for *achaar*.' Her eyebrows knit together as she tried to make sense of the expression.

'*Achaar*,' said Kamika.

Aasi brushed the girl's hair with her fingers.

'Pretty please,' said Kamika.

Aasi jiggled her purse. There might be enough for a pickle each. But first she slapped Kamika's backside. She said, 'Don't hide behind dirty dustbins!' to which Kamika laughed. 'I'm not making jokes. Dustbins have germs, they crawl with rats and worms. You want worms in your stomach, eating what little food I put in?'

Kamika's smile faded.

Aasi described black flies, laying eggs in Kamika's nostrils. Bugs crawling in her ears. Rats eating her toes. Kamika curled her toes inward. Goosebumps formed on her arms. 'Look!' shouted Aasi, grabbing an arm. 'Bugs are eating your skin!' Kamika stopped breathing. Her body swayed back and forth.

The pickle shop was crowded, but Aasi roared and customers backed away from the counter in fright. One woman laughed when she saw that the noise had come from a girl, but others began speaking insults and pinching Aasi's arms. The salesman placed two pickles into a plastic sack as someone stuck an elbow into her rib.

Aasi's lips burned as the pickle touched her tongue. Kamika's eyes watered until they resembled glass. Aasi finished her pickle first and poured what remained of vinegar and chilies into her mouth. 'Be brave,' she said, forcing Kamika to swallow what was left of her pickle. Kamika danced around, fanning her mouth with both hands. Aasi used the broken ankle bracelet for a percussion instrument.

'Now I must make a plan,' she said. 'Sit quietly and save your words for after.'

Kamika sucked in her lips.

If anyone could save Edward Rodgers, thought Aasi, it was the East Meets West Clinic. She considered making an offering for his good health, but marigolds were too costly. Besides, there was no time. So long as he remained unconscious, someone might steal the money from his pocket.

Money that was needed to pay Ramakrishna, the incense seller.

'If only we had incense sticks,' she whispered, 'we could light one to cleanse the air around Edward Rodgers. It's the bad air that has made him sick. He was hoping to escape Delhi and go to where the air is fresher, but he left it too late. It may be that his lung has collapsed. I have heard of this happening before, to an American who went jogging on a smoggy day.' Aasi took a deep breath, satisfied that her own lungs were in good working order.

The East Meets West Clinic was near the American Embassy, many kilometers away. It was where the Westerners went after hearing that government hospitals were full of germs, poorly trained doctors, and rusty equipment. Fall off a mountain, drown in the Ganges, get squashed by a bus, and a helicopter would swoop in and carry a Westerner to the clinic. But if an

Indian showed up at East Meets West, she was sent away.

Or so Aasi had been told.

There was a story about an Andaman Island mosquito - a whole swarm, actually - attacking a Dutch traveler. Before long, the traveler was delirious with fever. If not for East Meets West Clinic she would be dead. Then there was the Brit who walked barefoot and got a deadly infection in his big toe. The clinic saved an Argentinian bitten by a shark, a Canadian after falling from a rickshaw, and a Japanese man clawed by a snow leopard. Or maybe it was a bear; Aasi couldn't remember.

She pictured Mr. Wadhwa's scooter. A second chance at 50% profit might be enough to convince him to take them to the clinic.

They arrived at his shop to find the gate pulled down. Aasi rattled a padlock hoping to wake the shop assistant. The green scooter was gone; an oil spot showed where it usually stood.

'Mr. Wadhwa is home with his children,' she said. 'Two children, both girls. One small like you, one big like me. I think they are eating Shreemati Wadhwa's curries now, while watching cartoons from a DVD player...with a fan blowing.' She tried to picture the scene, while Kamika waited breathlessly for the next detail. But the Wadhwa home, which Aasi had never seen, remained blurry around the edges. 'Perhaps the family is riding around Delhi on the scooter, enjoying the nice breeze, Mr. Wadhwa steering with his wife seated behind and two girls squeezed between their parents.' It was a scene she witnessed many times a day, one that always left an ache.

She frowned. It would be hours until Mr. Wadhwa returned.

✳

Later, she woke when a policeman hit her with his *lathi*: a four-foot-long rattan stick.

'Move along,' he said.

'Where to, sir?'

'Out of my sight.'

Aasi rubbed the place where her shin stung. She wanted to fight back, kick him in the groin. Or, at the very least, speak a curse over him. Instead, she stood to her feet and bowed. 'Come Kamika,' she said, pulling the girl by the arm but making sure to keep both eyes on the stick.

'A man near the cinema will sell you a space for thirty rupees,' said the policemen. 'And a blanket for only twenty more.'

'And what is your cut?' said Aasi under her breath, regretting the words as soon as they'd slipped out. What if the policeman had exceptionally good hearing? What if he'd cleaned his ears that very day?

Luckily, the policeman's attention was diverted when a Westerner rode toward them on a bicycle. He was skirting potholes and debris, keeping his eyes on the road. He failed to see the policeman blocking the path. There would have been a collision had not the policemen drawn attention to himself by calling out a demand for an International Driver's License. Aasi and Kamika backed into a shadow. It was a made-up charge, if ever there were one; a license wasn't required to ride a pedal bike, even if the rider was from Pakistan.

The bicycle brakes screeched to a stop, but the cyclist kept both feet on the pedals, straightening his legs and balancing the bicycle by teetering left and right. The policeman said, 'Five hundred rupees,' putting out his hand.

The Westerner said, 'Screw you.'

Aasi cringed, waiting for the stick to fly and for bones to break.

In a flash, the Westerner sprinted past the policeman, turning his head backwards and laughing. The policeman didn't chase after the bicycle. He didn't even blow his whistle. Instead, he looked left and right, worried that a bystander might have witnessed this disrespect to his authority. Then he straightened himself with the help of the stick and walked on.

Aasi whispered, 'Next time a policeman threatens to hit me with a stick, I will repeat these two magic words. I've heard these words before but never knew what they meant. Now I know they are magic words.' Aasi loved the idea of curses and spells, as they held out the potential to make the world a fairer place. But a blessing, she knew, was the most powerful of all. She said, 'May you never be troubled by wicked men, Kamika.'

The girls watched as the policeman walked off in the direction of the railway station. 'Safe now,' said Aasi, even though the policeman was still in her line of vision. Someone had urinated on the spot where they were standing and she wanted to escape the smell. She motioned for Kamika to stay quiet as they worked their way to another shop entrance. Aasi whispered, 'I have spoken the magic words over the policemen. He will not bother us again.'

They stopped at a handcraft shop. The window display had been changed and now featured doorknobs and drawer pulls. Aasi put her face to the window glass, knowing that a clock hung above the counter. It had phosphorescent markings, which could be seen hours after the lights were shut off. The markings had dimmed and she had trouble making out the time. 'Half past five,' she said, yawning afterwards. 'Too late to sweep up at the Sujay.' Missing out on a microwaved bun made her stomach growl.

Chapter Fourteen

EVEN IN THE HALF-LIGHT OF DAWN, Jaya recognized the girls by the difference in their stature and the way they wore matching braids.

'Hey!' she said. 'You're the one who took me to that dirty restaurant.'

Aasi turned in Jaya's direction and smiled. Hoping for the opportunity to earn a few rupees, she said, 'Nice lady, you need ear cleaning? Hearing much improved after.'

'My hearing is fine, too good in fact. I need earplugs to sleep.'

'Very expert ear cleaning. First-class, using fine-point stick.'

'That restaurant,' said Jaya, 'you really shouldn't bring tourists there. The food is unsanitary and the place is a breeding ground for germs. The utensils aren't washed properly either.' She held up an index finger, getting ready to add to the rebuke. Instead, she sighed. 'Oh hell, it's not your fault I'm sick. I'm the one who put the food in my mouth. I bet your stomach is bullet-proof.'

'Is there blood in your *tatti*?' asked Aasi.

'Stool. I think that's the word you're looking for.'

'Stool meaning chair without arms.'

'The word has multiple meanings.'

'Blood is a bad omen meaning death is imminent, paining, too.' She said quickly, 'I recommend clinic. First-class clinic for Westerners with blood in stool. You will have no problem finding the way, I will be your guide. Best we take auto rickshaw, wouldn't you agree?'

'Well, the paining part is true enough,' said Jaya. 'But death?' A troubled look passed over her face. She'd read about amebic dysentery on the Internet and was planning to ask the pharmacist for advice. Maybe he would sell her an antibiotic.

As if she were a mind reader, Aasi said, 'The chemist shop is closed at this hour. While the clinic never closes' - Aasi added one of Miss Elizabeth's sayings - 'as a matter of fact.'

Jaya asked if the clinic was nearby. It wouldn't hurt to make an inquiry, she thought. Aasi explained that it was some distance away and would require an auto rickshaw 'at very little expense.'

Jaya bit her lip. 'It's probably a 24-hour bug thing, like what you get eating at Taco Bell. That's an American fast-food...' Her voice trailed off as she thought of the potential health risks.

Aasi jumped in with, 'Bugs are worse in India, lady,' launching into a story about a Swiss traveler felled by a rare and life-threatening ameba. 'An ameba as long as a saree - the equivalent to nine yarns.'

Jaya tried to laugh but it turned into a groan. Pain ripped through her intestine, originating at her bellybutton, ending at her groin, and causing her to double over. She knew she ought to be in bed, but after hours of tossing and turning she'd given up.

'Someone told me to eat white rice and bananas...' She

pictured an Indian hospital. A shudder went through her body. 'No, definitely not,' she said.

'We take rickshaw and you ask doctor. He will fix your stomach, no problem.'

'I'm not going to the hospital, end of conversation.' Jaya softened the statement by adding, 'How are *you* feeling? Here I am rattling on about my own problems.'

Her mother had always been kind to the homeless. Even the guy with the *Spare Change for Beer* sign got a coin whenever they passed by. A down-and-out saxophone player, who lived in his camper van, got a dollar. Two if he was playing John Coltrane at the time. Single moms received a hot meal and a pep-talk. Then there was the man who made a peace symbol out of pennies. He let Jaya decide where to put the coin: along the big round circle or on one of the straight lines. Years and years and the peace symbol was never completed. When Jaya asked why this was, her mother answered, 'He drinks, poor man. But it's good to be kind nonetheless.'

Jaya said now: 'I should have asked how you were feeling sooner. Only a few hours ago you were sprawled out on the road.'

Aasi saw her chance and took it. Her body swayed back and forth. The thong of her sandal came loose, but she ignored it. She took shallow breaths, clutching her chest. The few words she spoke came out as an unintelligible groan.

Jaya bit her lower lip and looked in one direction and then the other. 'Do I call 911 for an ambulance or what?'

Aasi's face lit up and she made the mistake of clapping.

Jaya stepped closer. 'That was a fast recovery.' She wanted

to feel the girl's forehead but thought better of touching the dirty face. 'Hungry is what you look, malnourished,' she said, with as much pathos as she could muster.

'You have Oreo, lady?'

'Sorry, no Oreos. I *do* have a cough drop.' Jaya tried to laugh but immediately her throat caught. This whole trip was to honor the memory of a woman who might not have bought the kid Oreos, but a Cliff Bar to be sure, a whole box. Reaching back into her bag, Jaya pulled out the guidebook. 'There's a breakfast place I've been meaning to try. Why not come with me?' She flipped through the pages. 'They say you can eat off the floor.'

'Pick a different place, lady, a place with plates.'

'It's not meant to be taken literally, it's a metaphor. Anyway, we don't *have* to eat off the floor if we don't want to.' Jaya laughed again, this time pressing a hand to her stomach.

Aasi examined the guidebook. 'Your guidebook is outdated, wouldn't you agree? Old and useless rubbish.' She clicked her teeth. 'Maybe you buy the newest edition and when you leave, give to me. I'm knowing the bookstore with the wholesale prices. Many books to choose from: *Lonely Planet, Rough Guide, DK Eyewitness Travel Guide*, and the best called *100 Coolest Things to Do in India*.'

'You're good, I'll say that for you. You don't miss a beat.'

Jaya found the restaurant review. There were four stars beside it, written with a green ball-point pen. The same stars appeared on stories she'd written as a child, on report cards, and on sticky-notes hung on the kitchen cabinets, usually accompanied by Deepak Chopra quotes. She closed the guide, using a finger as a bookmark.

'Are you coming or not?' she said.

Aasi bobbed her head from side to side. 'Tell me the name of the restaurant first.'

'Everest Café. Are they still in business?'

Aasi's eyes widened. 'Everest Café is *Lonely Planet* top pick for omelets! Omelets have eggs mixed in, you know. At Everest Café you are guaranteed happy. Only—'

'What?'

'If the owner is there, he will chase us away.'

'Let him try,' said Jaya.

'After,' said Aasi, 'I take you shopping for new guidebook. Or proper fitting trouser, something with a drawstring.' She lifted her top, showing Jaya what she meant. 'Or how about wrist-watch or doorknob? Many kinds in ceramic, glass, brass, wood, even. Does your house in America have doors?'

Before Jaya could change her mind, Aasi began walking toward the restaurant. The street was coming to life. Merchants arranged their wares and vegetable sellers stacked apples and potatoes onto slanted crates. Jaya had trouble keeping up with the girls. 'Hey, slow down,' she shouted. Her stomach couldn't take jolting.

'Hurry,' said Aasi, 'Everest Café is opening!'

'You hurry when the restaurant is closing,' said Jaya. 'Not when it's opening.' When she stopped to catch her breath, Aasi and Kamika waved her forward. Jaya was tempted to give them money, make her excuses, and return to the guesthouse. Or better yet - to California. Why had her mother asked this of her? It was all wrong, wrong, wrong. India was like the birthday gifts:

a batik-covered journal, the crystal pendent wrapped in copper wire, a mud bath at Indian Springs in Calistoga. 'No more wacky clothes, no more scented candles,' she told herself now.

Voicing it aloud made her tearful again. She paused in front of a stall where a shopkeeper was placing wooden boxes on a shelf. Each was encrusted with mirrors and colored glass, faceted like jewels. One was shaped like an urn. A table displayed bangle bracelets. Similar bracelets had adorned her mother's arms, arms that had become so thin the bracelets slipped off one by one. One of Jaya's last acts was to sponge off the tarnish marks they had left.

'Pretty,' she said, and the shopkeeper smiled.

'Hurry! They will sell all the omelets!' said Aasi when Jaya reached the Everest.

'Then we'll order something else. Parathas, maybe.'

Aasi circled behind Jaya, pushing at her back. A tiny hand tugged at Jaya's fingers. Stepping down into the sunken restaurant, Aasi headed straight for the waiter, almost tackling him. She fired off in Hindi and he handed over three menus. 'This one can't read,' she told Jaya, shoving a menu into Kamika's hands, 'but loves pretending.'

Kamika dropped the menu on the floor, staring at Jaya with eyes too large for her head. They sat at a low table on wicker stools. The ceiling was afloat with Tibetan prayer flags, flapping in sync with an oscillating fan. Jaya positioned herself so that the breeze cooled her forehead. Psychedelic swirls were painted on the floor, but scruff marks lessen their power to hypnotize. Even so, Jaya's head spun.

'Special of the day is lemon cake,' said the waiter, proceeding to describe the cake, as well as a wife, four children, and a widowed mother-in-law, all living in Nepal. Jaya was too sleep deprived to make the connection. *Did his wife bake the cake? The mother-in-law?* The cake had poppy seeds, that's as much as she was able to grasp.

'Bring omelet for lady,' said Aasi. 'Chapatti and dal for her' - indicating Kamika - 'and same-same for me.'

'Don't you want the omelet?' asked Jaya. 'You were so excited a minute ago.'

'Next time. Can we have Coca-Cola? We are each needing own bottle.'

'Live it up.' Jaya handed back the menu. 'And change the omelet to black coffee. Or better yet, ginger tea. Do you have ginger tea?'

'I have two daughters, like you,' said the waiter. 'Eight and six years old. Both are in school while my wife works our fields. Your daughters go to school?'

'These aren't my kids,' said Jaya.

'Five years,' said Aasi, shoving Kamika with a finger.

Jaya asked the girls for their names, explaining that she had a terrible memory. Aasi pretended to wipe a tear from a dry eye. Melodrama seemed to be the girl's forte, thought Jaya. 'What's the matter,' she asked.

'I am Aasi. And her good name is Kamika. Both mothers are lost.'

Jaya didn't believe a word of it. The mothers, she suspected, were hovering in the alleyway. She pressed her bag to her lap, wrapping the strap around a wrist. She sighed and said to herself, 'The penny man will never complete the peace symbol.'

Aasi said, 'May I please see your passport? This is good for passing time.'

The waiter stood in place, listening in on the conversation. Jaya said, 'Do you mind getting our drinks?' and he dragged himself to a refrigerator.

'Straws,' said Aasi, loud enough for him to hear. Turning to Jaya, she asked again to see the passport. Jaya removed it from her concealed pouch, making sure to keep it securely in her grasp.

'Gravely,' said Aasi. 'Sounding like grave, or gravy. Both words I know, but not gravely. What is the meaning of this word? Is this American name?'

'Gravely is an English name, I think. And there's no such thing as an American name, unless it's Native American like Pocahontas or Hiawatha or some such.'

'*Poc-ah-ontas* - true.' Aasi, examined the passport more closely. 'Written here you are born in New York, which is one of fifty states.'

'I was. But we moved to California when I was five, so I have little memory of New York. When my mother was a teenager, she ran away from home and hitched across the country to California, where she lived in a hippie commune. The police eventually caught up with her and shipped her back to New York, but it was always her dream to return to California.'

'Police whack your mother with stick?' Aasi leaned down and rubbed her shin.

'In those days they blasted people with fire hoses. Although, I guess, that happened more in the Deep South than in—' The girl looked confused, Jaya realized, stopping herself mid-sentence.

The waiter returned to the table with their drinks. Jaya gulped down the tea, burning her tongue. Aasi examined the straws, making sure that they hadn't been previously used. Once satisfied, she put them into the bottles.

'Do you know Arizona,' she asked, 'one of the fifty states? My mother is from Arizona.'

Jaya raised an eyebrow. This must be the ramp-up to some sort of a scam, one Ed Rodgers had failed to mention. A new spin on the email scam: an emergency plea from a friend's email address, begging the recipient to wire money to a foreign bank account. Jaya remembered the $100 her mother had lost that way. She said, 'I've never been to Arizona, not once.'

'This is very sad, lady,' said Aasi. 'On a schoolroom map Arizona is touching California. Same as India touches Pakistan.'

'But I'm from Northern California, which is far from Arizona. As far as India is from...Athens.'

Just then, someone called out a greeting to the waiter. Jaya watched as a grey-haired man stepped down into the café. A red vest reached to his ribcage. Hanging to his waist was a string of orange beads. She had seen necklaces like this before. A friend of her mother's wore one. When she was a child she thought they were cheese puffs. Where did all these hippies come from? There were hardly any left in California. 'A dying breed,' she said to herself and sighed. Californians dressed like hipsters now. They resembled lumberjacks, in flannel shirts and work boots. The last outing with her mother had been to the Haight-Ashbury, where Jaya pushed a wheelchair from Masonic Avenue to Golden Gate Park. They hadn't seen a single hippie, which took the life out of Jaya's mother. The whole way home, she had to use the oxygen tube.

The man looked at Jaya and turned up his nose. 'What's your problem,' he said. 'Some sort of White Savior Complex?'

'Excuse me?' Jaya's pulse raced. Could he not see that she was half Indian?

'Leave 'em be, *chéri*. You're only interfering with samsara.'

'Ignore that man,' said Jaya, motioning for the girls to turn their heads away. Kamika began fussing. Jaya wished there were a can full of crayons, along with those kid-distracting coloring books they had at American chain restaurants.

The waiter was back, salaaming with clasped hands. 'Good-morning Baba-ji. I bring your special and maybe today you help write letter to children in Nepal?'

Jaya tried to tune out their conversation by focusing on Aasi. The girl was reading from a crumpled sheet of paper. Jaya had missed the opening lines.

'Start from the top,' she said.

Aasi flattened the pages against the table and began again.

The Snake Charmer

ONCE UPON A TIME, there was a snake charmer and her baby.

Snake charming was the family trade: the mother came from a caste of snake charmers. When her baby grew to be an adult, she would be a snake charmer, too.

People loved watching the snake dance to flute music. They crowded around, dropping coins into a dish. So long as the charmer played the flute, the rattlesnake behaved, but if she stopped playing there was trouble. Not once did the snake charmer pause from flute playing, fearing that the rattlesnake would bite someone in the audience, or worse, the baby.

The charmer took rests but never slept. She swallowed food without chewing. While squatting above the toilet, she continued to play the flute. If she stopped, even for a second, the snake climbed her leg inch-by-inch.

One day the baby became sick. The charmer ran to a chemist, hoping for a pill to save the child. The snake followed behind. While the charmer spoke with the chemist, the snake jumped up and sank its fangs into her neck.

And she fell to the ground dead.

Chapter Fifteen

JAYA STIFLED A YAWN. She pushed away the tea glass. 'That's a good story, a little morbid though. I mean - the way the snake charmer dies like that. Don't most fairy tales have happy endings?'

Aasi opened the pages and scanned the two last paragraphs. The American was right. It would be better if the snake charmer were to escape death, and if the snake were to die instead. She had a memory of having written a different ending. This ending, she seemed to remember, was Miss Elizabeth's idea and not her own.

It was the last story Aasi had written before the school closed for good. At the time, Miss Elizabeth was trying to persuade Aasi to enter a girl's home in South India. She said, 'It's a healthy environment, in Kerela. Nicely situated on a hilltop with a lovely view of tea plantations. There are twelve other girls in attendance, several your own age. And the headmistress is a dear friend of mine, a native of Kerela. I've told her all about you, how promising a student you are. It's not a day school like this one, but a residential school. You'd have your own bed and three square meals a day. It will be like having a family.'

But Aasi had no intention of leaving Paharganj. This was where foreigners preferred to stay when they landed in India, and this was the hub to which they returned when the season changed from wet to dry, and when they moved from North India to south. Trains were continually arriving to the New Delhi railway station from Rajasthan, Varanasi, the Punjab, Goa, even from Kerela. There were hundreds of guesthouses, each room filled by a Westerner. It was only a matter of time before she found her mother. This certainty kept her alive, like food. Without it she would starve.

When she refused Miss Elizabeth's invitation, the teacher said, 'You'd be better to focus on your studies than on this ludicrous idea of finding your mother.'

A few days later, she returned the story to Aasi. It was marked in red pen, correcting spelling and grammatical errors. As usual, whole sentences were reworked. But for the first time, Miss Elizabeth had written a new ending.

Jaya winked conspiratorially. 'Let me guess. Your mother was the snake charmer in the story and *you* were the baby.' Then she laughed.

Aasi kicked the table pedestal. The soda bottles rocked like bowling pins. The tea glass tipped over and rolled to the edge of the table, but Jaya managed to catch it in time. She picked pieces of ginger root from her lap. The waiter rushed over with a towel.

'This is not my mother. This mother is dead!' yelled Aasi.

By now every table in the café was occupied. Books and smartphones were lowered as people turned toward the out-burst. Aasi was silent after that.

Jaya whispered an apology just as the food was delivered.

'Do you believe me - that my mother is living?' asked Aasi.

Kamika bobbed her head, willing Jaya to answer yes.

Jaya knew better than to argue. 'Sure, I believe you. Now eat up before your food gets cold.'

Aasi regretted having wasted the story - and so much time - on this American, who had done nothing to help her get to Edward Rodgers. Had she begun walking toward the clinic immediately, they might have arrived by now. They could have rested whenever Kamika tired. Aasi might have tried carrying the girl on her back.

Aasi said, 'Package, please,' but the waiter was busy taking another order.

'You're leaving me?' said Jaya miserably. Her eyes were cast down to the floor, which began swimming under her. Aasi was trying to say something, but the words sounded as if they were coming through a warped speaker. 'Water,' Jaya managed to say. Through her blurred vision she saw Aasi reach for the Sigg bottle.

Aasi shouted: 'Package!' then, 'Make way for sick lady!'

'You're leaving me?' said Jaya, fighting the urge to grab Aasi's hand.

Suddenly, the cafe seemed as if it had been submerged in deep water. Only the sound of chairs scraping against the floor and a voice saying, 'Is she alright?' kept Jaya at the brink of consciousness. For a moment, it felt as if her feet had left the ground. When she next opened her eyes, she found herself seated in an auto rickshaw.

Someone said, 'East Meets West Clinic. Delhi Cantonment.'

Jaya's bag was pressed into her lap. She wondered if she was hallucinating when she heard her mother say, 'Hold tight to your bag so that no one steals.'

She was glad that her mother had taken charge again.

Aasi cried, 'Go faster!' pointing to a gap between two lorries. They drove along the rim of the road, competing with bicycles and push carts. She offered a prayer to the goddess occupying the dashboard: Parvati adorned with tinsel. Leaning over the seat, she said, 'How is lady holding?'

'Dizzy and thirsty,' said Jaya. 'My water bottle! I think I left it back at the restaurant.'

'No worries, lady. Clinic will attach water hose to your blood vein. A Dutch lady showed me the mark on her hand after leaving this clinic. Before she was so thirsty. After, she need to use toilet constantly.'

'I think you mean intravenous, not hose.' Jaya tried to sit up, but the rocking motion of the rickshaw made her head spin again and she leaned back against the seat.

'I remember now, "intravenous," ' said Aasi. 'This is what Dutch lady said. We saying *nason mein* in my language.'

Whenever the driver slowed, Aasi yelled at him in Hindi. This seemed to work and he accelerated, veering around potholes and pedestrians. They hit a speed bump and Jaya's head slammed into the canvas top.

'Are we almost there?' she asked.

'Halfway,' said Aasi, who was seated upfront. On the edge of the driver's seat with Kamika on her lap.

Jaya's hair was wet with sweat and her clothes were soaked through. Aasi reached behind the partition and fanned Jaya's face using her small hand. 'Better?' she asked. 'You have malaria or Japanese Encephalitis, as a matter of fact. I knowing a Danish lady who expired from this. You use mosquito net? There is a shop with good selection. All colors and prices. They'll make a deal for you.'

'We should have waited for an air-conditioned taxi,' said Jaya when the rickshaw came to a stop at a traffic signal.

Aasi's attention was focused on keeping the rickshaw out of congested traffic. The driver needed constant prodding. They circled the statue of Baba Gandhi, leading the people on a march to the sea, and Aasi knew that they were nearing the clinic. As soon as they saw the gates, the driver announced the fare. By the time they had come to a stop, Aasi had halved it.

Jaya ripped the hidden purse from her waist, dropping it onto the seat beside her. Aasi reached over and picked it up with shaking hands.

'Find him the right amount,' said Jaya.

Aasi opened the purse and let out a gasp. It was full of new and crisp rupees. 'Lady, you watch so later you don't say I steal.' She pulled out a 500-rupee note and then shoved the wallet into Jaya's bag. The rickshaw driver looked on hungrily but Aasi crumpled the note into her hand.

'*Namaste*,' said a security guard, checking each occupant in the rickshaw. He opened the gate and waved them through. The rickshaw sped up an incline to the main building. They passed gardeners, pulling weeds and trimming bushes. The driver tooted the horn at a peacock, sunning itself in the middle of the narrow path. It hissed and opened its feathers. They drove under a canopy of mimosa. Aasi was relieved to find that the temperature had dropped.

'Good place to recover energy inside,' she told Jaya.

Chapter Sixteen

AT THE TOP OF THE HILL A white mansion came into view: tall columns and a veranda with wicker reclining chairs. Aasi's one wish was to be allowed inside. She closed her eyes and imagined her mother waiting to welcome her. But when she opened her eyes again all she saw was a nurse dressed in white, stepping out from behind a double door.

The nurse barked a command and an orderly rushed to help Jaya from the rickshaw. He returned a minute later with a wheelchair. Jaya was dumped into the seat and whooshed up a set of plank boards.

The nurse looked at Aasi and said, 'You must wait outside.' To the security guard, she said, 'Let the children wait in the garden,' pointing to a bench.

Aasi heard water trickling from a fountain into a pool. Around the stone edges birds drank, sang, and splashed. 'As you wish,' she said, taking Kamika's hand.

There was no sign of Edward Rodgers. Aasi scanned the grounds, afraid that she'd see a freshly dug grave, but found none. Westerners preferred burial over cremation, she knew. She hoped this meant that he had survived.

Meanwhile the driver had pulled the rickshaw beside her, keeping his eye on the crumpled rupee note in her hand.

'What?' she said, trying to convince him that he had already received his fare. The argument was settled when the driver reached for the note, tearing it in two. Aasi looked at the small piece that remained in her hand. Seeing that it was useless, she threw it at the driver. He spat on the ground and shoved the torn pieces into his pocket. Then he pushed the rickshaw in a circle until it faced downhill.

The driver mounted his seat and popped the clutch. It was only then that Aasi remembered having placed her bag on the storage ledge. She reached for it as the engine choked to life and the rickshaw jerked forward, the back tire rolling over her toe. She tried to think of an appropriate curse, but the pain was overwhelming and she gave up.

'Foot is paining. Oh, so badly,' she told Kamika, planting herself on the bench. Blood pooled under the nail and her foot throbbed. After a deep breath, she took in the surroundings.

The peacock waddled up, letting out an eardrum-splitting cry. It closed its feathers and let them rest along the ground. Aasi found the food package in her bag, leftover rice and dal. She threw grains of rice at the peacock and it lurched out with its beak. Birds darted from trees and fought for the stray grains. Kamika shimmied alongside and reached her hands into the package.

'This is an auspicious day, Kamika,' said Aasi, even though the pain in her big toe was growing worse. Kamika grinned back with rice stuck between her teeth. Aasi's eyes drifted closed and before long she was dreaming. For once her dream wasn't much different than the world around her.

✳

The nurse shook Aasi awake. She had grey hair tied sloppily into a bun. Aasi was about to recommend a place where henna was sold, but the nurse rushed in with, 'Your friend will be fine. Nothing we don't see every day.' She removed a pack of cigarettes from her uniform pocket. Aasi made room for her on the bench.

'She will live - the American lady?'

'She needs rehydration and rest, is all,' said the nurse.

'Are you British?' The nurse reminded Aasi of Miss Elizabeth, the missionary teacher.

'Irish,' said the nurse, after blowing smoke from the side of her mouth. She laughed. 'I quit years ago, I did. This is a wee taste.'

Together they watched a bird dive into the pool. It was only then that Aasi noticed the fish swimming in and out of the reeds. She was about to throw a few grains of rice into the pool when the nurse stopped her. 'They eat algae, not rice,' she said. Out of the corner of her eye Aasi saw the gardener approach, waving his hands franticly.

'It's all right, Raj!' said the nurse, and the gardener went back to pulling weeds. 'He's very protective of his fish, you know. They've each got a name.' She stared into the distance, with the smoking cigarette held close to her mouth. 'I got my start at an orphanage in Sri Lanka. Mind you, this was when we still called it Ceylon, like the tea. Still got a soft spot for orphans, I do.' She made a fist, touching it to her chest as if that was where the soft spot was located.

'I'm not an orphan,' said Aasi. 'My mother is lost.'

'I've heard that one before.' The nurse shook her head, at

the same time crushing the cigarette with the heel of her white orthopedic shoe. Speaking her thoughts aloud, she said, 'Everyone's got a story.'

'I work for the American lady,' said Aasi, hoping to be allowed to stay.

'Good thing. She'll need help. Runs to the chemist, help with meals, of course. But you'd better walk the straight and narrow. I'm a proponent of discipline and order. And I've got eyes at the back of my head, remember.' She tapped her hair bun. 'Nurse Mary-Louise Patel, that's my name. My husband is the chief physician. First sign of trouble and we'll send you out on your ear.'

Aasi pressed her palms together. 'I will be a faithful and loyal servant, honest, and hard-working.'

'Maybe a day or two, at most. Nothing a little saline solution can't cure.'

'*Mata-ji*,' said Kamika, her eyes fixed on the nurse.

The nurse responded by pinching the girl's cheek.

'Will there be a salary?' asked Aasi.

'You'll have to take that up with your employer. Now follow me.' She stood and reached out for Kamika's hand. Aasi was surprised to see the girl go along willingly. She followed behind, asking if they would be allowed to sleep on the bench beside the fountain. The sound of running water would lull the girls to sleep.

'We'll see about that,' answered the nurse. 'We might even do you one better. But first things first. The two of you need a scrubbing before you step anywhere near my patients.'

They walked to an outbuilding, which served as a staff

changing room. After examining the girls' hair for lice, the nurse pulled back a curtain, revealing a water sprocket piped high on the wall. She took a whiff and said, 'Smells a bit like a terrarium.' There was a bar of soap on the floor, which she handed to Aasi. Then she went to a laundry bin filled with crumbled uniforms, lifting a green nurse's uniform and holding it to Aasi's front. 'That will suit. Your old clothes will go into the incinerator.'

'No!' cried Aasi, thinking that she'd be a laughingstock back in Paharganj. The green dress was the ugliest thing she had ever seen, styled in the Western fashion.

'Everyone will think you're a nurse trainee,' said the nurse. 'People have tremendous respect for our profession.'

Aasi had begun to panic. The uniform smelled of sweat and disinfectant. She backed into the wall trying to avoid it.

'Stop fussing now,' said the nurse, grabbing the hem of Aasi's top. 'I'm not putting *you* in the incinerator.'

'Smells bad!' cried Aasi. 'Smells like pyre dogs.'

A tug-of-war ensued and the seams of Aasi's top torn open in the process. Once she had succeeded in removing it, the nurse held the garment above her head and out of Aasi's reach, saying, 'Our hospital has a reputation for being immaculately clean, spotless in fact. And I'll not have anyone - and *definitely* not a street urchin - bring ill-repute upon our professionalism.' She puffed out her chest before adding, 'I'll have it known that we launder daily, using boiling water.'

Aasi let out a mournful wail.

'For Pete's sake, I'm not putting *you* in boiling water!' said the nurse. 'Stop with the dramatics right now or you'll be out on the street.' She tapped a foot. 'Your choice.'

'Don't look,' said Aasi, clutching her bare chest.

Nurse Mary-Louise covered her eyes as the girl began removing her pajama bottoms, first untying the string at the waist and then working an ankle-tight hem over her dirt- incrusted heel. Glancing through her fingers, the nurse spoke her thought aloud, 'She *might* actually be older than I'd thought.' She watched as Aasi hid the bottoms behind a barrel. 'You best wash your hair,' she barked, 'and your privates, too.'

Aasi yanked the shower curtain closed. When the water touched her body, she screamed in agony.

The nurse found Kamika sitting outside on a rock. 'You're next up,' she said, this time in unaccented Hindi. She lifted a tattered top over Kamika's head, pinching her nose with the free hand. Kamika sniffed under both armpits and giggled. The nurse fished around in the laundry bin for another uniform, settling on scrubs and a sash. 'We'll have to take a scissor to the hem, but this should do.' She handed the girl a washcloth. Kamika looked at it not knowing what it was.

Aasi shouted, 'Soap is stinging eyes!'

'Let this little one join you,' said the nurse, gently pushing Kamika into the shower stall. Stepping over to the laundry bin, she pulled the pajama bottoms from where they had been hidden.

After the shower, the girls began searching for Edward Rodgers.

In the first room they found a middle-aged Norwegian, who explained that he was recovering from a vasectomy. In the next room they met an American boy with a compound fracture. He was happy to describe the break - the way the bone had pierced through his flesh, jutting out just below the knee. He asked if the girls wanted to sign the cast, handing Aasi a black marker. She wrote her name just as Miss Elizabeth had taught her to, with a swirly capital followed by its lowercase counterparts. She guided Kamika's hand as it formed her name in Hindi कामिका .

Before leaving the boy, Aasi asked if his mother, by any chance, had a rattlesnake tattooed on her leg.

A staircase led to the roof, where the girls had a bird's-eye view of the grounds. 'Only gardeners and a delivery boy,' said Aasi. Kamika kept tripping on the hem of her scrubs. Aasi stopped to tuck the fabric into the belt, tightening it until she got to the last notch and Kamika began whimpering. They searched for their old clothes, but to no avail.

In the room at the end of the corridor lay a woman who had just come out of surgery. 'Acute appendicitis,' said Nurse Mary-Louise Patel in a whisper. She held up a jar, showing the girls the organ that had been removed. Aasi said, '*Ungalee*,' meaning finger, and the nurse corrected her, ushering them from the room. The patient, she explained, had not yet come out of anesthesia and should under no circumstances be disturbed.

There were five rooms remaining. Jaya slept in one, two were vacant, and they were told to stay away from the fourth. 'This patient took LSD,' said the orderly, 'and has lost her mind!'

The last room was locked from the inside. Aasi tried to peek through the keyhole but someone had stuffed it with cotton gauze.

'I have lost my 50%,' she told Kamika. 'My fortune is no more.'

Chapter Seventeen

JAYA WAS HOOKED UP TO an intravenous bag, lying on a narrow bed with the sheets wrapping her torso to the mattress. Her face had taken on the appearance of a Grecian theatre mask: white and waxy. At least, this is how it looked viewed through a mosquito net. A mirror hung from the opposite wall, mottled with age. The whole scene brought back memories of her mother's last days, after they'd moved her to a hospice facility.

She watched as a nurse filled a pitcher from a plastic water bottle. The cuffs on her uniform were frayed, but clean and starched. The nurse examined a glass in the dust-speckled light and pronounced it clean. 'One really can't be *too* sure,' she said, satisfied. After that she tucked in the edges of the mosquito net.

As soon as the nurse left the room, Jaya reached under the net, going for the pitcher.

The room resembled a library, although the shelves were empty of books. The walls were paneled, with decades of high-gloss varnish. Plaster laurel branches decorated the ceiling. 'No,' thought Jaya, taking a deep breath. 'It isn't anything like the hospice.' The lingering memory made her sad. She heard the oncologist's voice, *It's like home, isn't it?* When the hospice wasn't in the least like the geodesic dome.

It was during these last days that her mother asked that her ashes be scattered on the Ganges River. 'It will be my last gift to you, Jaya,' she had said. 'Or a parting shot, however you choose to look at it. I worry that you'll end up a recluse, holed up in the geodesic dome without a friend in the world, getting fat on Häagen-Dazs and Twinkies, working remotely, your only human contact via cyberspace. A modern-day Miss Havisham; J.D. Salinger without ever having written the Great American Novel. Promise me you'll go to India, promise me on my death-bed.'

Jaya sighed and tried to focus on the present. Beside the bed sat a Bakelite telephone, like something in a 50s film. She picked up the receiver and a woman's voice said, 'Hello, may I help you?' After mumbling an apology, Jaya hung up. A minute later, an orderly ran into the room asking if she needed assistance.

'My mistake,' said Jaya.

He backed out slowly, expecting Jaya to change her mind.

She sat up in the bed, trying to sort out her feelings. This setback would mean that she'd have to change her return flight. For a moment she was panic-stricken, certain that the ticket was non-changeable and non-refundable. Then she relaxed, remembering that she'd purchased the add-on insurance for such an event as this. She leaned into the pillows, thinking how pleasant the starchy smell was. Everything around her was clean: white enamel freshly painted over the chipped bed frame, sheets bleached and ironed crisp. She'd have to contact the neighbor back in California and ask him to continue watering the plants. Other than that, there wasn't anything Jaya needed to do.

She was enjoying herself, if the truth be told. When she'd first entered the hospital, a swarm of nurses surrounded her wheelchair. And even though they spoke a language she couldn't understand, Jaya felt sympathy in every syllable.

'It's so quiet here,' she whispered, as if she'd wake someone in the next room. Enveloped in a white mosquito net, she felt as if she were in a womb. 'So much quieter than Paharganj, almost *too* quiet.'

Out of instinct, she reached for the remote control and surfed channels until she found a music video station. A sick room didn't seem complete without a *little* background noise. She couldn't see the screen without adjusting the net, but that wasn't why she had turned on the television. Her mother had never been able to fall asleep without music playing. In the end, Jaya had been the one to find the requested CD and adjust the volume.

Aasi pressed a finger to Jaya's neck vein, and said, 'Only sleeping, not expired.' She looked around the room. 'Too plain. Boss will recover rapidly in a pretty room.' This is why people died in government hospitals, or so she surmised: grey walls without decoration. She told Kamika, 'I was once a patient after being hit by an Ambassador car, the heaviest of all taxis. Unconscious for many days and all because of grey walls.'

It was the thing she loved about Paharganj. The Main Bazaar was full of color, with shops displaying tapestries and spices, sarees and flowers. Why, there was one shop that sold mosquito nets in every color of the rainbow... if only this American lady had known. And during the festival of Holi, when everyone threw brightly colored powder at each other, one merchant let Aasi take a handful for free, a reward for recommending his shop. Last year she had chosen pink, the year before blue.

'Flowers are needed,' said Aasi. 'For both color and smell.'

'Have as many of these as you like,' said the gardener, laughing. He pulled a dandelion from the lawn. He even provided a jar.

They found a marble bust, covered with leaves, and dragged it to a tap. Aasi made Kamika scrub until the stone was free of dirt. An ear was broken off and part of a crown as well. Aasi noticed an inscription at the base of the statue: 'George VI,' she said, pronouncing the Roman numerals as letters. Together they made a chain of dandelions to place around the neck. They carried the statue to Jaya's room, with the gardener bearing the brunt of the weight.

'He will protect the American from evil spirits, intent on snatching her soul,' Aasi told the gardener. He looked at the statue in awe.

After a few more additions, she was satisfied. 'The room is looking first-class. The patient will recover nicely.'

Only once did Nurse Mary-Louise peek her head in, requesting that they quiet down. She returned a few minutes later to strap a belt to Jaya's limp arm, explaining that this was how to read blood pressure. 'A little low,' she pronounced, 'but not dangerously so.'

Aasi washed Jaya's brow with cooling water. She taught Kamika how to tuck the edges of the mosquito net under the mattress. Then it was time to fetch meals, in case the patient woke hungry. 'We'll use money from the purse,' said Aasi, matter-of-factly, but she didn't want to be accused of stealing. 'Best we ask for receipts,' she added.

The guard stationed at the front gate recommended a clean restaurant, one safe for a Westerner's weak stomach. 'No one has gotten sick eating there. There are no complaints. Even the doctor eats at that dhaba stall, it is so clean.'

He directed the girls to a dhaba stall around the corner and they trotted off, making sure to lift the hems of their uniforms from the ground. Aasi walked lopsided, trying to keep pressure off her left foot. After being told there were no omelets, she picked samosa, dal, and chapatti. The proprietor filled a box with white rice and invited them to sit at a table. Aasi was amazed at the difference a change of clothes made; before, he might not have served them.

'We must hurry back to boss. Very important work to do,' she said.

Along the way, they bought bottles of Thums Up and aspirin tablets wrapped in silver foil. Aasi bought a package of Himalaya throat lozenges, knowing how much Westerners liked this brand.

Jaya woke when they returned to the room.

'How are you feeling?' asked Aasi. 'Hungry?'

'Famished,' said Jaya. 'Like I could eat a cow.'

'Not in India. The cow is sacred.'

'Whatever you have. Crank me up, would you?'

The bed had a handle on the side and Aasi exhausted her strength turning it. 'This is an excellent bed,' she said. She filled a water glass and lifted it to Jaya's mouth.

'Who are you, anyway?' asked Jaya. 'Aren't you those girls

from Paharganj?'

'Save your energy, lady. Trust you are in good hands.'

'Oh, I remember now. It's just that you look different some-how...'

'New suit.' Aasi wrinkled her nose and picked at the front of her dress. 'Ugly, wouldn't you agree?' She reached over and put a hand on Jaya's forehead, as she'd seen the nurse do. 'I think you are suffering. Yes, I am 100% sure.'

Trying to keep from giggling, Jaya said, 'Are you a doctor now? You look awfully young to be a doctor.'

'Save your breath, lady. Shake head yes or no. I understand American head shaking.' Aasi's head wobbled left to right, repeating the action with her interpretation of the American counterpart: forward and backward. 'Do you want something to eat?'

She opened the packages one by one, and the room filled with the smell of coriander, cinnamon, and curry. Kamika was ordered to fetch a plate and fork. She returned out of breath, carrying a plastic tray with all sorts of utensils and bowls, including a butcher's knife.

A young nurse came back to take Jaya's blood pressure, pushing the girls aside.

'Blood has increased,' said Aasi, 'due to excellent care.'

The nurse took note of the decorations and proclaimed the room cheerful, but mentioned that the calendar they had nailed above Jaya's side table was for the wrong year. '2002,' she said before leaving, '—although such a nice photograph of Munnar!'

Aasi filled a bowl with rice and dal, rolling two chapattis and placing them on top. She draped a towel on Jaya's lap. 'I will feed you. Open your mouth.'

'Aren't you going to eat, too?'

'A servant eats after her boss.'

'Are you my servant? I'm so confused.'

Aasi took the opportunity to tell Jaya about Indian hospitals.

'You mean to say they won't provide meals?' asked Jaya.

'Never. A servant is needed to fetch bandages and medicines from the chemist. If something is removed' - Aasi let her hand waver over Jaya's torso - 'the servant will find a pickle jar to put it in.'

Jaya knitted her eyebrows. 'You mean the appendix?'

'Yes, appendix. This needing special jar. I know the best shop. I will make you comfortable. Fluff pillows, chase away mosquitos and flies. You need help, I will run for doctor. You want more water, lady?'

'They don't have a staff to do this?'

'No, boss.'

Jaya considered her options. In the short time she'd been in India, nothing even remotely resembled the world she had always known. She'd heard India described as 'Third World,' and had taken this to mean poor and underdeveloped. Now she wondered if the term was a metaphor meaning a *totally different world*. A world apart, one with its own norms and values. And hospital policies. She remembered a quote from Margaret Mead she'd used in her thesis: 'Anthropology demands the open-mindedness with which one must look and listen, record in astonishment and wonder that which one would not have been able to guess.'

Maybe the girl was telling her the truth. It made about as much sense as anything else she'd encountered in the past two days.

Aasi interrupted her thoughts, saying, 'If you not believing me, ask the head sister. The grey hair one. She will tell you.'

The girl was convincing. And, more importantly, familiar, unlike anything else in her surroundings. Jaya said, 'Well, maybe you're right. I'll probably need someone to run errands. But I won't be having surgery, not in India anyway. I've got travel insurance. If this were something serious like appendicitis - which I doubt - they'd medevac me to Tokyo.' She chewed on her bottom lip. 'Tokyo or Bangkok, I have to look again at the contract. But even if I *did* have an organ removed' - she laughed nervously - 'I certainly wouldn't want to save it.'

She put her chin in her hands, with her elbows resting on her raised knees. 'Okay, I'm obviously in over my head here, and it's possible that you've saved my life with your quick action.'

Aasi bowed. 'I will be faithful, loyal, honest, hard-working, clean and—' She tried to think of a few more adjectives.

'It's not a permanent job, you realize. I'm flying home in a week.'

'I will work as long as needed. After this I go back to Paharganj.'

Jaya tried to eat a few bites. 'I think my stomach has shrunk, I swear.'

'Should we consult with doctor?' Aasi's head bobbed knowingly. 'Shrunk stomach is meaning imminent death.'

Without answering, Jaya fell asleep. Aasi cranked the bed

flat and made sure that the sheets were tucked around Jaya's arms and chest, and that the mosquito net was in place. Her only regret was that she hadn't broached the subject of a salary.

The girls sat cross-legged on the floor and ate their second meal of the day. 'This is where we will sleep,' said Aasi, knocking her knuckles against the hardwood floor. 'In case the patient wakes in the night needing help. We will take turns sleeping.'

'*Accha*,' said Kamika, wide-eyed.

'You are talking well,' said Aasi. 'Before long you will be making sentences.'

They swept rice from the floor and tidied the room until there wasn't a speck of dust. They chased away spiders after destroying the webs, and caught mosquitos as they worked their way through the net. Aasi took the dirty bowls to the kitchen, where a woman volunteered to wash and return them to the shelf, first offering apples from a bowl.

Kamika had already stretched out on the floor. Aasi sat in an armchair and kept her eyes on Jaya, making sure that she breathed. A television was mounted to the wall, almost near the ceiling, and she examined the remote control. After a few false starts, she had the television switched on and the volume turned to the lowest bar. Skipping through channels, she stopped on a cartoon. In this way, she passed the hours happily. Hopefully the American wouldn't recover *too* quickly. She almost regretted having made the room so pleasant.

A nurse returned hourly to check blood pressure and temperature. Aasi offered to do it herself, but the nurse explained that the skill required matriculation at a technical college, naming the one she had attended.

Aasi knew what the nurse was thinking. It was true. She knew nothing but reading and writing. The school she'd attended wasn't at all technical, unless she counted the headmistress's laptop which was kept locked in a cabinet. Miss Elizabeth taught using textbooks, spiral notebooks, lead pencils, and crayons. And never eBooks, although many of the Westerners had switched to the device. Miss Elizabeth had a shelf full of books, all with aged pages, by the writers Elizabeth Gaskell, Wilkie Collins, and Anthony Trollope. 'God forbid,' Miss Elizabeth would say whenever Aasi suggested they read *Twilight*, *Karma Cola*, or *Shanteram*.

Aasi knew that she'd never be allowed to touch the blood pressure monitor or the digital thermometer. The nurse exited the room with her nose in the air, carrying both instruments in her front pockets.

Chapter Eighteen

EARLY THE NEXT MORNING, Jaya woke to the cry of a squawking peacock. Her throat was parched and she had trouble swallowing. Sitting up in the bed, she pushed the mosquito net aside and blinked. 'Where am I?' she asked herself, coming up blank. She felt a tug on her hand and noticed that it was wrapped in surgical tape, attached to a tube that snaked its way to an IV bag. She rose from the bed, grasping onto the stand and wheeling it around in a circle. By then, she had begun remembering. Her stomach, she was pleased to find, had stopped doing cartwheels. Jumping jacks but not cartwheels.

Aasi was asleep in a vinyl covered armchair. Jaya looked around the room for Kamika and found her circled up under the bed.

The pitcher was empty and she went in search of water. She heard clanging noises that reminded her of college cafeterias and walked in that direction. There she found a woman flinging a pail of dirty water out an open door.

The kitchen made Jaya suspicious. 'Excuse me,' she said, 'but is it true that the hospital doesn't provide meals for its patients?' The woman turned her head and stared at Jaya with vacant eyes. Jaya pointed to the stove, but the woman had lost interest.

'Water?' said Jaya. She remembered the Hindi equivalent, '*Pani.*'

The woman pressed a button on a water filter mounted above the sink. A yellow light came on and the machine began beeping. The woman continued picking bugs from a pile of leafy vegetables. Soon water was spouting into the sink.

'*Pani,*' said Jaya again, accompanying the word with a rasping gasp.

The woman reached for a cup.

It was hot in the corridor and Jaya thought it might be cooler on the veranda. Another patient sat in an armchair reading. Jaya trembled when the girl grinned. Her mind flashed to a scene from *One Flew Over the Cuckoo's Nest*. The girl was reading a blank journal and there didn't appear to be a pen in sight.

'Excuse me for disturbing you,' said Jaya, adding under her breath, 'not that *I'm* disturbing you, but something sure is!' Without waiting for a reply, she darted back into the building, pulling the IV stand behind her.

A man wearing a white doctor's coat, a stethoscope wrapped around his neck, walked toward Jaya with his eyes on his smartphone. Two steps before bumping into her, he looked up.

'Pardon,' he said.

'Are you the doctor?' asked Jaya.

'Dr. Vikram Patel.' He reached out a hand. 'How may I help you?' He stared into Jaya's pupils, checking to see that they were dilating properly. His fingers moved from Jaya's palm to the pulse on her wrist.

'I'm feeling much better,' she said. 'I'm on a tight schedule, with a flight home in a week and lots to do beforehand. So maybe someone can take this IV out?' She looked at her hand and felt queasy. She'd always been a wimp when it came to needles.

'I think you'd best stay another day,' he said. 'Dehydration is quite dangerous, life threatening in some cases.'

'Is it? Life threatening?'

'Quite.'

She began to feel dizzy but decided against telling him.

'Come into my office,' he said, and Jaya followed him down the hallway to a room at the end of the corridor. It was crammed with bookcases, floor to ceiling. Books were stuffed into the shelves at odd angles, along with papers, envelopes, and dirty coffee mugs. An antique table was placed below a multi-paned window; the window glass was ancient, distorting the view of the garden. Jaya noticed a Ganesh statue enclosed in glass, with strings of fresh marigolds hung over the case. The flowers, along with incense sticks, lent the office a spicy aroma. Dr. Patel invited Jaya to take the swivel chair on the visitor's side of his desk. A laptop computer seemed to be the only nod to modernity.

'Nice office,' said Jaya, examining a wall of framed diplomas. 'John Hopkins Medical School. But you're from here, aren't you?'

'Born and raised,' he said. 'Although I was educated in the States and practiced in the D.C. area for several years before returning home. McLean, Virginia, to be exact. Oh, how I miss the Smithsonian. But not the winters.' He lifted a crystal ashtray filled with little candies and caraway seeds, the kind Indian restaurants provided near the cash register. Jaya took a pinch to be polite; the mixture tasted of sugared anise.

'Thank you,' said Jaya. 'Actually, that's one of the reasons my mother moved us from New York to California - the winters. She died recently of breast cancer. Two weeks ago. Right before she died, she begged me to have my breasts removed. My grandmother died of breast cancer, too. I guess my chances are astronomically high.'

'Are you asking for a referral?'

'I mean, it seems pretty extreme, don't you think?' She cradled both breasts, feeling their heft. The idea of losing them brought tears to her eyes.

'Let's concentrate on getting you better,' said the doctor. 'You're young. Take time with your decision. When you get home, make an appointment with a good oncologist. And in the meantime, why not do a daily self-examination? It will put your mind at rest.' A nod of his head and Jaya began to relax.

'I'm lucky to have found you,' she said.

'Indeed you are.'

'I've been meaning to ask, only I haven't wanted to be rude...but what exactly do your head movements mean - yes, or no?'

'Yes *and* no. Plus, maybe. Stay in India long enough and you'll get the hang of it. It took my wife years to finally under-stand.'

'Your wife isn't from India?'

'Ireland. Although she's been practicing in India nearly as long as I have. She first volunteered with Mother Teresa. In fact, somewhere here we have the cross of St. Brigid, Ireland's patron saint of healing.' He rummaged around until he found a small cross made of woven reeds. 'I don't know how it ended up in the vase. It really ought to be hung on the wall.'

'Are most of the nurses nuns? I noticed that they call themselves sisters.'

Dr. Patel rocked his head. 'No, not in the religious sense. The term is left over from the period when many nurses were in fact nuns. Most of our staff are Hindu. With the exception of my wife, of course. She has remained a Catholic due to her great esteem for Mother Teresa, and more recently for Pope Francis.'

Jaya yawned involuntarily. 'Oh, my. I'm so sorry. I'm still tired, even after sleeping for the first time in days.'

Dr. Patel reached behind him, to a Victorian era roll-top desk with pigeon-holes, where he found a prescription pad. He scribbled and said, 'This will help. There's a pharmacy around the corner. Left out the front gates.'

'Thank you,' she said, looking for a pocket. She couldn't remember when she had gotten into the hospital gown. The prescription was made out for five milligram Diazepam tablets. Maybe I've lost weight, she thought hopefully, given that the doctor judged her to be a five-milligram body rather than a ten.

'One tablet about half-an-hour before bedtime,' he said.

'Then, it's true - patients need to buy their own medicine and meals? That's what someone told me. But maybe I'm being taken for a fool. It wouldn't be the first time.'

'What you've heard is correct,' he said. 'Although when there is no family or friends present, one may employ a boy to run errands for a small sum. I realize this isn't the custom in the States, but it works quite well here in India.'

'Does it?'

'In the United States, patients routinely complain about hospital food. Especially about Jell-O and boiled chicken livers. Here, we never have that problem. You may eat whatever you wish, so long as it's not too spicy.' He tapped the edge of the desk. 'For now, broths will be best. Vegetable broths would serve nicely. Maybe a few chapatti. Limited oil. Tell the shop - limited oil. Ghee is too heavy for amebic dysentery patients.'

Jaya's jaw dropped.

'We did a stool analysis and the results were conclusive.'

'I don't remember giving a stool sample.'

'We managed. Are you still being troubled by diarrhea?'

Jaya blushed. 'Is this normal? I mean the runs...constantly?'

'Quite normal. We have you on an antibiotic. It should do the trick.' He sucked in his lips and added, 'No curds for the time being, and *absolutely* no fruits. And no alco—'

'I've taken the liberty of hiring someone to run errands.'

'Ah, very wise. That way there will be no waiting. Already we have several patients who have no one to help.'

'That would describe me exactly, the last in my family line. I asked because, well, I don't want to interfere with the proper running of the hospital.'

'That won't be possible. This hospital is a well-oiled machine. Did you know that we are approved by American insurance carriers? Blue Cross/Blue Shield, United Healthcare, *Cigna*, even.' He smiled proudly. 'Had you gone to a government hospital, your carrier would have most assuredly rejected the claim.' He rifled through an oak file cabinet and handed over a three-fold brochure, first pointing out the clinic's website address.

'Your hospital came highly recommended,' said Jaya.

'By whom?' He leaned in, waiting for Jaya to formulate an answer.

'By my caretaker,' she said, thinking that the word servant, which Aasi had used to describe her role, might sound a bit patronizing coming from her lips.

Dr. Patel glanced at his wristwatch, stood, and walked briskly to the door, explaining that it was time for his morning rounds.

But Jaya remained seated, tightening her grip on the chair's wooden armrest. 'Then I have your approval for my caretakers to...to stay at the hospital? So that they're on hand for errands, and such.'

'They?' he asked, raising an eyebrow above his owlish glasses.

She raised two fingers and wiggled them as if they were finger puppets.

Dr. Patel nodded his approval and Jaya breathed a sigh of relief, following him into the corridor. Standing at the end of the hallway, backlit by an open door, were the two caretakers. They reminded Jaya of Girl Scouts who had yet to grow into their uniforms. Their hair was swept back into schoolmarm buns. As the doctor passed by, both girls bent reverently.

'What will I use for money?' whispered Aasi when Jaya got closer. 'To buy medicine when needed. And for nourishing omelets." And then, with her finger on her chin, she added, "Best you give me your ATM card and passcode. Easier for you.'

'I'm not an idiot,' said Jaya. 'I mean, I'm *really* not.'

They returned to the room and she handed over a 100-rupee note. When Aasi leaned down to show Kamika, Jaya snuck the travel purse under a pillow.

'I want a full and accurate accounting each day,' she said.

Aasi brushed a finger over the note, letting it rest on Mahatma Gandhi's face. 'I will purchase a ledger from the stationery shop,' she said enthusiastically, followed by a whisper, 'Only I have not learned accounting. I can copy numbers in the ledger. Only this.'

'Forget the ledger book," said Jaya. 'A verbal account will be enough.' She'd already filled in three ledger books, one at the Sujay guesthouse, another at the Jyoti Palace, and one upon entering the hospital.

'I can read stories,' said Aasi. 'From my book called *Grimm's* or a story of my own. Very good spelling and grammar. A+ stories.'

'That would be sweet.' Jaya felt weepy again, remembering the times she'd lied to her mother in order to skip school. Always the same excuse: a stomachache. Her mother had seen right through her. And yet she would sit beside Jaya's bed reading Dr. Seuss. And now when she had the mother-of-all stomachaches...

She leaned into Aasi and gave her a peek on the cheek. The girl smelled of soap and cut grass, and something else. 'Have you been into my cough drops?' she said.

That afternoon, Aasi read one of her stories. She spoke softly and Jaya drifted in and out of sleep, lulled by the rhythm of the words.

The Girl and the Daboia

THERE ONCE WAS A GIRL who was afraid of everything: spiders and worms, and especially snakes. She lived in terror of snakes, afraid that they would find her in the night and wrap their slimy serpent bodies around her neck, choking her to death.

Her fear was not imaginary; a deadly, five-foot long Daboia tormented the village. It swallowed rats whole, strangled grown men, and carried away babies in its stomach. The snake had fangs big as a tiger's. It terrorized the surrounding villages too, going from house to house in search of prey.

The villagers tried to stop it. They built a stone wall - the snake climbed above it. They lit bonfires - the snake laughed as it wiggled around the burning embers. They tried shooting it with arrows, crushing it with boulders, piercing it with lances, but the snake was too fast.

The girl had nightmares. She awoke screaming and grasping her throat until her mother calmed her with hugs and glasses of warm milk chai. Then, one fitful night, the girl had a nightmare in which she was transformed into a rattlesnake more deadly than a Daboia. With her powerful jaws she crushed the Daboia's skull. The girl woke with the taste of snake blood in her mouth. She knew that the dream was an omen.

But could a girl turn into a snake, she wondered?

Then one day, while browsing the marketplace, she came upon a tattoo shop. Enquiring within, she asked if it were possible to change one's appearance into a rattlesnake. 'No problem,' said the shop owner, 'but it will cost a fortune, take many months, and be painful.'

'I am willing,' said the girl, in the hearing of the entire village.

The villagers took up a collection. People sold their precious possessions: gold dowry jewelry, jade statues of Durga, cars and motorbikes, furniture and steel kitchenware.

For months the tattooist worked on the girl's body. First her arms were made to look like yellow, black, brown, and white scales. On the way home that day, she encountered the Daboia.

'You're not a snake. You're a girl with snake arms,' it said.

Next, the girl's back was tattooed. The Daboia mocked, displaying its back as it slithered away.

The tattoo artist began working on the girl's legs - first the left leg, then the right. But the snake wasn't fooled. That very night it strangled a grandmother, the village matriarch.

The people were furious and worked harder to defeat the Daboia. The village blacksmith fashioned fangs to fit over the girl's teeth. The ophthalmologist crafted green glasses with slits for the pupils. The beauty shop sharpened the girl's fingernails to a point. The jeweler fashioned a rattle and attached it to the girl's ankle. Eunuchs taught the girl to move correctly. Then the village chemist made a capsule of deadly poison: the venom of a hundred rattlesnakes. He instructed the girl to tuck it below her tongue. She had only to bite down on the tablet, he said, and then into the Daboia.

When the tattooist finished drawing scales on the girl's toes, her own mother almost killed her with a pitchfork.

That night, the Daboia returned to the village.

The girl danced toward it on her belly, hissing and rattling her ankle. They met in the village square, below a Banyan tree.

The snake said, 'Who are you? This village belongs to me!'

The girl said, 'I am your mortal enemy, that's who.'

They were about the same size, both in length and width. The snake jumped at the girl. She used her arms to wrestle it to the ground. As the deadly tongue flashed out, the girl bit down on the capsule and rattlesnake venom dripped into the snake's open mouth.

The snake died instantly. The girl too.

The villagers mourned the girl for many days. They carved a life-size statue of a girl-snake and placed it below the Banyan tree. Night and day they lit candles, burned incense, and brought offerings to their newest goddess. And the goddess protected the village from everything vile and deadly, so that children slept in their beds and feared for nothing.

Never again did a snake dare enter the village.

Chapter Nineteen

THAT NIGHT JAYA DREAMT OF RATTLESNAKES. When morning came, she woke to find the bedsheets soaked through with sweat. The girls were asleep on a floor mat, and so she went in search of an orderly, hoping to have the sheets changed. She wouldn't have known it was a hospital were it not for a gurney in the corridor, and signs pointing in the direction of toilets, lab and x-ray rooms. She located a nurse in a room a few doors down, spoon-feeding a clean-shaven man. Jaya wondered what the patient had done to merit special attention.

He greeted Jaya with: 'Hey, what's up?' rubbing his bald head where a tan line ended. 'We met at the train station.'

'At the pharmacy, actually.' Jaya looked down at her hospital gown, aware of the fact that she wasn't wearing a bra. 'It's not the most flattering,' she said.

'Not that I'm any judge,' said Ed Rodgers, who was wearing an identical gown. The nurse poured another spoonful into his waiting mouth, lifting his chin and wiping it with a hand towel. She still hadn't acknowledged Jaya's presence.

'This is the life, idinit?' he said.

Jaya let the nurse know about the soaked sheets. At the same time, Ed swatted the nurse's backside, causing her to giggle flirtatiously. Jaya cleared her throat and repeated the request.

'Which room?' said the nurse grudgingly.

'Down the hall. In what I believe was the former library.'

Ed laughed. 'Quite a place. And wait 'til you get the bill. Motel 6 charges more.'

The nurse, meanwhile, began rearranging a tray table, tossing used facial tissues into a trash can and checking to see that there were still some in the box.

'Really, I could use your help,' said Jaya.

Without making eye-contact, the nurse answered by pressing a button on the oak paneled wall. Before long, an orderly came to the door and she followed him out of the room.

'Take a seat,' said Ed, once they'd left. 'I could use the company.'

Jaya drew the IV stand beside her. 'I saw them put you in the ambulance, you know. You didn't look good. As a matter of fact, I figured you for dead. I'm glad to see you're alive and kicking.' To her untrained eye Rodgers seemed perfectly healthy. With his head shaved, he reminded her of Bradley Cooper in *Silver Linings Playbook*. As she sat, Jaya said, 'Partying a little too hard, were you?'

He snickered. 'Who me?'

'Yeah, you.'

'Takes one to know one.'

'I don't partake in drugs of any sort. A little Valium for sleep is all.'

'Just one itsy-bitsy pill. I got it,' he snickered again. 'Incidentally, they have 12-step meetings every Monday. You're welcomed to join in. Some old fart comes and gathers us in what was once the morning-room. Claims he took to the bottle during Indira Gandhi's reign. Things were rough then, if you didn't know.'

'What happened to your—' Jaya rubbed the top of her head.

Ed imitated the gesture. 'Turns out I had lice, insult to injury. Could've killed them with wintergreen alcohol. But no, I wake up to find my precious locks have been shorn. The nurses even shaved my pubic hair. Crabs, apparently.'

Jaya reflexively scratched her head, thinking that as soon as she got back to the Jyoti Palace she would ask to be moved to another room. The only time she'd gotten lice was in kindergarten, and it wasn't an experience she cared to repeat. Pushing away the impulse to scratch her crotch, she said, 'What was this place, anyway?'

'British Officer's Club from the ol' Raj era. They even have a pub out back, although the taps haven't run since Independence.'

'Which is probably a good thing in your case.'

'I'm not an addict, recreational use is all. So, yeah, maybe I got carried away with the cheap hashish and opium floating around. I was headed to Nepal to clean up. Then, "What the heck," said I. "One last time." It was either that or flush the stuff down the toilet. I don't like having it on my person, not with the cops wanting to shake you down all the time. And besides, flushing the stuff puts it into the aqua filter. Not good for pregnant women, kids, and whatnot. Doc suspects I bought uncut heroin.'

Rodgers reached under his mattress for an embroidered pouch. When he zipped it opened, Jaya said, 'Should you be doing that?'

'Lock the door,' he said. 'The headmistress gets a whiff and she'll bounce me.'

For some crazy reason, Jaya did as he asked. The instant he lit up, someone began slamming a fist against the door, yelling, 'Open immediately! I know what you are doing, Mr. R! Trouble, nothing but trouble you are!'

'That's her, Nurse Ratched. She's married to the doc, so she thinks she's something." He waved a hand dismissively. 'Ignore her.'

Jaya let go of the handle and walked over to the bed.

Nurse Mary-Louise shouted through the door, 'I'm going to fetch the key!'

'You're not a cooperative patient,' said Jaya, laughing.

'Let that never be said of me.'

'Yet you have a way with nurses, the younger ones particularly.'

He finished rolling two joints and handed one to Jaya. 'They say it helps with nausea,' she said. 'When my mom was in chemo she had me score some from her dealer, this college student who also sold refabricated iPhones. He had me meet him behind a certain bar, a place called Smiley's. This was after medical cannabis was legalized in California. We could have bought some with a doctor's note, but my mom didn't have insurance and already the medical bills were piling up and she was talking about having to take a mortgage on our geodesic dome. So that was me - arranging a clandestine meeting with this skuzzy college guy. I was scared to death of being arrested. But it helped my mother, so who was I to judge? And, okay, I *did* take a puff or two during a particularly stressful time between stage three and four.' Jaya raised a shoulder.

'They can't expect me to withdraw from everything all at once,' said Rodgers. 'It would kill me.' His shoulders relaxed as he exhaled.

Jaya took a deep draw and choked. 'What is this? It doesn't taste like pot.'

'Mostly cloves. I got the mix from an Ayurveda medicine man. It's supposed to help with detox. I tried to explain all this to the doc, but it was a no-go. He's a conventional medicine man. Western trained. He loves to push pharmaceuticals. But they *do* hold yoga classes in the ballroom every morning at six am, so that's one thing.'

'Do you go?'

'Nah.'

'When are the 12-step meetings?' she asked. She had once attended ACON - Adult Children of Narcissists - at the encouragement of a friend. The group met in the basement of a Methodist church. It turned out that Jaya was allergic to the kind of mold that grew under wall-to-wall carpet.

Nurse Mary-Louise slammed on the door again. They were both silent, sucking on their joints. The nurse tried one more time at the doorknob before giving up.

'Better hide this someplace,' Rodgers said, handing the pouch and lighter to Jaya.

She managed to stand on a chair, although the IV feed was stretched to its length and it tugged uncomfortably at her hand. Tucking the pouch on the top of a window valance, she said. 'How's that?'

'Defeats the whole purpose having to suck it down like this. My Ayurveda man says you got to take it nice and slow, with deep breathing exercises in between tokes.'

Jaya opened a window and tossed the burning stubs just as a key slid into the lock, dislodging a cotton ball. Nurse Mary-Louise ran to the bed wagging a finger. 'Mr. R., you'll be the death of me, you will!' The younger nurse stood behind, making googly eyes at Rodgers.

'Time for my hourly spanking, I'm afraid,' he told Jaya. 'Better leave if you don't want to see my exposed butt.' Bending a finger, he directed the nurses to come forward.

Chapter Twenty

WHEN A WATER JUG TIPPED OVER, Aasi went for a towel. She knew where to find one, having scouted out the hospital the previous night while the duty nurse napped. She'd found closets containing cleaning supplies: mops and buckets, cases of bleach and floor wax. These she had taken a cursory look through. Glass-fronted cabinets stored sterilized surgical instruments, bottles of anesthesia, and pain killers. She rifled through a cabinet filled with rubber gloves, cotton swabs, and tongue depressors, which she mistook for ice-pop sticks. One room had nothing but patient records and X-rays.

None of this held her interest like the locked drawer.

The day before, Aasi overheard a British patient ask to settle his bill. White gauze was taped to his knees and elbows, and skin on the his legs and arms was flayed and scabbing, as if he'd had a motorbike accident. This was confirmed by the motorcycle helmet tucked under his arm, dented beyond repair. He wanted to pay with cash and a junior nurse rang for her superior. Nurse Mary-Louise came carrying a key, which opened the center drawer in a metal office desk. The drawer resembled an old-fashioned cash register, with slots for notes of various denominations and a place for coins. The junior nurse wrote a receipt and gave the top slip to the patient and a carbon copy to Mary-Louise, who placed it in the drawer before locking it again. From that moment, the drawer had become Aasi's obsession.

Today she passed the drawer with only a glance, running straight for the linen closet, where rasping breath emanated from within. Aasi expected to find the old cleaning woman when she opened the door, but it was Rodgers she found instead. Fondling one of the nurses.

Aasi had probably laid eyes on her friend before but had failed to recognize him without his long, cumin-colored hair. His skull, she thought, was shaped like a lichi fruit. The technical college-trained nurse glared at Aasi and said, '*Arey, kya!*' The blood pressure instrument was still sticking from her pocket. Her hair was loose and her uniform buttons were open to reveal a pink bra. Aasi thought, Now it's your turn to feel ashamed!

Rodgers let his hands drop as he tried to decide what to do with the spectator.

'Get lost kid,' is what he finally said.

'Nag Champa?' said Aasi, placing both hands on her hips. 'You promised, Edward Rodgers. Not a maybe, but a 100% promise.'

A smile stretched his clean-shaven cheeks. 'Get a load of *you!*' he said.

The nurse buttoned her uniform and stormed off. Aasi stepped into the closet. 'I am pleased you are not expired,' she said. 'I was thinking you are gone to be with your god.'

' "Gone to be with your god," that's rich,' he said with a chuckle. 'I've had a slight setback, is all. As it turns out, a defibrillator works wonders.' He pounded his chest and then pushed Aasi into the hall, saying, 'Wouldn't do to be caught in the supply closet with a minor.'

Aasi suggested they sit in the garden, where the sound of flowing water would further revive his health. Although once she got a look at him in the daylight, she saw that he was healthier than ever. He'd gained weight, especially in his cheeks, which no longer looked gaunt. She asked how he managed to get food.

'The nurses are at my beck and call,' he said.

'I will happily be at your beck and call,' she said, hoping to double her salary.

'There is one thing...'

'Your wish, my friend.'

He leaned down and cupped her ear, whispering, 'I could use a little ganja. Take the edge off. Help me relax.'

Aasi narrowed her eyes. 'Why you tell me this?'

'Don't give me that look. I need a couple of ounces is all... nothing illegal.'

He touched Aasi's hand, but she pulled it away and slid to the end of the bench.

'It's legal in Colorado,' he said.

Aasi tightened her arms around her chest.

'That's next to Arizona. Where your fairy-tale mother hails from.'

'Arizona,' she said, and then caught herself. She didn't like where this was heading. There was a story going around - a Turkish traveler who gave birth in a prison cell full of rats. And all because someone talked her into carrying a suitcase full of ganja from one hotel to another.

Aasi looked into Rodger's pleading eyes and found they were the same as Kamika's when she was hungry: '*Please*,' they said, 'I beg you!' She found herself weakening.

'I'll make it worth your while. Easiest money you ever made.'

She closed her eyes and tried to bring up an image: a prison cell full of snakes. They slithered around the bars, crawled up the walls, and hung from the ceiling.

'No!' she shouted.

Rodgers jumped back, raising his hands in defense. 'Whoa, girl, calm yourself!' Reaching into his pocket, he pulled out a 5000-rupee note and squeezed it into Aasi's hand. She tried to make a fist but couldn't. She had never held such a large note. When she put it to her nose, it smelled of fresh ink. Holding it up to the light, she tested to see if it was counterfeit, as she knew there were notes of this kind flooding in from Pakistan. The watermark of Gandhi's face appeared to be genuine and the metallic strip perfect. Aasi pressed the note to her lips, imagining how much dal it would buy. Mutton korma, even.

'I know a guy in Paharganj, perfectly legit,' said Rodgers, resting his back against the bench. 'Use half for the pot and keep the rest.'

Aasi was relieved; buying from a steel shop was not illegal. Perhaps she'd misunderstood. 'You want big pot or little pot, with or without lid?'

Edward Rodgers corrected her. 'Pot. Marijuana. Ganga. Same-same.'

'Oh,' she said, struggling which way to go. Visions of snakes and rats faded as she rubbed the note between her fingers, testing the paper again. She was certain it was authentic.

Rodgers instructed her to run and get a pen and pad from his room. He would write down the address. Draw her a map, even. She wouldn't have to take a bus, he added, promising to pay for an auto-rickshaw. When she hesitated, he said, 'Make that an air-con taxi. You can travel in style like Shah Rukh Khan, that Bollywood star.'

'What about your promise to buy case of Nag Champa?' she asked. 'I had everything arranged with Mr. Wadhwa. Then you get sick and forget.' She slid to the end of the bench again.

'Okay - I'm a man who keeps his word. How much will that set me back?'

'Help me figure math. One hundred boxes at half off shop price.'

'Shop price to tourists or locals? There's a big difference. All depends on your bargaining power.'

'Price for Americans.'

'A little birdie tells me you're taking advantage of my generous nature.'

As hard as it was, she threw the rupee note into his lap. If she didn't settle with Rodgers now, later he would be too stoned to remember his promise.

'Fine,' he said, 'you got me. Say a dollar a box times a hundred. What's the exchange rate these days?' He looked into the distance, chewing on his lower lip. 'Last I checked it was 55 rupees to a dollar.' He used his fingers to calculate the price and came up with two thousand rupees. Hearing the number made Aasi lightheaded. Rodgers reached into his wallet and handed over another note. 'Bring me the change. Ask my friend to give you 4000 thousand rupees of his special.'

'His special ganja?'

'Just say *special*. He'll get it. Now run along.' He waved a hand dismissively. 'And get me a couple packs of Wrigley's spearmint gum, the one in the green package. Think you can manage that without moral qualms?'

She didn't know what a *qualm* was, but wouldn't give Rodgers the satisfaction of admitting it. The money had somehow found its way into her bag. Rodgers was no longer paying attention to her. He was scratching the inside of his arm, at a row of scabs.

'You depend on me,' said Aasi.

'Glad to hear it.'

Back in the room, Jaya slept flat on her back. Aasi gently wiped dribble from the side of Jaya's mouth and covered her toes with the end of the sheet. After mopping up water, the only thing left to do was fill the jar and rearrange the flowers.

Kamika was riveted to a cartoon featuring Ganesh and his father Shiva. Aasi knew she would cry when Shiva cut off the boy's head, but there was nothing to prevent that. She turned up the volume so that Kamika's eyes would stay fixed to the TV as she tiptoed from the room.

Jaya woke and began reading *Eat, Pray, Love*, the only English language book in the hospital's dog-eared collection. She raced through the section on Italy, skipped the part about India, and was just beginning the Bali chapter when Dr. Patel entered with his wife, Nurse Mary-Louise. Kamika trailed behind, holding onto the hem of the nurse's uniform.

They removed the IV from Jaya's hand, swabbing it with

alcohol and covering the small needle prick with a bandage.

'You are free to go,' said Dr. Patel. 'Make sure to drink plenty of fluids. We'll give you a prescription for 400mg metronidazole tablets.'

'That's it then?' Jaya was half hoping that they'd insist she stay.

'We don't want to spoil your holiday,' said Nurse Mary-Louise.

'It's not exactly a holiday,' said Jaya.

'Vacation,' said Dr. Patel, 'that's what Americans call it.'

'I stand corrected,' said Nurse Mary-Louise.

'We hardly ever take a vacation,' said Dr. Patel, telling Jaya about their plan to cruise Antarctica once they retired. The anticipation of all that ice, he said, helped get his wife through the hot season.

'We Irish,' said Nurse Mary-Louise. 'Back home there are ten days of sun out of a year if we're lucky and everyone complains. But during the monsoon season, I start dreaming about a holiday to Kilkenny.'

'Or the Gobi desert,' said Dr. Patel, laughing.

'Anywhere but here.'

'My mother and I used to go to the wine country,' said Jaya, 'to the wineries with free tastings, and cheese and crackers. Or we'd hike in the redwoods. That was before she relapsed. I never once imagined ending up here.'

'Well, we hope this illness hasn't spoiled your impression of our country,' said Dr. Patel. 'It's possible to get sick anywhere. I was once violently ill after eating shellfish at the Jersey shore. This at a seaside restaurant where one would expect a fresh catch. Then there was the outbreak of E.coli O26 at Chipotle.

Why, just a couple of years ago, in the United States of America, what with all those health codes, several people died eating cantaloupe!'

'I think she's heard enough, Doctor,' said Nurse Mary-Louise turning to Jaya. 'The clothes you came in, dear, are hanging in the wardrobe. Keep a fresh plaster on the puncture mark until it's completely healed, why don't you?'

'Band-Aid,' said Dr. Patel. 'That's what we call it in the States.'

Nurse Mary-Louise rolled her eyes and said, 'There's always the danger of staph infection.'

'*Listeria monocytogenes*, that was the culprit in the cantaloupe incident,' said Dr. Patel, rocking his head. 'It mostly effected the elderly, pregnant women, and those with compromised immune systems.'

'I'll stay away from melons,' said Jaya in all seriousness.

Once they'd left the room, she began dressing. There had been no mention of the girls, she realized. Kamika followed the nurses around like a groupie and they seemed to return the affection. Someone had given her a doll. She was wearing traditional Indian clothes again, a long top, studded with beads, and matching pants. The cleaning woman was teaching the girl to use a whisk broom, and the head gardener let her scoop leaves from the pool using a long-handled net.

'Well,' Jaya said aloud. 'It's working out for the best. They're a lot better off here than living on the street.' Aasi could keep the money and that would settle things between them. The only thing left to do was settle the bill and say her goodbyes.

Ed was out on the veranda and gestured for Jaya to sit

beside him. A nurse brought a glass of milk chai and he ordered another, even after Jaya protested. Together they watched as a bird swept down and stole a toast crumb, then fluttered away. In the distance, Kamika ran circles around the fountain, using the long-handled net like a butterfly catcher. Jaya pushed her glasses to the bridge of her nose and saw that the girl was laughing.

Ed removed the pouch from his bathrobe pocket. 'I'd offer, but I'm running low.'

Jaya told him that she'd been released, waving a receipt to prove it.

'Good for you,' he said, scattering tobacco onto a rolling paper.

'I'll have to put off the trip to Varanasi a day or two while I get my strength back. As much as I'd love to get out of this city.'

'The Taj Mahal makes for a nice daytrip,' he said. 'You might be disappointed though. People usually are. It's a lot smaller than it looks on postcards.'

'Smaller than on a postcard?'

He handed her the chai, insisting that she drink up. 'Gita will be back in a jiffy with another. And, hey, maybe you'd do me a favor?' He asked Jaya to bring his backpack, which had been left behind at the guesthouse. 'And couple John Le Carre novels wouldn't be turned away.' He offered money for the paperbacks, but Jaya said she'd get it when she returned.

It felt good to be needed again.

The chai was syrupy sweet and Jaya returned the glass to the tray. 'Maybe it *would* be nice to get out of Delhi and see the countryside,' she said, as if the idea of visiting the Taj Mahal was entirely his.

'You can't come all the way to India and not see the Taj Mahal,' he said. 'The town is a tourist trap, so don't bother. Unless you're the type that goes in for overpriced, kitschy souvenirs.' He looked at Jaya appraisingly. 'Just don't fall for the elephant ride. It's a rip-off.'

She asked how he funded his travels and Rodgers answered vaguely with 'this and that,' at the same time opening his silver cigarette case. Jaya wondered what 'this and that' included; the cigarette case, she noticed, was engraved with initials that weren't his.

'And, besides,' he went on, 'my travels have been suspended for the time being.' Pinching the beadie between two fingers, he wheezily inhaled until the tip sparked with embers. 'But maybe this is exactly what I needed. The place is something along the lines of an ashram, wouldn't you say? But without having to sit ramrod straight all the goddamn time.'

'Shangri-La,' said Jaya, motioning toward the garden. 'That's what my mother would've called it.'

'You talk about your mother a lot.'

'I came to India to scatter her ashes in the Ganges.'

'That's heavy, man.' Angling his head, he exhaled smoke while inclining his body toward hers.

'You don't know the half of it,' she sighed.

Rodgers nodded slowly and rubbed his chin. Jaya wondered if this was what grief support groups were like. Taking a deep breath, she looked up at the sky and tried to decide where to begin.

'The bitch is,' Ed said, 'I'll have to rebook my train ticket.'

Jaya's lower lip began trembling. 'Oh?' she said.

'It's nothing short of a miracle I got a berth in a sleeper car. This is like, seriously, the worse time to be going north. I'll be lucky to get a seat in third-class. I mean, normally I don't mind slumming it but not when I'm recovering from a serious illness.'

'Illness?' she mumbled. Is that what he called this?

Rodgers moved the tea set to the ground and rested his feet on the rattan table. Then he began waxing on about the rigors of budget travel. 'I once travelled on the roof of the train. All the way from Kolkata to Banaras - that's Varanasi, to you - me and a thousand Indians. Almost got decapitated by a low hanging electrical wire. By the time we arrived, I was covered head to toe in soot.'

He looked to Jaya for sympathy.

'At least you *had* a head,' she said.

'Those wood benches in third-class are murder. And my back is already killing me due to sleeping on crappy mattresses. I'd need a dose of diamorphine to survive the trip, and no way is the doc gonna give me a prescription. Says he's on to me, quote unquote.' He shook his head mournfully, but then smiled suddenly. 'Hey, maybe the doc'll hook me up with a masseuse.'

'That nurse of yours should be game,' said Jaya, but Rodgers didn't seem to be listening. If I suddenly dematerialized, she though, he probably won't notice.

'My prediction,' he went on, 'is that I'll end up flying to Kathmandu. Which sucks, because I'm trying to keep a low footprint and all.'

'We have solar panels at home,' she said weakly. 'And a composting toilet.'

The nurse returned with a second glass of chai, letting her hip brushed against Rodgers's side. Jaya used the distraction to make an exit.

Chapter Twenty-One

AASI KNEW HOW IMPORTANT IT WAS to return before Jaya woke. If the American noticed her gone it would mean dismissal. She ran lopsided, keeping pressure off her wounded toe. This caused the thong of her flip-flop to break where it had been mended with electrical tape. One slipper was useless without the other and she threw both into a bush.

That's when she realized how ridiculous she looked wearing the ugly green dress. She smiled. It was a nice to have money in her possession for a change. There was a shop at the edge of Paharganj selling panjabi suits at a discount. She would stop there first.

At the rickshaw stand, drivers stood licking paan from leaves. The man in charge spat red saliva on the ground and waved toward the first rickshaw in a row of identical vehicles. After giving the driver directions to the shop, Aasi climbed into the back and elevated her foot to the seat. The toe was twice its normal size and she tried to put it out of her mind. She had never ridden in the passenger seat and wanted to enjoy the journey. As the rickshaw passed a billboard advertising the Bank of Baroda - a happy, and obviously prosperous, couple playing with their toddler - Aasi considered the possibility of opening an account of her own, one that came with an ATM card. It was clever, she thought, to forgo the expense of an air-con-taxi.

She rested against the seatback and let her eyes drift closed. Next thing she knew, the driver was poking her. She gave him twenty rupees and he began complaining.

'No point throwing words to the wind,' she said, and hurried into the shop.

Rodgers's friend lived down an alley beyond the Sujay guest-house. Joe, the manager, and his wife were standing at the entrance. The wife was greeting a guest with that fake smile of hers. She took one look at Aasi and lunged for the girl's braid, saying 'What are you doing, you evil child? Where did you steal those garments?'

Aasi tugged at the braid, losing a valuable hairband in the process. Without looking back, she ran down the alleyway, skirting around a street sweeper and making her way to Rodgers's friend. At the left-luggage shop, she stopped to catch her breath. As instructed, she asked the manager to point her to a man named Zulfikar Ali.

Attaching a tag to a backpack, he said, 'Zulfikar Ali? What do you want with him?'

'I have important business with Zulfikar Ali,' she said.

'Nothing good can come of it, I'm sure.' He hesitated and then called for his assistant, telling him to take charge of the desk. Aasi followed him around the corner, to a dark and narrow path smelling of chicken droppings. Wire cages were stacked near a door, each one crammed with hens. Aasi cringed feeling dirt push between her toes. Someone threw dirty water from a window and she jumped out of the way. They stopped at a door pasted over with an advertisement for Vodafone.

'Here?' she asked.

'Upstairs, top floor you'll find him. What business could you have with that man? A nice girl like you...'

'You call me nice girl. You are very kind, sir.'

Stepping into the vestibule, she heard a television muffled by a closed door and the cry of a baby wanting attention. She felt calmer suddenly. It was a normal building where families lived. When she turned to acknowledge the left-luggage manager, he was gone. She began climbing the stairs. Except for a light filtering through a shattered window, the stairwell was dark. Glass shards twinkled in dust-speckled light.

She could go no further barefoot.

She found her way back to the Main Bazaar, which was filling with afternoon shoppers. Her stomach rumbled and she surprised Mr. Aggarwal, the jhajariya seller, by offering to pay for sweets. He happily fished some from the hot oil, laying them in a bowl made of dried leaves. Aasi saw that he had given her two pieces for the price of one.

He said, 'Your fortune has changed, I see!' His wife grunted her disapproval. 'May the gods continue to smile upon you,' he added.

'You are most kind. I will pray for your good health and pros-perity, Mr. Aggarwal-ji.'

She made her way through the crowd, headed to a certain shop. Along the way she finished eating, only to find that the sweets had failed to silence her stomach. Nearby was a samosa seller, the one with the freshest offerings. Aasi fought to the front of the line. The seller handed over a bowl with samosa and chana masala, adding a hot pepper to the top when Aasi complained that the dish was incomplete. She gave him one of the rupee notes and he asked for something smaller, saying that he couldn't make change. Handing over a different note, Aasi made sure that the samosa seller returned the correct amount and that her bag was securely knotted afterwards. The whole time, she scanned the crowd for thieves. She knew most of them by sight.

This was the first meal in ages that she hadn't had to share. But much to her surprise, by the last two bites she began wishing Kamika were there to finish. When she thought about Zulfikar Ali and the task in front of her, the final chana bean got lodged in her throat. She swallowed hard, hoping this would also give her courage. Now that she had begun spending Rodgers's money, there was no turning back.

'After I purchase new slippers,' she said aloud. 'After this.'

She threw the bowl into the gutter.

A cart stacked with potatoes parted the crowd, revealing a shop where hundreds of slippers hung from clips. From where she stood, Aasi was able to get a whiff of buffalo hide. Men's slippers lined the left-side wall. Ladies' slippers - far more beautiful - lined the right and back walls. One pair caught Aasi's eye and she approached trembling. Had there ever been any-thing to compare? she wondered. Each shoe was embossed with golden songbirds. The toes curled to points, each adorned with a red pompom. She flexed the soles - they were delicate yet strong. Shoes like that would last a lifetime, she thought. A price sticker was glued to the heal, but she was afraid to look.

'May I help you?' said a shop assistant.

'What is your best price for those?' she said, squeezing her eyes tight and holding her breath.

'Two hundred for you.'

Aasi was sure he had given a fair price, but she said, 'One hundred,' thinking how impossible it would be to repay Rodgers should she lose courage. The shop assistant saw how much she wanted the shoes. He unclipped them, sliding one onto Aasi's foot. She stifled a cry, thinking that maybe open toe slippers would be better. But once they were on her feet, she said, 'One hundred twenty is my final offer. I am a poor girl, as you well know.'

'One fifty is a very good price, *na*. I will only earn twenty-five rupees. I have children to feed, *Kum*.'

No one had ever called Aasi *kum* and her heart warmed at the honor. She was a different person wearing these shoes. The leather was soft against her feet. Her belly was full, her body clothed in a brand-new Panjabi suit, thousands of rupees waited in her bag. For the first time in her life she was able to be generous. 'I will give you your price, *Sri*.'

He clasped his hands and hurried to the desk to prepare a receipt. Aasi told him it wouldn't be needed. Then she broke the spell by reminding him who she was. His eyes opened wide with surprise.

'Have you found your mother at last?' he asked. 'How wonderful!'

'No,' she said sadly. 'But I have done well in business.' She turned away as she opened her bag, so that he couldn't see exactly *how* well and raise the price. 'Here you are, *Sri*. Only remember - should my luck change and you see me wearing these slippers while begging on the street, you will know that I have attained them by honest means.'

'May your good luck never change. May you return to buy many fine slippers.'

'May it be as you say.' She put her palms together. 'And may your children never hunger.'

'These slippers will do well when you do acrobatics. They will not fall from your feet they fit so perfectly. If I didn't know better, I would say they were custom-made.'

She jumped from the top step. And just as promised, the slippers stayed firmly on her feet.

She began walking toward Zulfikar Ali.

Chapter Twenty-Two

JAYA LULLED IN BED THE NEXT MORNING, listening to the air-conditioner hum and wishing that she didn't have to get up. The owners of the guesthouse had switched her to a different room. She fluffed the pillow, thinking, 'Lice free,' and then smashed her face into it.

She'd meant to visit Ed in the hospital before leaving for Agra, but now there wouldn't be time. 'I'm not Ed's caretaker,' she told herself. The hotel owners would send his backpack to East Meets West Clinic if she asked.

At a nearby market she bought a bag of cashews, banana chips, vanilla digestives called *Parle-G*, and a big bottle of mineral water: a snack for the drive to Agra. The shop next to the grocery displayed used books, neatly wrapped in cellophane, and she bought two John Le Carre paperbacks - *The Constant Gardener* and *Tinker, Tailor, Soldier, Spy* - feeling less guilty about letting Ed down. The hotel owners welcomed her back, asking if there was anything they could do to make her stay a success.

'Everything's good,' she said. 'Thanks for changing my room. It's even nicer than the last one. Very Zen-like. If I could have the key back...I forgot a couple things. My sunglasses and sunscreen. I'm going on a daytrip to the Taj Mahal.'

'Oh, you will not be disappointed!' said one of the owners.
'You don't think?'

'But you ought to have booked with us. I hope you selected the deluxe bus.' After examining the voucher, he pronounced, 'Yes, everything is in proper order,' flicking his finger against the word SUPER DELUXE LUXURY VAN written in the upper corner.

The minivan was almost full and Jaya was forced to take a place at the back. She laid a shawl over the seat before sitting. 'This is super deluxe luxury?' she said. The upholstery was ripped and the interior smelled of burnt oil and strawberry disinfectant. The taste of Parle-Gs rose up her esophagus. She willed herself not to vomit again.

Elbows jostled for position and her kneecaps were pressed to the seatback in front of her. She was squeezed between two men. The one to her left took a flask from his backpack, offering Jaya a drink.

'What is it?' she asked.

'Vodka.' He pronounced the word the way she supposed it was meant to be: *Vud-ka.*

'Better not,' she said. 'queasy stomach.'

He passed the flask around. Jaya considered asking the driver to let her out. It was a three-and-a-half hour drive to Agra. She closed her eyes, leaning her head against the headrest.

'From Ukraine,' said the man. His breath smelled like a liquor cabinet and Jaya backed her head away.

'I'm from California,' she said without enthusiasm.

'You come along with us. We be your protection.'

'That's nice of you, but really, I don't need protection.' It wasn't true, but it sounded good. Jaya tugged at her shirt, making sure that her cleavage was hidden. She pulled at her skirt until the hem covered both knees.

'Never meet person from California,' he said, touching Jaya's arm.

'We're probably not much different than Russians.'

'Ukraine.'

'Ukraine, sorry. *Perestroika* ...yes, I remember from history class.'

The whole van burst out in shouts of *Perestroika! Perestroika!* The one girl in the group twisted in her seat and said, 'Don't mind them. They are harmless.' She rebuked the others in Russian and they simmered down. Jaya was grateful for her presence. They were a motley bunch: a cross between hippie and gangster. Some of the men had bandanas tied around their heads or biceps. They had pierced noses and pins in their eyebrows. She wondered if it was a tribal thing: neo-Genghis Khan, maybe.

The girl was clothed in a cotton dress that needed ironing. Her arm was covered in a parrot tattoo, and there were small circles tattooed above her eyebrows and below her chin. She was pretty. Delicately boned, like a Bolshoi ballerina.

'I know a girl who tells stories about tattooed women,' said Jaya, remembering Aasi's fables.

'You like?' The Ukrainian girl raised her elbow to the seatback that separated them. 'I had it done in Goa. By a Brit named Patrick. You know him? Beautiful work, yes? He is not finished.' She drew a finger over a section near her elbow where there were outlines in black ink.

'It must be painful,' said Jaya.

'I take something to knock me out.'

Jaya tried to remember the story Aasi read yesterday. Something having to do with a rattlesnake. The girl's stories always featured snakes and tattoos. A weird sense of responsibility came over Jaya, an impulse to rescue the girl. She took a deep breath, hoping to regain the sense of freedom she felt right after her mother died.

'I think I'll listen to music,' she said, stuffing earbuds into her ears. She lifted the iPhone, hoping they'd take the hint. The van was swelteringly hot and she asked the man next to her to open a window. Another passenger shouted at the driver, demanding that he turn on the air-conditioning. The window wouldn't budge, but cool air began blowing in Jaya's face from a ceiling vent. She skimmed her playlist.

Before long, the men on either side were sleeping. Their heads kept drifting toward Jaya's shoulders and she had to periodically pushed them off.

The van stopped alongside the road, at a ramshackle structure that served as a snack bar. The driver shouted, 'Ten minutes!' and then disappeared behind the building. Jaya shook the Ukrainian girl, seated in front of her. The girl yawned and slid the door open. It felt to Jaya as if she'd opened a furnace.

The Ukrainians piled out and began franticly lighting cigarettes. They shoved a pack at Jaya and she politely declined, asking, 'Did the driver mention where the bathrooms are?'

The tattooed girl jutted her chin toward a shack at the side of the building.

The stink assaulted Jaya with every step nearer the shack, but her bladder was about to burst and there didn't appear to be another option: the landscape was devoid of trees. In anticipation, her bowels began rumbling.

She rattled the door but it was locked. A sign hung from a rusty nail: *Please do not throw the toilet into the paper.* She snapped a photo with her iPhone, thinking that she'd send it to her mother. Then she bit her lower lip and deleted the contact. There would be many moments like this, she thought, small erasures until there was little evidence that her mother had ever existed. She wiggled uncomfortably and knocked at the door again. It threatened to come off the hinges.

One of the Ukrainians exited, pinching his nose. He said something in broken English, holding the door open. A woman scurried over with her hand out. 'She wants five rupees,' he said.

'Okay, sure,' said Jaya, fishing through her bag. She handed over the coin and stepped inside. It took a minute for her eyes to adjust to the darkness, but she began to make out a hole in the floor. Feces coated the rim. Horseflies buzzed around the confined space, trying to get up her nostrils. 'See what you've put me through?' she said, talking to her mother again, 'Happy?' She slammed a fist against the wall.

Water flowed into a plastic bucket and a bowl floated on the surface. She lifted the bowl and splashed water onto the toilet rim. Ceramic footrests indicated where she was to straddle the hole. Jaya was glad to be wearing a skirt.

She walked back to the minivan and found the doors locked. From a makeshift bench - a plank resting on soda crates - the Ukrainian girl called Jaya over, pointing to the place beside her. She was drinking orange soda from a bottle and offered a sip. Jaya declined but took a potato chip. The plank bent under their weight, and Jaya noted that she was disproportionately responsible.

'Better to go in nature,' said the girl, pointing to a scraggly bush Jaya had failed to notice earlier.

'Now I know.' She took another chip. A soda was a good idea, she thought. 7-up helped settle the stomach. The girl's bottle was sweaty with condensation. 'Save my seat,' she said.

At the counter, empty soda bottles were stacked beside an ice chest. The toilet-toll woman was serving behind the counter. She flipped the cap on a Limca - after Jaya asked for a 7-up - and handed over a straw. Jaya lifted a bag of Doritos and the woman called out a price.

'Prescription medicine,' said Jaya when she sat down again. She placed a pill on the tip of her tongue and took a gulp of Limca. 'I have amebic dysentery, well, *had*. But I'm on the mend. I wouldn't advise eating here.'

The Ukrainian girl offered another chip.

'I have my own,' said Jaya. 'I don't want to spread disease. Don't you hate when people do that? I mean, like when they offer you a bite from their fork and only afterwards mention that they have herpes.'

'Pardon?' said the girl.

'Or they get cancer and don't tell you until they're at stage three. So, like, you don't have a chance to be extra nice during stage one through two.'

The girl squinted her eyes against the sun.

By then, the driver was standing beside the van. He wiped his mouth and said, 'Time to go!' Jaya was the first back at the van and took shotgun. Her feet hit into a backpack and she tossed it to the seat behind. One of the Ukrainians looked on scathingly, but she said, 'I'm recovering from a *serious* stomach illness. Trust me, you don't want me to throw up.'

The driver wouldn't leave until Jaya draped the seatbelt strap around her. The buckle was broken. 'Police,' he said, and shifted into gear. A statue of a Hindu deity, mounted to the dashboard, looked on disapprovingly.

'How much longer?' she asked.

'One hour.'

'I must have slept on the way.' It felt as though her jetlag was over. Something poked her hip and she reached down to find a guidebook wedged between the stick shift and seat. She pulled it out and opened to the index. The pages were greasy with food slime.

'Agra,' said the driver, pointing to the road ahead.

'Yes, I know.'

Jaya found pages recommending eateries near the Taj Mahal and scribbled notes in a Moleskin notebook, along with a map, approximating the path from the Taj entrance to a restaurant recommended for its brick-oven pizza.

'Pizza in India,' she said. 'Go figure.'

She made an X to indicate a luxury hotel that might offer a clean toilet.

An hour later, they pulled into a dirt parking lot. The driver said they could either wait for a trolley bus or walk downhill to the entrance gate. There was the elephant option, too, but Jaya remembered Ed's advice and declined. The driver warned everyone to return to the van at the designated time. He would return to Delhi with or without passengers, he said.

Men swarmed around the group. Each offered his services as tour guide, displaying credentials in loose-leaf binders, along with testimonials from satisfied customers. One shouted in Russian, another spoke pidgin French. The Ukrainians began negotiating and Jaya ducked out of the huddle and jogged toward the entrance. A persistent guide trailed behind, asking that she name a price - *any price*. Another man ran alongside, holding a miniature Taj Mahal carved out of sandstone. It had an electric cord and two wires where a plug ought to have been. She brushed him off with a wave of the hand.

'Please, lady. It lights up at night,' he whined. 'Only 500 rupee. Cheap, cheap!'

Halfway down the hill she stopped to catch her breath. She had only jogged a short distance but it felt as if she'd done the Ironman. Her head pounded and she drank every drop in her water bottle before continuing on.

She passed a pack of monkeys, sifting through a dumpster. The males had swollen testicles that looked as if they'd explode. One mounted a tired female, who looked around for sympathy. Jaya averted her eyes and veered toward the grandest of several entrance gates, one that resembled something from *Arabian Nights*. Her steps echoed under an archway and she stopped to rest in the shade.

Two lines formed at the entrance gate, one for foreigners

and one for nationals. There were also two prices, one considerably higher than the other. A German couple, with matching Leica binoculars strapped around their necks, stood at the back of the line for foreigners. They asked Jaya to take their photograph, handing over a Hasselblad DSLR Camera. 'I'm not the best photographer,' said Jaya, but they wrapped their arms around each other and smiled, preparing to be photographed. She snapped ten rapid-fire shots and returned the camera. They began deleting all but one photo.

When it was her turn at the ticket counter, Jaya handed over the voucher.

'750 rupees,' said the ticket collector, sliding the voucher back at her.

'But I've already paid for the all-inclusive tour.'

'Take that up with your travel agent. 750 rupees, madam.' He stroked his chin. 'A thousand rupee extra for use of video camera.'

True, the iPhone did have video capabilities, but Jaya wasn't about to admit to it. She handed over a 1000-rupee note, thinking what a sucker she'd been. Again. In return, she received a ticket with a glossy picture of the Taj Mahal.

'Familiarize yourself with the rules,' said the ticket collector, pointing to a sign. She read down a list: *Strictly prohibited! Eating and smoking, arms, ammunitions, fire, smoking, tobacco products, liquor, eatables (Toffees).* She wondered why exactly toffees had been singled out.

The first view of the Taj Mahal brought an ache of loneliness. Jaya wanted to grab someone's hand. She thought about Ed, then Yoel, trying to choose between them. There were couples everywhere, taking pictures of each other with the Taj Mahal for a backdrop. A couple reclined on the dry grass eating toffees (or something resembling toffees, Jaya thought). They kissed fugitively, hidden beneath a blanket.

'Were you here,' she asked her mother, 'before me?' Funny, she thought, but she had never seen photographs of her mother's trip to India. When she got home she'd search for some. There were photo albums high up on a bookcase in the hallway, but she'd assumed they were pictures from her own childhood. Her mother had had a whole life before giving birth, she realized now. To Jaya, they had always been a single entity.

The Taj Mahal looked like a mosque and she wasn't sure why this came as a surprise. A man approached, saying, 'Excuse me.' For a second Jaya thought he wanted her to take his picture. She looked around for his mate but found that he was alone.

Sucking in her stomach, she said, 'Yes?' trying for a beatific smile.

He tugged at the name badge clipped to his shirt pocket, identifying himself as a government sponsored tour guide. I'm pathetic, she thought as she accepted his services. The fact was, she craved his company. He wore white slacks and a black shirt opened at the neck, revealing a hairless chest. He carried a long-handled umbrella. When he popped it open, Jaya saw that it was paneled with rainbow stripes. He held it over her head.

'Are we expecting rain?' she asked. There wasn't a single

cloud in the monochrome sky.

'To protect your delicate skin,' he said, lifting an eyebrow. He stood a respectable distance apart, with his arm fully extended as he held the umbrella.

'That's very kind, but I'm hoping to get a tan. Where do we start?'

'Do you prefer the best for last, or the best for first?'

'For last.'

He turned toward a complex of buildings and they walked along a brick path lined with hedges. Green-winged birds floated above and the whole scene was sickeningly romantic. 'Parrots,' he said. 'I think there are no parrots in your home country.'

'Only in cages.'

He laughed and beckoned Jaya to follow him. 'I am a university student. History. Usually I say this right up front, only you didn't give me the opportunity.'

'Please forgive me,' she purred.

'All is forgiven, madam!'

'*Madam* makes me feel sooooo old.'

'Only when applied to elders. May I call you by your given name?'

He led Jaya to a complex of ruins. She was shocked by the amount of garbage thrown about; this was a UNESCO World Heritage Site, after all. He said, 'Jaya, these palace buildings were at one time cooled with ice from the Himalaya. The first recorded air-conditioning. They were grand, but as you see, they have fallen into disrepair.'

'There's not much left.'

'You said you wanted the best for last,' - he raised a perfectly arched eyebrow again - 'and this is the worst. Shall we move on?'

A minute later they gazed together at a mosque, not the Taj Mahal but something smaller. Jaya said, 'The king was Moslem, I take it?'

'You refer to the Mughal emperor, Shah Jahan. The Mughals ruled North India until the British exiled the last emperor following the Mutiny of 1857. Indeed, they were Moslems. You have read J.G. Farrell's *The Siege of Krishnapur*? It was winner of the Booker Prize.'

'You are very well read, I see.'

'One might say. My studies focus on Raj history: the despicable British Empire in India. Maybe you've read William Dalrymple? He's very popular with English speaking holiday-makers. I would have thought—'

'I'll check him out.'

'Dalrymple's formidable work is *The Last Mughal - The Fall of a Dynasty, Delhi 1857*. Have you read this one perhaps?'

'No, I can't say that I have. But after your recommenda-tion—'

'My ambition is to become India's William Dalrymple. Pop historians they are called, meaning best sellers. Whereas most academics can expect nothing more than an article or two in a scholarly journal. If they are lucky, a teaching post.'

'I studied anthropology in college, so I understand.'

'Maybe you are thinking this is presumptuous on my part, but as the saying goes, "One must aim high to reach great heights." Don't you agree? My dissertation will delve into the fascinating history of the East India Company. This will, I believe, attract an English-speaking audience as well as an Indian one.' He held onto Jaya's elbow as they took two steps upward, whispering, 'It is Friday, Jaya, and we are not permitted to enter the mosque.'

'Because I'm a woman?'

'Because you are an infidel. I too am one, being Hindu.' He gave a few more details about the building - height, width, building materials - before saying, 'Shall we proceed to the main attraction?' As they neared the Taj Mahal, Jaya realized that her pulse was racing. It was the most ethereal building she had ever seen, even though the iconic pools leading up to it had been drained of water. She only wished that her tour guide would shut up with his detailed description of the construction. During a rare pause, she said, 'It's a sad story... I mean about his wife dying.'

'Romantic, no?' he said. 'If one adds the romantic angle to history, one is certain to attract a larger audience.'

'But a tomb. There's nothing romantic about a tomb. If I'd known beforehand, I might not have come. It's sort of like visiting a graveyard when you think about it.' She paused for a moment, thinking about her mother's ashes stuffed into a cardboard box. The Taj Mahal was a step up, she had to admit.

The tour guide clapped his hands enthusiastically. 'As for the romantic perspective, the poet Rabindranath Tagore described the Taj Mahal as "a teardrop on the cheek of eternity." Rudyard Kipling wrote that it was "the embodiment of all things pure." One never tires of contemplating it.'

He walked briskly to where a group of people were

removing their shoes. Reaching into his pocket, he retrieved a pair of white socks. 'My mother cleans them every evening, you have nothing to fear. The marble tiles are very hot in the sun. Unsuspecting tourists, those who have rejected the services of a knowledgeable guide, have been known to received second-degree burns.' He bent down and untied his lace-up shoes. Jaya kicked off her sandals and pulled the socks over her feet. They buckled at her ankles. Not the most attractive look.

'As I said, Miss, the Taj Mahal was built to house the tomb of Emperor Shah Jahan's second wife, Mumtaz Mahal. Her name means "Chosen of the Palace." They were betrothed when she was merely fourteen years of age, but married five years later on a date selected by court astrologers to ensure a happy marriage. She died after giving birth to their fourteenth child. Are you married yourself, Jaya?'

'Never.'

'And no children?'

'None whatsoever.'

'Not one, Miss?'

Jaya wanted to scream, 'I'm totally alone in the world!' And it was true, she thought. The only child of an only child of...

'Sorry to bring up a painful subject,' he said, before launching back into his travelogue: 'Construction began a year after Mumtaz Mahal's untimely death in 1632. It took twenty-two years to complete. What we are about to see is a decorative mausoleum, as the emperor and his wife are buried underneath, a location we will not be permitted to enter. How are your feet - not too hot?'

Jaya wiggled her toes in answer. There wasn't much to see once they got close to the building. She felt sorry for poor Mumtaz Mahal, with her fourteen pregnancies, swollen feet, stretch marks, and, no doubt, a dropped uterus. Everything was conspiring to send Jaya into a slump.

That is, until her tour guide said, 'Jaya, perhaps you will consent to marrying me?'

She asked him to repeat the question.

'I am offering to be the husband you lack, Jaya.' Clearing his throat, he added, 'To take away your shame.'

'Why?' she said, genuinely puzzled.

'Because there are many opportunities for scholars such as myself in America. Whereas, here in India I will likely remain a tour guide for the rest of my life.'

'I appreciate the honesty,' she said, 'but can't you do better? A woman wants to feel cherished. Worshiped even.'

'We will grow to love each other. This is the way in our culture.'

Jaya belly laughed and he looked down at his stocking feet. 'How many times have you tried this on women tourists?' she asked.

'Is my delivery at fault - must I use flowery words?'

'It doesn't work this way in my country. People spend time getting to know each other first. You know, *dating*? We take Enneagram tests to see if we're compatible. Then we live together a few years before crafting a prenuptial agreement.'

The tour guide knit his eyebrows together.

The truth was, Jaya had always been a hopeless romantic. In middle school she secretly envied Evangelical Christian girls who received promise rings from their fathers. Girls who believed in the One True Love. But Jaya's mother did everything to squash that. 'Jaya,' she'd said, 'if you're waiting for Prince Charming to come along with a size 10, double E-width, glass slipper, you'll be waiting forever.'

'Look, I don't even know your name,' Jaya said now.

'It's on my badge. Didn't you read? My name is Anupam.'

'Look, Anupam. I'm not about to marry someone so he can get a passport. It's illegal for one thing. The INS will see right through you.'

'I'm gravely disappointed. *Crestfallen*, even.'

She found her wallet, thinking, 'Do I really look that desperate?'

'Five hundred rupees is the government price,' he said.

'You sure about that, Anupam?' She raised a mimicking eyebrow. 'How about two-fifty?'

'Maybe you have a friend in America, one seeking a husband?'

She handed over three hundred rupees and told him to keep the change. His face brightened slightly. He asked if she'd like to visit his family's shop, where one could purchase a hand-painted reproduction of the only existing image of Mumtaz Mahal.

Jaya declined and they parted ways.

The minivan returned to Paharganj and Jaya dragged herself back to the guesthouse, stopping along the way to browse in shops whenever her energy slacked. She kept a lookout for Yoel, hoping to see a familiar face. It seemed that while she was away a whole new crop of travelers had arrived. They looked dazed and overheated, but eager. Jaya failed to understand why anyone would come to New Delhi voluntarily. Only a last wish, a death bed wish, could have compelled her to come.

'Nice trip?' said the hotel owner.

'Magical,' she said, taking the key from him. He smiled as if she'd given him a personal compliment.

The elevator was out of order and she hiked up four flights, sweating profusely in the windowless stairwell. She stopped at each floor, clutching her sides and breathing heavily. By the time she reached the top floor, she was dizzy. Maybe I should have rested today, she thought. She came out between potted ferns and made her way around a balcony. It opened to a courtyard below. Across the expanse, she saw that her door was ajar. She dragged herself to the room, fearing the worst.

'You scared me!' she said to a housekeeper. 'I thought someone had broken in.'

The housekeeper flattened the white bedspread with an open palm. Jaya was happy to see that she'd let the air-conditioner run. The room was spotless. There was a spray of flowers in the vase beside the bed. Her clothes were neatly folded and the cardboard box was now sitting on top of the television. Jaya laughed. Her mother had never liked television. She called it 'The Boob-Tube.'

'Madam needing anything,' said the housekeeper, pointing to the phone. Jaya slipped rupees into the woman's hand and then made sure that the door was locked behind her.

The bathroom was sweltering. A small window had been left open, one facing onto a side street. Outside, brightly colored garments hung from clotheslines. Jaya drew the curtain and began undressing. She had lost weight since coming to India, but the sweat-soaked fabric clung to her body like a wetsuit. 'After a nap,' she said, 'I might buy myself an Indian outfit.' She imagined herself in a cotton dress over baggy drawstring pants. Aasi would be able to recommend a shop.

She sucked her bottom lip. 'Really,' she told herself, 'I did the right thing by not bringing them back to Paharganj.'

Under the cool spray, Jaya began to feel human again. A shiver ran down her body when she stepped back into the air-conditioned room. She toweled off and then laid on the bed naked.

Sometime later, she jumped from the bed taking a defensive posture. It was only after coming fully awake that she managed to shake off the nightmare. Something about snakes, that's all she remembered. She tried to grasp onto the dream before it was gone completely.

That was it! Aasi was being swallowed by a snake.

'Relax,' she told herself. She'd never been one to read portents into dreams. That was her mother, with a 'dream journal' next to her bed.

Besides, Jaya told herself, I'm not responsible for Aasi. Same as: I'm not responsible for the homeless people who beg for spare change, or the saxophone player who sets up in front of the bank with his hat in front of him. Still not convinced, she said aloud, 'And I'm not responsible for global warming either, because I don't have a car.' Then, realizing that she'd inherited her mother's Subaru station wagon, she corrected herself. 'A car with 145,000 miles on the odometer. A car that spits out black smoke.'

Only a rumbling stomach was able to interrupt this depressing train of thought. The guesthouse, according to the guidebook, had a decent rooftop restaurant. Rather than risk getting sick again, Jaya decided to have dinner there.

The sun was setting over Delhi as she was ushered to a table. The restaurant was otherwise empty. The temperature was dropping but the humidity hung on grudgingly. There was no menu, the waiter explained, before sounding off specials. Jaya asked him to let the chef pick, so long as it was vegetarian and not too spicy. He promised something 'delightful' and vanished behind a screen. Pots and pans began rattling in the kitchen, which was really just a hut set on top of the roof.

It's pleasant up here, she thought, watching as lights came on all around the city.

The waiter returned to the reception counter and put a CD into a player. Soothing music blended with the sounds of the Main Bazaar below. 'You like?' he asked.

'Tabla,' she said, without elaborating. After this trip she would donate her mother's CD collection to Goodwill. Her taste ran more to Top 40. Coldplay if she were feeling especially daring.

'Do you have a wine menu?' she asked, even though the doctor had advised against drinking alcohol while taking metronidazole.

The waiter glanced at a refrigerator. 'We offer Kingfisher beer. Or if you prefer, Foster's.'

Jaya searched her memory for a story, something she'd read about the 19th Century explorer and ethnologist, Sir Richard

Francis Burton, who was credited with having discovered the source of the Nile. And who drank a bottle of Port wine a day, believing that it warded off stomach ailments.

Who was she to argue with Sir Richard? 'Foster's sounds great,' she said.

A couple appeared at the top of the staircase, both out of breath.

'G'day,' said the man. 'They're open I hope?'

Jaya laughed. 'They are. And you'll be happy to hear they serve Foster's beer.'

'Everywhere in India. That piss Aussie beer. Why can't they import Cooper's?'

'You got me,' said Jaya.

'Mind if we sit here?' said the woman, fingering a chair at the nearest table.

'Be my guests,' said Jaya. The truth was, she was glad for the company. The Australians appeared to be normal. They didn't have piercings or tattoos anyway, and they'd combed their hair. The woman was wearing perfume that wasn't patchouli.

'American or Canadian?' said the man, 'I mean, it's obnoxious the way everyone assumes American when there's a vast country to the north where people also speak English.'

The woman jumped in before Jaya could answer. 'We're originally from Melbourne, but we live in L.A. now. John's a location scout. Did you see *The Best Exotic Marigold Hotel*?'

'I'm afraid not,' said Jaya, 'We don't even have a television. And the closest theater is in San Rafael, which is a bit of a drive. Sometimes we stream PBS.'

'We?' said the man.

The waiter returned. 'Malai Kofta, chef's best all-time recipe!' The chef stepped from behind the screen, waiting to see Jaya's reaction. He wiped his apron and returned to the hut satisfied.

The Australian woman eyed Jaya's dinner. 'It's said that a kitchen producing a good Malai Kofta can make anything. You know, the gold standard and such. You'll have to tell us how it is.'

Jaya waited for the waiter to pop the cap on a Foster's. The Australians continued to look on. 'Delicious,' she said, after licking the fork. The dish resembled two pointy tits with raisins for nipples. Jaya's face flushed with embarrassment. She wished the Australians would stop staring. 'Not that I'm an expert because, honestly, I've never had Malai Kofta before. Never even heard of it. Is it supposed to be sweet?'

'London is the best place for Indian food if you ask me,' said the Australian man.

'But the best Indian meal we ever had was in Dublin, believe it or not. What was the name of that place, Audrey?'

The woman tapped a finger against her mouth. 'Veda!' she said, pleased with herself. 'The Irish have stepped up their game. Used to be boiled mutton, potatoes, and soda bread. Washed down with a Guinness.' She looked into her partner's eyes: 'Ya' reckin' we share the Malai Kofta?' He answered by squeezing her hand.

Jaya felt lonelier than ever.

The wind picked up, blowing napkins across the roof. The umbrella above Jaya's head snapped in a gust of wind. 'I hope it's not going to rain,' she said.

'This time of the year? Not a chance. Not until mid-June.' He pursed his lips.

Jaya reached into her bag for the William Dalrymple book she'd purchased on the way back to the hotel, the only one of his books she could find at the used bookshop. It opened to an essay entitled *At the Court of the Fish-eyed Goddess.* The title reminded Jaya of Aasi's story: A girl who ends up a snake goddess. She pictured Aasi at this very moment, chatting companionably with Ed.

The Australian woman interrupted Jaya's thoughts, wanting to know what she was reading and if it was any good. Jaya showed her the cover and said, '*The Age of Kali: Travels and Encounters in India.* The author was recommended to me by an Indian scholar. I can't really say yet if it's any good or not.'

'Oh, then don't let us interrupt you,' said the man, who turned his eyes back on his girlfriend, or wife, or whoever she was. They seemed to be having a staring contest. Then they were kissing. Just lip pecks, but...

Jaya raised the book so that it blocked her view of them.

A phone rang at the reception desk. The waiter answered it and began speaking in a rising crescendo. Jaya didn't understand anything he said, but he was obviously agitated. She couldn't help but notice that he was looking at her the whole time. After returning the receiver to its cradle, he hurried over to the table, saying: 'Madam, the police are in the lobby asking for you.'

'But why?' she said.

'I don't know, madam. You must go to the lobby without delay.'

'Exercise extreme caution with the police,' said the Australian man. 'You should see how they shake down a film crew. Unscrupulous. I kid you not, we have a line item in our production budgets titled Baksheesh to Police and Government Officials.'

Setting down her fork, Jaya took a last swill of beer. 'It's got to be a mistake.' She lifted her bag from the chair, tucking it under an arm. Her knees were wobbly.

Back in the lobby, Jaya peeked from behind a life-sized statue of a baby elephant. Two policemen stood at reception. One examined the ledger book, copying information into a spiral notepad. The other paced back and forth between the desk and the orange sofa, turning with military precision. He took a breather to examine the motivational poster, smiling in appreciation. One of the hotel owners spoke to the policemen in an unctuous tone, offering refreshments and suggesting that they take a seat.

'We will remain standing,' said the senior of the two. Both wore uniforms but only his had epaulettes.

'As you wish,' said the owner, before spotting Jaya. 'There she is, at last!'

The senior policeman turned on his heels. 'You must come along to the station - we have taken your daughter into custody.'

'My daughter?' Jaya was confused and relieved, all at the same time. Clearly they had the wrong person. She could return to the rooftop, finish her meal, maybe order dessert.

The junior policeman took the spiral notepad from his breast pocket, flipping to the appropriate page. 'Your daughter is named Aasi Gravy, correct?'

'Not Gravy. *Gravely*,' she said. A knee-jerk reaction to always having her name mispronounced. Then raising her voice until it cracked, 'You must believe me, Officer. Aasi isn't my daughter. Why, I'm only twenty-one and she's thirteen.'

'You can make your report with my superior, Mrs. Gravely. I have orders to escort you to the station.'

'Honestly, I don't have a daughter.'

'Your daughter, madam, has been arrested for buying illegal substances.' He stretched his lips against his teeth, taking the posture of a drill sergeant.

There was little point in resisting, but Jaya did anyway: 'Can't we call your superior and straighten out this blatantly obvious mistake?'

'Impossible,' he said.

'Seriously - I don't *have* a daughter!' Somewhere in the back of Jaya's mind was a memory of Aasi telling her about police corruption. Ed had said something along the same lines. And the Australian. If the policemen even hinted at *baksheesh*, a little bribe, she would gladly give it. But they weren't doing that and her thoughts took a dark turn: What if she disappeared? Who would call the American Embassy on her behalf? Did they have Miranda Rights in India? Probably not.

Trying not to panic, she said, 'Okay...but first let me get a few things from my room. Prescription medication, for one thing.'

The senior policeman motioned for his subordinate to accompany Jaya.

'Is this really necessary?' she said, thinking, If he searches the room and finds the Valium, I'll use Dr. Patel's prescription to explain the pills.

They began hiking the staircase.

The officer shouted, 'Bring passports along! Yours and your daughter's.'

The junior policeman, at least, was the silent type, which allowed Jaya time to strategize. They arrived at the room and he watched as she inserted the key into the lock.

'I'm going to take a quick shower and change into something fresh,' she said.

A dark cloud passed over the policeman's face. Before he had time to protest, Jaya closed the door and bolted the lock.

She grabbed two pairs of panties and a spare bra from the neat pile, stuffing them into a daypack. Next went four Cliff Bars and the Moleskin journal. The idea of handing herself over to the Delhi police made her nauseous again.

Taking the guidebook, she entered the bathroom and let the shower run full force. She located a list of embassies and consulates. The call was answered after one ring. At this hour, she was expecting a recorded message.

'You've reached the American Embassy after our normal business hours. May take a message?'

'Thank God, you're human,' said Jaya, explaining her situation. Nodding at the response, Jaya found the Bharti Airtel SIM number scribbled in her Moleskin journal.

'Should I give you *all* the numbers? There's an awful lot of them.'

'The last ten, please.'

After they hung up, Jaya turned up the ringer volume, staring at the phone and willing it to ring. She realized with a pang, that her mother wasn't around to give advice. 'If ashes could speak,' she said with a sigh.

It wouldn't be long before the policemen forced her from the room. She slumped on the toilet. She checked the phone battery and found that it was fully charged.

It was then she heard someone say, 'Run!' The voice seemed to come from the vicinity of the cardboard box, which she could see through a hole where a doorknob should have been. But the voice might have come through the wall - from a flat screen TV in the next room.

She said in jest, 'If you're here Mom, knock three times,' then began weeping.

Her cloths were damp by then, the shower had turned the bathroom into a sauna. The space was dark until a streetlight switched on. It reminded Jaya of the Point Reyes lighthouse beacon on a foggy night. She bit her lip.

'Maybe it's a sign,' she said, exhaling.

Leaning out the window, she discovered a fire escape. When she rattled it, a screw came loose but it was otherwise sturdy. It led down to overflowing garbage cans. She opened her bag and considered if there was anything else she needed to take. Two Cliff bars and a John Le Carre paperback were sacrificed for space, but a minute later she had the cardboard box stuffed into the daypack.

With her mouth pressed to the door, she said, 'Just a minute!' receiving a frustrated grunt in reply. In a flash she was squeezing through the window frame. The iPhone made a bubble ring-tone. Jaya balanced precariously, digging around for the phone and then wedging it into her bent neck. She said, 'Hold a sec,' and wiggled out, swinging a leg over the rusty railing.

A voice said: 'Hello - hello? Miz Gravely? This is Megan Loomis, American Embassy...are you there? Do I have the right number?'

Jaya wasn't surprised to find her voice shaking. She was breathless too, free-falling four flights and then jumping six feet to the pavement, up and over the garbage bins. She landed in a pile of sand - yet another construction site.

'Miz Gravely, are you all right? Are you in any sort of danger?'

'I'm here,' said Jaya, putting the phone on speaker. 'But I'll have to call you back. Give me five minutes.'

'The answering service told me you called needing help.'

'I do. I'm in the middle of an escape, actually. Is this your personal number?'

'Oh, heavens,' said the woman with a drawl. 'Yes, this is my cell. But can you at least tell me where you are and if you're in a safe place? You *are* an American citizen, correct?'

'Five minutes max, stay by the phone please.' Jaya hung up and slid the phone into a pocket. Right then she needed to concentrate on finding an escape route.

She was standing in an alleyway. Other than a mother and two children circled up on a flattened cardboard box, the alleyway was deserted. Her attention was drawn to a propped door, to the voice of an overwrought actor wailing through surround-sound speakers. She stepped inside the darkened space and found herself near a movie screen, the biggest movie screen she had ever seen, bigger even than an IMAX

Theater's. The seats were half empty. A figure rushed at her and she jumped back.

'*Aaisakreem*,' he said, pulling an ice-cream pop from a cooler.

'*Jee nahin, Dhanyavaad*,' she said, something she'd learned from Aasi.

The ice-cream seller gestured toward an empty seat, and she considered taking it, then changed her mind. This would be one of the first places the police would search. The exit door was still propped open and the film illuminated every face in the audience. The film cut to a dance scene and everyone in the audience began singing along. Everyone but Jaya. 'I have no chance of blending,' she whispered.

She got her bearings. The theater fronted a crowded street, which was good. But the lobby would be empty, making her exit obvious. She ducked and ran across the width of the theater, to an exit door opposite the one she'd entered. An usher saw her approach and swung the door open.

Once she reached the street Jaya slowed to a walk, hoping not to draw attention to herself, an impossibility given her Danish stature and Western dress. Women called out, offering tapestries and brass bells. A man blocked the path, unfurling postcards. She was encouraged to visit Kashmir. Someone tried to hand her a menu for a tandoori restaurant. Jaya passed by without making the usual excuses. When a small hand tugged at her pocket, she brushed it away. The whole time her eyes scanned the road looking for a rickshaw. Several breezed past.

At the end of the block she spotted a rickshaw stand and began sprinting, imagining that at any second a police club would strike her head. 'What have I done?' she said to herself. 'What a dumb-cluck fool thing to do.'

She dove into a rickshaw, bruising her knee in the process.

The driver said: 'Where going?'

Jaya said, 'United States Embassy. You know where that is?'

He twisted his face into a grimace.

Leaning out, Jaya called: 'Does anyone speak English?' Two men ran over, sticking their heads into the rickshaw. 'Can you please tell the driver I need to go to the American Embassy.'

'American Embassy,' mimicked one of the men.

'USA, madam?' asked the other.

'Yes, USA.'

They began a harried conversation, none of which Jaya understood. Soon the rickshaw was surrounded, everyone in a loud and heated discussion. She tried to get the driver to start moving, but he was caught up in the conversation. Finally, a consensus was reached and people went back to their business. Jaya yelled out a thank you, '*Dhanyavaad*.' The rickshaw driver turned the ignition key and they left the curb with a jolt.

'That couldn't have taken more than five-minutes,' she said, reaching into her pocket for the iPhone.

Her hand came out empty. The other pocket held nothing but a Himalaya brand cough drop.

Covering her face, Jaya began weeping.

Chapter Twenty-Three

AASI LEANED HER HEAD AGAINST the cement wall. Grey, she noticed. She had been close to getting away, but the new shoes slowed her down. Her big toe hurt more than ever. If only she had chosen runners - the American brand Nike, perhaps.

The scene played over in her mind: Zulfikar Ali demanding the money, grabbing at Aasi's bag, and ripping the strap that wrapped it around her neck. They fought a tug-of-war and Aasi won. Ali was weak from drugs, famine-thin, with bruises below his eyes. He spit out the price and they exchanged notes for two plastic bags. The larger one contained dried, crushed leaves. The smaller was filled with chalky powder.

Aasi said, 'Is this the special?'

A toilet on the floor above flushed and Zulfikar Ali laughed. Half his teeth were missing and the rest rotten. Aasi should have seen this as a warning, she should have run right then. But sewage water rushed down a pipe in the wall, footsteps moved across the ceiling, and Aasi was momentarily distracted.

She said, 'Very good, *Sri*,' as policemen appeared from nowhere.

Maybe they'd been hiding in the next room, she thought now, trying to remember the order of events.

They hit at her arm and head with sticks and she fell to

the ground. They yelled insults, calling her a liar and worse: a drug-smuggler. They searched her bag and tore at *Grimm's* until it was nothing but confetti. Strange, because she couldn't remember having put the two plastic bags behind the lining where a seam was ripped.

'Heroin,' they said, meaning the white chalk.

Zulfikar Ali walked away after handing over the money. His laugh echoed through the hallway. Aasi heard glass crunching below his feet. A small boy peeked his head into the apartment and screamed. Aasi rubbed at her eye, which was swelling so that she could no longer see clearly.

She saw the policemen sneak Rodger's money into his pocket.

That's when she decided to run.

On the second landing her back was pressed to the floor by a knee, both wrists clamped with handcuffs. As they pushed her to the police wagon, she cried out her innocence. Spectators wagged their tongues in disapproval. She hoped her mother wasn't there in the crowd watching. What shame she had brought upon her dearly beloved parent.

Aasi's new shoes - the slow shoes - stayed on the whole time, getting only a few scruff marks. For that much, she was glad.

Sometime later, she found herself in a jail cell.

Fourteen people were crammed into the cell, along with three babies. Aasi recognized a woman as a Paharganj beggar. The way she held the baby, forgetting to cradle its head, told Aasi all she needed to know. Babies sold for less than a cotton saree. The woman made a living by pleading for powdered milk, using the baby as an excuse for needing it. As soon as the carton was in her hands, she sold it back to the merchant. The same box circulated dozens of times while the baby went hungry. Aasi had seen this woman stealing from shops. Things she could tuck into the folds of her saree: trinkets and bangle earrings, bars of soap and deodorant.

Now she had stopped pretending that the baby was hers. It laid on the cement floor with its cloth nappy soaked in urine. When it whimpered, the woman kicked it with a heel.

Aasi made her way to the baby, careful not to insult the other women by stepping over their legs. These are the kind who scratch out eyes, she thought. When she lifted the baby, the beggar turned away. The poor thing flopped in Aasi's arms, its eyes blank even when she cooed like a mother bird. The nappy wafted of ammonia.

'Girl,' Aasi decided.

Besides urine, the nappy was full of poo. She gave the beggar the evil eye and whispered her most potent curse, certain that it would rot the woman's intestines. Then she stepped over the beggar's legs.

There was hardly enough room for squatting and not enough to lie down and rest. Someone had stolen what little space Aasi had claimed for herself. Her new slippers, with the tasseled points, came to good use then.

The baby made sucking sounds and Aasi said, 'Sorry, honey, no milk in these breasts.'

A woman on Aasi's left bragged about having stabbed a man.

'Where is your knife now?' said Aasi, so that the woman would know she wasn't afraid. Surely the police had taken the knife, just as they'd taken everything Aasi possessed. Even the ankle bracelet was gone, the one thing she had of her mother's.

The woman seated on the other side was old, with a dried-up face. She pulled at the baby's toe, trying to make it smile. 'I have a son and two grandsons,' she told Aasi. 'My husband is expired.'

'They take care of you, *Dadiji*?'

'My son married a bad woman, an evil woman.' She tickled the baby's feet. 'I have a hard life because of this.' Aasi asked how she had ended up in jail, surprised to find her there. The daughter-in-law, the woman said, wanted to kill her. She put poison in her tea, but the old woman poured it into the gutter. She brought a scorpion into the shack, but the old woman crushed it with a frying pan. Early that morning, while the old woman slept, the daughter-in-law set the shack on fire. Four adjoining shacks burnt down, too. The old woman was accused of misusing the gas ring. Meanwhile, her son had stood by mutely.

'Seventy-two years old this year, I know how to light a stove.'

'Oh, *dadiji*,' said Aasi, 'I am sorry for your trouble.'

The old woman tilted her head, letting Aasi know that there were no words to describe her misery.

The baby's head fell backwards and Aasi cradled it with a palm. Its kohl-outlined eyes refused to focus. Aasi's beautiful new Panjabi suit was wet where the nappy rested.

'What happens now?' she asked the old woman.

The woman responded by tightening a shawl around her shoulders, making sure to cover her head.

The stabber said, 'They will assign us a government lawyer, but not until after a hearing with a judge. Then they will set a date for a trial and that might take years. Best you hire your own solicitor. Otherwise, you will spend the rest of your days at Tihar Jail. It's not so bad. The matron organizes meditation for the prisoners. Things could be worse.'

Aasi couldn't imagine how. The only solicitor she knew was an Iranian who had passed through Delhi many months before.

A while later, Aasi was escorted from the cell. A lady in a bronze-trimmed saree explained that she worked for the police. Her name, she said, was Inspector Kumar. Sindoor had been applied to the part in her hair, and a bindi to her forehead. Aasi wondered if she had children. Inspector Kumar spoke English. Aasi couldn't understand why.

Then she remembered telling the policemen she was American.

She tried to answer with an American accent, shaking her head the right way and letting her body hang loose. It wasn't easy given how terrified she was. Her mouth tasted of blood where she'd bitten the inside of her cheek.

They entered a windowless room. A table and two chairs filled the space.

'I need the particulars of your birth: birthdate, your parent's names, etc.'

'Arizona,' said Aasi, because she couldn't very well say, 'First day of Diwali.'

'What are your parent's names? We'll need to contact them.'

The first thing that popped into Aasi's head was, 'Jaya Gravy, Jyoti Palace guesthouse.' The American was kind: three meals in as many days. She complimented Aasi's stories. She hadn't crossed the street, ducked into a coffee shop, or hailed a taxi when she saw the girl coming. And she had offered employment; no one had ever done that. Edward Rodgers sent her on errands, which wasn't the same.

But it was more than that. Aasi fantasized about being Jaya's daughter. They had imaginary conversations, discussing mundane topics like household chores and shopping. She imagined a bedroom of her own in Jaya's California house. The walls were orange, then green, then purple. Jaya wasn't the first tourist to play the role. In a month, she would be replaced by someone else.

Inspector Kumar wrote JAYA GRAVY on a form, in block letters using a black pen. It was too late to take back the words.

'How can we reach your mother?' asked the inspector. 'Where is she staying? In a flat or in a hotel?' She left the room, returning with a soft drink, an American Coke, although the label was in Arabic and it had been bottled in Saudi Arabia.

'Apply that to your eye,' she said.

Aasi pressed the can against her eyelid. 'What will happen to me?' she asked.

'Nothing good,' said Inspector Kumar, same as the left-luggage manager. She continued filling out the form. Even upside down and with one eye, Aasi was able to read the words: *Heroin .25 grams. Hashish .50 grams.* 'It's not enough for a smuggling charge. If your mother gets a good solicitor, he'll plead for extradition.'

'Extradition?'

Inspector Kumar explained the term, then placed the pen on the table and stared without blinking.

'My mother is not drug user,' said Aasi.

'Who then?' Grabbing Aasi's arms, Inspector Kumar yanked until the pale undersides faced up. 'No needle marks,' she said to herself. Then with a raised voice: 'Who sent you to buy drugs?!'

Aasi looked down at the floor and kept silent. She was already in trouble with Edward Rodgers - losing his money *and* his drugs. If she spoke his name they would arrest him too. Moving only her lips, she said, 'Arē nahīṁ,' with a moan. Luckily, Inspector Kumar couldn't lip-read.

'Tell me exactly what happened, everything leading up to your arrest.' The inspector's fingers flexed above a laptop keyboard, waiting for Aasi to begin.

'I start at left-luggage shop, asking the way,' she said, deciding it was best not to mention the East Meets West Clinic. 'Then I became afraid of broken glass. Bad to step on glass, wouldn't you agree? I was needing to buy new slippers.' She showed Inspector Kumar her feet, as if to prove the story true. Inspector Kumar's fingers never stopped typing for a moment, taking down every detail of the story. Then Aasi mentioned Zulfikar Ali.

'Excuse me? Would you repeat that?' said Inspector Kumar.

'Zulfikar Ali,' said Aasi.

'And did the man answer to that name?'

'Yes. I ask if he is Zulfikar Ali and he answer yes.'

The laptop closed slowly. Inspector Kumar squeezed her eyes tight. Next thing Aasi knew, the inspector was pounding on the door. It had been bolted from the outside. She said, 'Wait here.' The door shut behind her with a bang. What choice did Aasi have but to obey? She drank the Coke, trying to calm herself by concentrating on the bubbles. Her stomach tumbled like clothes in a Maytag dryer.

The Inspector returned finally. 'Ṭhīka hai, back to the holding cell,' she said.

'For how long?'

'Until we decide what to do with you. There's the possibility that you'll be sent to Borstal School in the interim.'

'School?' said Aasi. 'They teach maths?'

'It's a youth detention center. I have no idea what the curriculum includes, but I'd assume maths were part of it. If anything, it would be a temporary arrangement. I doubt there'd be time to learn the multiplication table.'

'Don't you want me to finish the story?'

A wall phone rang. After she hung up, Inspector Kumar said, 'Good news. We have located your mother at the Joyhi Mahal.'

This is when Aasi started wailing. Like a widow tied to a funeral pyre, she thought later.

Inspector Kumar slapped Aasi's face. 'Stop that right now!' she said, shaking the girl's shoulders. Aasi's cries got louder. Inspector Kumar looked as if she would slap the girl again, but instead she reached out with a hug. Aasi's cries were stifled against Inspector Kumar's cushiony bosom.

Chapter Twenty-Four

THERE WAS NO SENSE IN GOING to the Embassy if it was closed. What Jaya needed was a phone. She tapped the driver's shoulder and told him to go to the East Meets West Clinic instead. He pulled up alongside a car and motioned for Jaya to speak to its occupants. The back window rolled down and an older woman leaned her head out, offering to help. Her hair was wrapped in pink silk, which wafted in the breeze. She brushed strands from her mouth and smiled. All Jaya wanted to do was crawl into her lap.

'My driver doesn't understand English,' Jaya shouted.

'No problem,' said the woman, cupping an ear.

'Could you tell him I need to go to the East Meets West Clinic on Nyaya Marg Road? Near the American Embassy.'

'American Embassy,' said the driver complaining.

'*Not* the Embassy, *Ji*,' said Jaya, 'East Meets West.'

The woman called out instructions, but the driver refused to listen. They had come to a traffic circle and the car veered to the right and raced away. The woman waved an arm out the window. Red and gold bangle bracelets gleamed in light cast by a streetlamp.

'Fine, American Embassy,' said Jaya, resigned to finding her own way to the hospital. The driver looked angrily into the rearview mirror, as if she had questioned his professional skills. She smiled back. What was the use of arguing?

They parked next to a barrier. 'Wait,' she said, getting out of the rickshaw.

'You pay now!' raising two fingers.

'Wait,' she said again, 'We're not stopping here.'

'You pay now!' He had his hand out.

Jaya found two hundred rupees in her skirt pocket. Before she had taken three steps, the rickshaw had made a U-turn.

On one side of a blue gate an American seal was mounted to the wall. On the other side were the words, *Embassy of the United States of America.* Even though Jaya had never been much of a patriot, had never registered to vote, served on a jury, or cared much for 4th of July fireworks, she found solace in these seven words. On the other side of that wall was home soil.

The problem was, they'd topped the wall with spikes.

A security guard stood beside neatly manicured bushes. He was wearing a baseball cap and a blue shirt with epaulets. He looked on lazily as Jaya approached. She wondered if the baseball cap was worn in homage to the American sport.

'When does the embassy open?' she asked.

'Nine in the morning.' He pulled at the end of an oiled mustache.

'Look,' she said, 'I've lost my phone, or maybe it was stolen. I don't know which. Could you—'

'Nothing to be done at this late hour.'

'You see, I was in touch with someone from the embassy. A woman with a Louisiana accent? Then I lost my phone, so—'

'Very sorry, embassy closed.' He consulted his wristwatch and said, 'Return at nine.'

'Would you be so kind as to call the emergency number for me?' Jaya removed the guidebook from her bag and opened to the appropriate page. The guard looked as if he suspected a terrorist plot. Jaya found her passport, pointing to the gold seal on its cover. 'Please,' she said.

He turned away.

She shouted, 'Call the *freaking* number, would you!'

The guard sucked at his mustache, refusing to make eye contact. Realizing that if she were to continue arguing he might call the police, Jaya returned to the barrier.

In the guidebook she found a map of greater New Delhi. The Embassy was marked as well as the clinic, just a few blocks away. She slung the daypack onto her shoulder; it seemed to have gotten heavier.

The road was pitch-dark. She walked pass the Myanmar Embassy, then the Russian Embassy. Consulting the map, she saw that she had come to Shanipath Road, with its grass median. Turning right, she walked past the Embassy of Netherlands, where the gate opened for a car. At this point she was beginning to recognize things: an Axis Bank ATM, the Canadian Embassy, a mimosa tree.

The hospital security guard recognized her. He stepped into his booth and pressed a button that sprung open a door at the side of the gate. Solar lamps, now dim, lined the driveway leading up to the front porch. Frogs croaked, and Jaya had to jump from the path of a sprinkler. She leapt again when a snake slithered across the grass, but it turned out to be nothing but a stick.

She thought of Aasi then.

Without a phone she wasn't sure what time it was. The front door was locked and she spoke into an intercom without getting a reply. A minute later she was buzzed in by a woman holding a mop. Behind the cleaner, Jaya saw that the floors were wet. Bleach burned her nostrils. The cleaner smiled and said something incomprehensible, although Jaya was almost certain it was meant to be English. The woman gave up and leaned the mop against the wall, escorting Jaya to the nurse's station. Grabbing Jaya's hand, she placed it on an old-fashion desk bell. Then she returned to her mop, singing as she went. Jaya rang the bell again and a nurse appeared from behind a door, rubbing sleep from her eyes.

'Doctor is not here,' she said, yawning.

'Yes, I understand.'

'Madam is sick again?'

'Something like that.' Jaya clutched her stomach.

She heard a British voice say, 'Today in Syria two militants—' She looked down the corridor and saw that the voice had come from Ed's room. 'I'll visit my friend,' said Jaya. Stepping into the room, she noticed that Kamika was curled up on the floor. Ed was sitting in a chair with his legs propped up. The television was tuned to the BBC news.

'How are things in Syria?' she asked.

'They suck.'

'How about with you?'

'Better than ever.' He put a finger to his lips. 'The kid is sleeping.' Then he turned his attention back to the television.

The room was dark except for flickering images of war and destruction.

'Can't you find anything cheerier?'

'Not in English I can't.'

'You mind?' Jaya placed her hand on the chair. Ed pushed it toward her with his foot. She stared stupidly at the television, not sure where to start.

'Have a pleasant day?' he said after a beat or two. He looked to either side of her and added, 'Did you bring my back-pack?'

'No, sorry. I'd meant to, but... I do have a John Le Carre for you.' She removed the cardboard box containing her mother's ashes, placing it on the bed. The paperback had gotten crinkled and she straightened the pages before handing it to Ed. 'I hope it's one you haven't read. There wasn't much of a selection. I bought two, but I'm not sure what happened to the other one.'

'Tinker, Tailor,' he said, looking at the cover. 'A good one. I've read it already, but it's been a while.'

'I spent the day at the Taj Mahal,' she said.

'How is the good old Taj?'

'A little depressing. It's a tomb, you know. But then I guess many of the Wonders of the World are. The Great Pyramid of Giza and the Mausoleum at Halicarnassus. I might not have minded so much if it weren't that—'

Rodgers flipped through the paperback. 'What was the other one you bought?' he asked.

Trying to keep her voice steady, Jaya said, 'Can I use your cell?'

'Sure.' He moved his eyes to the metal table beside his

bed. 'It's in the drawer.'

'What's your passcode?'

'Give it to me.' He pressed his thumb to the screen.

Jaya took it back and opened the guidebook. The number was underlined in smudged eyebrow pencil. She cleared her throat and said, 'American Embassy? It's me again - we spoke earlier. I need you to connect me with the agent. She called but I lost my phone. Better yet, give me her number.' Jaya paused and then whispered to Ed, 'He won't give it.' Muzak began playing through the phone's speaker and Jaya turned down the volume.

'What, did you lose your passport?' asked Ed.

'Do you have anything to eat?' She was feeling the urge to binge. Although that usually involved pints of Häagen-Dazs and Hostess cupcakes.

'Check in the fridge.' He waved a hand in that direction.

Jaya kept the phone pressed to her ear as she walked to a mini refrigerator topped with a microwave.

'Nice set up,' she said.

'Yeah, this place is decent,' - he took in the wood paneling and parquet floors, his face as smug as a lord in his manor - 'if you have to be in the hospital.'

The bulb lit up when Jaya open the refrigerator, but then went out inexplicably. She opened and closed the door a few times before it went on again, revealing paper bags each holding take-away containers. She was still on hold. Muzak switched to Justin Timberlake. Jaya found rice in one container and cauliflower curry in the other.

'Want any?' she asked.

'Nah.'

Jaya noticed that her hands were shaking. She said, 'I had a totally lame tour guide who tried to proposition me,' hoping to get her mind off her troubles.

'You mean, like, for sex?' They made eye contact.

'No, more like a marriage proposal.'

'Don't take it personally. Happens to American women all the time. The minute they get the green card, they're like, '*Outta here.*" '

Jaya sighed, turning her back. Tears welled in the corners of her eyes and she brushed them away hoping Ed hadn't noticed. She shoved the curry and rice into the microwave as the phone alerted her to the fact that someone was calling on a second line. She shouted: 'Hello! Jaya, here!'

Kamika sat up, rubbed her eyes, and then went back to sleep again.

The voice on the other end of the line was familiar. Redolent of mint juleps and Spanish moss. Jaya saw that her hands had steadied. She stepped into the hall.

Ed called after her: 'You're going to have to do something with the kid. She's cramping my style.'

Jaya returned to the room, ready to tell Ed everything that had happened. But before she could begin he said, 'Did you at least bring me the Wrigley's Spearmint?'

'I don't remember you asking for gum,' said Jaya. 'But so much has happened between here and there no doubt it slipped my mind. Sorry...I'd meant to bring your backpack. I'm sure the hotel owners will be happy to send it over. They're very accommodating.'

'Turn up the volume, you'll want to watch this. The show is sick, man.' The title credits began playing for a series called *Locked Up Abroad*.

Jaya groaned.

The episode featured a woman from Argentina who had attempted to smuggle drugs out of Indonesia. She'd been sentenced to execution. Her hair was stringy with grease and she kept having to re-pin her head scarf. She claimed to have converted to Islam. Every one of her sentences ended with '*Inshallah*.'

'God, how awful,' said Jaya. 'I really need to get out of Delhi.'

'Hang loose for a couple days and we'll go up north together,' said Ed. 'Then overland to Nepal, like I told you.'

Jaya pressed her fingernails into the flesh of her hand. How could Ed have forgotten about her plan to scatter her mother's ashes? The ashes were sitting right on his bed. 'No Nepal for me,' she said, turning her face away.

Rodgers turned his attention back to the program, which had resumed after a commercial break. 'Stupid if you ask me,' he said. 'The conversion story doesn't wash. Obviously it's a ploy to gain her captor's sympathy. Doesn't change the fact that she got caught with the goods. I mean, what kind of idiot goes through airport security with heroin in their luggage? Swallowing the stuff, at least, makes sense. Although there's always the chance the packet breaks in your stomach and you die.'

Jaya licked curry from the dish. She was still hungry.

Ed looked around the room. 'Where's the other one?'

'Other what?'

'The other girl. I thought she was with you.'

'You mean Aasi. Well, Aasi has been arrested. For having drugs, I think. The policeman said "illegal substances," but that must mean drugs.'

Ed spun in his chair. 'And you're only mentioning this now?'

The Argentine prisoner said, 'I regret what I did. It goes against everything I believe in. *Inshallah*.'

'Shut it off,' said Ed. Jaya was holding the remote.

'There's nothing we can do tonight,' she said. 'And if you must know, the police came to my guesthouse to question me. Apparently, Aasi told them I was her mother. I have no idea why. She must have told them I was staying at the Jyoti Palace.' Jaya's eyes opened wide. 'God - I hope she didn't mention this clinic!' Her eyes focused on the door.

'Do you mind if I lock it?' she said.

Ed sank back in the chair and said, 'Whoa, not good.'

'Now you know why I was on the phone with the American Embassy.'

'True. Now I know.'

Jaya walked back to the refrigerator. She found a package of cookies and half a banana, brown where it had been cut. 'Do you mind?' she said, lifting both.

'So, what did the embassy people have to say?'

'We'll meet in the morning. Meanwhile, I'm to keep a low profile.'

'Wait - I'm confused here.' He was waving his hands about franticly.

Jaya told him not to get worked up. That everything was under control, not that it was. She was grateful for his concern.

'It's a simple mistake, obviously. I tried to explain that to the police.'

'They let you go, just like that?'

'Not exactly.' She shoved the banana into her mouth.

'I can't understand you,' he said.

She swallowed and then launched into the story. Ed was speechless but communicated by twitching his eyebrows and lips. The only time he spoke was to say, 'You didn't mention me, did you?'

'Why would I do that?' asked Jaya.

There was a minute or two of silence. Jaya was exhausted and flopped onto the floor beside Kamika.

When she woke hours later, Ed was gone.

Chapter Twenty-Five

AASI WAS BACK IN THE CELL, rocking the baby in her arms. She tried to remember what it was like to be one herself: A blue room, a peaceful sea, mangos sitting in a wood bowl, a snake tattoo on her mother's leg. This is all she remembered, as hard as she tried.

Some days she was sure her mother had brown hair, but the next day the hair would change to red. Or was it pink? Aasi's mind played these tricks with every detail. Were her mother's eyes brown or blue? Whenever Aasi thought of her mother, she was sitting cross-legged on the floor so that her calf showed the yellow, black, and white scales of the rattlesnake tattoo. Sitting on a yoga mat, she thought now.

If only the picture would come into focus.

Aasi was certain her mother spoke English. Or was she con- fusing her with the American travelers she had spoken with since? None had had the same gentle voice. Jaya couldn't be her mother - not with black hair, straight like an Indian lady, and shaved legs. Aasi remembered the pale hair on her moth- er's legs, soft like a newborn rat. Hippies were the ones with tattoos covering their limbs. Jaya's was so small it looked like a birthmark.

Why couldn't Aasi remember the day she was taken from

her mother? 'Only kidnapping makes sense,' she told the baby. 'Cooo,' she whispered.

She closed her eyes and imagined the scene.

This time, the kidnappers came in winter, when people dragged their charpoy beds back inside and were sleeping beside electric heaters. She pictured others huddled below cardboard and scrap tin, around fires they'd lit using old newspaper. Shop attendants slept on the floors where they worked, with the doors shut against the cold.

Aasi opened her mouth, miming a scream. Her mother's scream.

In her mind's eye the scream bounced off window glass. Rickshaw drivers, coiled on their bicycle seats, lifted their weary heads before going back to sleep. Her mother kicked at the kidnappers. The tiny bells on an ankle bracelet failed to send up an alarm. Her mother managed to cry out a name - 'Aasi!' - before the kidnappers stuffed a towel into her mouth.

That's when the clasp on the ankle bracelet broke. It must have been then.

Aasi opened her eyes, wondering if she would ever see the ankle bracelet again.

The memories were clearer after her mother was gone. There was the lady with the mole on her face. Aasi had a vague memory of walking backwards with her eyes fixed on the lifeless body, then turning at the door and running barefoot from the slum.

But how did she get to New Delhi? Did she run all that way?

She would never forget the house full of beggars. Some

had been lamed on purpose, eyes gouged out with sticks, legs cut off, arms bird-thin. Aasi wished she could forget the babies in glass bottles, fed with straws until they were so big their bodies cracked the glass. After that they were freaks, with legs bent backwards and hands resembling bird claws. By the time Aasi came to live in that place, she had grown too large to fit into a bottle. The man explained that the babies had bad karma, that he was helping them to a better existence. 'Next life will be Brahmin caste,' he promised.

He had the children beg outside hotels, where business-men sometimes gave coins from foreign countries. Aasi once received a coin from New Zealand, impressed with the image of a long-beaked kiwi. American coins were the most coveted of all. These she hid from the boss.

The children begged until they'd collected enough money for their supper. Always the same: watery dal and rice with mag-gots; never chutney, never spices. 'Enough,' Aasi said one day, tired of bland food, of the boss, and of bottle babies.

That's when she came to Paharganj, although she had no memory of the journey. It's where Aasi befriended a hippie for the first time.

His name was Moonglow, which wasn't his real name. Moonglow was a hippie name, he said. He let Aasi touch his dreadlocks, but not the ring that looped through his lip. He was patient, listening to Aasi even when she had to revert to a lan-guage he couldn't understand. He saved the leftovers from his meals, seeking her out with grease-stained packages. A comb, a tube of antibiotic cream, and a walking stick were three of his many gifts. He had only recently returned from trekking and no longer needed the stick. The handle was carved into a lion's head.

'No use carrying a comb,' he said, rubbing a dreadlock between the palms of his hands.

Moonglow came from Oregon, one of fifty states in America. Aasi asked him to name the others. He began with Alabama and then said, 'Arizona.' To Aasi the word sounded like a perfectly pitched Tibetan singing bowl.

Ar-ahh-zooo-naah!

'I think this is where my mother is from,' she said, and asked Moonglow if he would help to find her.

'What's your mother's name?' he asked. 'I could look her up on Facebook.'

'I don't know. Can you say a few American names?'

Carol, Lisa, Sue and Beth... Moonglow knew many American names. And yet, none of the names made the hairs on Aasi's arms stand up again.

'Maybe your mother's name was Arizona.' He'd met someone named Virgina and another called Montana.

'Nahīm,' she said, 'No.' English was coming easily, as if it were her mother tongue.

One day they were sitting together in a park littered with plastic water bottles and food wrappers. Moonglow was trying to figure out the notes for a song. He hummed a note and then put a flute to his mouth. Even though he'd taken lessons with a master in Benares, Moonglow played the notes off-key. A waste of money, Aasi thought. The notes hurt her ears.

'You hearing song on radio?' she asked. It sounded familiar.

'No, it's a Bob Marley song.'

'You knowing words to song - English words?'

He began singing.

While he sang, Aasi was able to picture her mother's face. Even the nose came into focus, with a silver nose-screw on the left nostril. When she explained this to Moonglow, he said, 'Dude, I think your mom must have been a hippie. That's cool - way cool.'

'Then you be knowing her!'

'Doubtful. There's a lot of us out there.'

After he said this, Aasi wanted to throw herself in front of a train. She had never come so close to finding her mother. Disappointment was easier when there was no hope before it. She tried to picture her mother's face again but drew a blank.

A short time later she met Miss Elizabeth. 'Same as the queen,' the Englishwoman said. 'If you want to speak properly, you'll attend my classes. Every morning at eight sharp. Miss one class and you'll have to begin again at the start of the next month. English is not a subject to be taken lightly. Begin by dropping the *ing* ending in certain applications, a common error. For example, you will say, 'I know English' instead of 'I knowing English.' Until you know that much, you certainly *do not* know English!'

The first book Aasi read from cover to cover was *Grimm's Fairy Tales*. Her favorite story was 'The Three Snake-Leaves.' Before long she began making up her own stories, which always featured snakes. Miss Elizabeth didn't approve of snakes. They gave her the shudders, especially the one in *The Book of Genesis*.

'The serpent is the symbol of the Devil,' said Miss Elizabeth.

'Why would my mother tattoo the Devil on her leg?' asked Aasi.

'Just another one of your fairy tales.' Miss Elizabeth picked up a red marker. 'Snake, by the way, is spelt with a letter *n*. Otherwise the word refers to a Japanese alcoholic beverage called *sake*.'

Later, after Miss Elizabeth made a gift of *Grimm's* and the used bookseller refused to buy it, Aasi had the idea for her first business. Asking Westerners to donate used books was easier than begging or doing backflips. Before trading a paperback, she read it, copying new words into the blank pages at the beginning and end of *Grimm's*. Soon she was able to speak fluently with Westerners.

'During all that time,' she told the baby now, 'I never touched drugs. Not unless I was cleaning Edward Rodgers's chillum, that is.'

Aasi woke to find that the old woman had been taken away. The baby was gone, too. In her frustration, she kicked the metal bars. A guard passed on the other side and she asked to use the toilet. He pointed to a bucket in the corner of the cell.

'But it's running over,' she said.

He walked on.

Her neck was sore and the bruised eye had swollen shut. The only consolation was that she was able to flex her toe without much pain, although the toenail had turned black and blue and would likely fall off. Stretching from side to side, she grabbed her foot and held it in the air. Orange rays came through the barred window, making a striped pattern on the wall. At least now there was room in the cell to lay down.

A guard opened the cell door and shouted for everyone to get up. She led the women into an open courtyard, where they walked on a path made of bone-white gravel. When no one was looking, Aasi ducked behind a bush. After walking a few more circles, her toe began hurting again.

They were taken to a hall and told to sit on mats. In the center of the circle were three large pots. All they had to do was wait for the server to come to them. The pots went around twice.

Jail is not bad, she thought. Her stomach had rarely been this full.

It was only after finishing that she noticed a Westerner, sitting opposite in the circle and eating with her fingers like everyone else. Her head was shaved except for a braid hanging from the crown. She had tattoos on her throat: black spirals and lines. There was one on her head, too. On a bare arm, another tattoo wrapped completely around like a permanent bangle. She wore brown shorts and black lace-up boots. Two T-shirts - one black, one grey - hung from her skinny body. Aasi made eye contact. What had she done to end up here? she wondered, deciding on gold smuggling, the most exotic of all crimes. She pictured a backpack loaded down with gold jewelry, statues, and even a gold crown. When the meal was finished, Aasi made a dash across the space.

'Where are you from?' she whispered, so that the guard wouldn't hear.

'*Kahkoy*?'

'Don't you speak English?'

'Little.' From the way she said *le-tal* Aasi guessed she was from either Russia or Ukraine. 'You have *advokat*?' the girl asked.

'Avocado?' said Aasi.

'*Advokat.*'

Aasi shook her head, not understanding. Then she got it. *Advokat* was probably the same word as *advocate*. Language was funny like that, she knew. Words jumped from one to another, often meaning the same thing. Take the words pizza or television, information, omelet, or taxi.

'Have *sigareta*?' said the girl, pretending to put one to her mouth and suck.

'No cigarette,' said Aasi.

The girl's face fell and her eyes stared into space. '*Eto piz`-dets*,' she said. Aasi tried to explain that she didn't understand Russian, but the best she could do was to say hello a few times. At least this made the girl smile.

'*Bardák*,' the girl said, and Aasi realized that the one good thing to come of jail was the possibility of learning Russian. By now they were walking single file back to the cell. Someone had emptied the bucket and mopped the floor. The girl took a rag from her back pocket and dried a spot big enough for both of them to sit, a place along the wall so they might rest their backs.

The girl yawned, indicating boredom. Aasi couldn't blame her. There was nothing to do except sit and wait for something to happen. Their eyes stopped on places around the room, but they weren't looking at anything but their own troubles. Whenever the girl spoke, Aasi pretended to follow along by making sympathetic expressions. Several times the girl asked a question, her voice raised at the end of a sentence.

'I'm not understanding,' Aasi kept saying. After a while she gave up.

There was a long silence before Aasi began a story of her own. The story had been confiscated along with everything else, but she knew it by heart. It featured a Russian traveler and that's why she chose it.

The Russian Girl
and the Snake

THERE WAS A GIRL named Olga. She lived where the sun rarely came out, in a town where snow refused to melt and the streets were covered in ice. Electric heaters were useless against the cold. Olga dressed in furs and wore socks, a hat, and gloves. She slept below piles of blankets. Even so, she shivered constantly.

Her friends told stories of a place called Goa, with white sand beaches and never-ending sunshine. They returned home tanned from head to toe. In Goa, they said, tourists went naked. They let their nipples point to the sun while they danced on the beach with Hula Hoops.

These stories came as a shock to Olga. Her esteemed mother had taught her modesty. Yet she went to Goa anyway.

Day after day, Olga sat on the beach clothed in furs, sweating for the first time in her life. But when she considered removing her clothing, she would hear her mother's voice say: 'Child, do not be like these scandalous women.'

The Goans felt sorry for Olga, although they respected her at the same time. They brought coconuts, telling her to sip the juice through a straw. They brought buckets of water drawn from the well, ladling it into the girl's thirsty mouth. They invited her to sit below palm trees during the hottest point in the day.

One day a man joined her under a palm tree. 'I can help you,' he said. 'Come to my shop.' He handed over a business card with his shop number.

Olga reached the shop in an awful state, fainting near the door. The man carried her inside, laying her on a table. 'This is the perfect time to work,' he thought.

When Olga woke, she felt cool for the first time since coming to India. 'The shop must be air-conditioned,' she thought. But as her hands ran down her stomach, Olga realized that she was naked. As she searched for her furs, she let out a scream, thinking she'd seen a snake when it was her own reflection in a mirror.

The man returned to the shop. 'What do you think of my work? I picked a rattlesnake, the deadliest of serpents,' he said.

'Where are my clothes?' asked Olga.

'Into the dump. You won't be needing them.'

When Olga returned to the beach, the tourists ran away scared. She had the beach to herself. All day she lay coiled in the sand, soaking up the sun. She swam in the sea naked. The local people were grateful because the beach had returned to its peaceful ways. They continued to bring Olga coconuts and curries, hot and spicy.

She was never cold again.

Chapter Twenty-Six

JAYA HAD ALWAYS BEEN THE punctual type, but today she intended to arrive at the embassy before the doors opened. The embassy representative, Megan Loomis, had arranged to meet at nine in the morning. Jaya estimated the walking distance from the clinic to the embassy to be about ten minutes, but she hadn't counted on the sun being so strong that early in the day. Only by taking detours was she able to keep under shade.

At a traffic intersection, she saw a man selling something that resembled barbeque potato chips. It made for an odd breakfast, but Jaya was famished. The chips were spicier than she expected. She chugged from a plastic water bottle until her mouth stopped burning.

Her Prada knockoffs were ornamental - useless for filtering light - and they weren't prescription. What Jaya needed, she realized, was one of those silver foil windshield shades. She had seen Japanese travelers in Paharganj wearing moistened terry cloth towels on their heads. Indian women preferred umbrellas, which Jaya had only ever considered for rain. She wore a lungi - a gold trimmed cotton shawl that Ed had left behind - wrapped around her head and shoulders to keep the sun off her neck. When she saw her reflection in a window, she thought, I look like Christiane Amanpour reporting from Islamabad. Already she had wet patches under her armpits and where the underwire bra met her shirt. It didn't help that she was carrying the cardboard box. She shifted the daypack. Its straps were leaving nasty red marks on her shoulders.

The guard had been replaced by American soldiers, tall and buff, berets tilted jauntily on their buzz-cut heads. One invited Jaya to wait, tapping the face of his chronometer. She leaned against a wall and watched as the shade receded inch by inch. A half-hour later, she was instructed to put her bag through a metal detector. By then, a long line had formed behind her.

She entered the embassy to find a receptionist behind bulletproof glass. Jaya spoke into holes drilled into the scratched barrier. Must be the heat, she thought, because normally she was good with details but couldn't remember Megan's last name. 'Megan Something,' she said. 'I'm Jaya Celestial Gravely, as you can see on my passport.' She put the passport into a sliding drawer. 'Megan is expecting me.'

'You must be referring to Loomis. Let me see if she's in yet.'

'Any luck?' said Jaya, after the receptionist returned an earpiece to its cradle.

'I'm afraid not. But you are invited to proceed upstairs to the visitor's waiting lounge.'

The drawer was thrust back at Jaya and she retrieved her passport.

The waiting lounge was decorated with an American flag in a brass flag stand, plastic seats in red and blue, and floor tiles a shade of grey-blue. A photograph of the POTUS hung on the wall. Next to that was another portrait, someone Jaya didn't recognize but assumed was the Secretary of State.

She smelled a coffee pot before seeing it. It was placed on a folding table, along with powdered creamer and white sugar.

'Oh hell,' she said, pouring herself a cup.

She sifted through a stack of magazines and began leafing through *Time*. Her eyes gravitated to the text, trained to find typos. There was a *Vogue* in the pile: the September issue featuring wool and fake fur. The air-conditioning wasn't on and she used the magazine to fan herself.

Across the room was a flat-screen TV, the remote balanced on the thin-edged top. Jaya flicked the power button and surfed channels until she found the BBC news Asia edition. The newscaster was giving an update on the earthquake in Nepal.

That made Jaya think of Ed. She still couldn't understand why he'd left the clinic in such a hurry, without saying goodbye or leaving a note. Maybe he'd found a last-minute airline ticket to Nepal, one of those flights that required him to be at the airport at three in the morning. Ed had taken the John Le Carre novel, which was no surprise. But he'd also taken Jaya's guidebook, which was down-right baffling.

The news broadcast cut to scenes from the earthquake: a crumbed temple, paramedics carrying a child, piles of bricks where there had once been an apartment building. The city still hadn't recovered from the devastation.

Jaya thought, Tickets to Nepal are probably going cheap. What with tourists afraid of an aftershock.

She debated with herself. Was it a good idea to trust the American Embassy? She imagined shuffling through an airport with chains clamped around her ankles, handcuffed with twist ties and chaperoned by an FBI agent carrying a Zero Halliburton case. Or maybe she would end up on *Locked Up Abroad*.

The BBC cut to an interview with a mountain climbing guide who had been up at Everest Camp 2 when the quake hit. They switched to a Red Cross worker alongside a spokesman for Doctors Without Borders. Jaya tried to convince herself that her own troubles were nothing in comparison.

A man stepped into the room and took the seat next to her, first lifting his trouser leg so that it broke correctly at the knee. He was wearing a seersucker jacket over matching slacks. He cleared his throat. In anticipation, Jaya shut off the television.

He said, 'Hot out there.'

'Hot in here, too. You'll notice in about a minute.'

'Can't they pay the electric bill?'

'Budget cuts, I guess.'

The man laughed. 'Where are you from?' he asked, holding up his hand. His fingernails were buffed to a shine. 'Let me guess, say something.'

'Oh my *gud,* get *outta* 'ere.'

'New York. Too easy.'

'That's where I was born. I don't really talk like that...I was imitating someone.' She hugged the daypack to her chest, feeling for the edges of the cardboard box.

'I'm from Boston, myself,' he said.

'What brings you here? If that isn't too personal a question.'

He launched into a story about his passport having been stolen from his hotel room. He blamed housekeeping. 'Should have kept it on me, I know, or put it in the hotel safe.' He threw up his hands in resignation. 'The hotel manager denies it was their fault. Says the staff is "unimpeachable." '

'Stay there often?'

'What, the Delhi Regency? No, this is a first. *And* a last. I usually book at the Oberoi but with the trade show in town—'

A conversation that normally would have bored Jaya was having a calming effect. She asked, 'What kind of trade show?'

'Crafts. I'll tell you though, everyone's going to China these days. I don't know what's to become of this country if the government doesn't get it together with exporters. I mean, first the rigmarole of a business visa. Then they want you to register with the police. They used to ask for an HIV test. I mean, seriously? I'm a businessman, f'crying out loud - I don't have time for that. Now the Chinese on the other hand. How about you? What brings you to India?'

Jaya's stomach began tumbling and she said, 'Oh, this and that.'

'I'll probably be here a while,' he said, 'Waste the whole day. Fresh passport picture and all, identity check, you know the drill. They wanted me to bring along another American, one who could vouch for me. But I still have my wallet, right?' He threw up his hands again. ' - with my driver's license and credit cards.' He reached for the wallet, then changed his mind.

The room had filled, with every chair taken.

'Oh, well,' said Jaya, throwing up a hand, 'guess I should take advantage of *Vogue* while the going's good. She hefted *Vogue*. He lunged for *The Economist*.

As soon as the conversation ended, Jaya began stressing out again. Could the embassy really protect her from the Delhi police? She found a pen and began scribbling notes on a Versace ad. At the top of the list she wrote: *Ask Megan Loomis to recommend an attorney.* Hopefully, the embassy provided this service, something along the lines of a public defender. She hadn't exactly been accused of a crime, not yet anyway, but she wanted to be prepared. It would be her word against the police. Or her word against Aasi's. Jaya sucked at her lower lip. She wrote: *See what can be done for Aasi.*

As she scribbled this last action point, Megan Loomis walked into the waiting lounge. She was scanning the room and chiming out, 'Jaya Gravely?'

'Over here, Megan!' Jaya waved her hand in a concentric circle.

'Call me Loomis.' She was wearing a pinstriped pantsuit with the jacket sleeves rolled to the elbows.

Jaya tore the Versace ad from the magazine. She said, 'What a relief!'

'I skipped breakfast so as I could get here early.' Loomis held up a paper bag. 'Samosa. Enough for both of us. You want to come to my office?'

Jaya nodded. The exporter lifted *The Economist* as a way of acknowledging their fleeting connection.

Loomis went on, 'Just got off the phone with a co-worker, the one who'll be liaising with the police. We should hear back from her before long.' She swiped an identity badge over a scanner and a door popped open.

Jaya followed through a set of glass doors and down a corridor lined with the portraits of former American ambassadors. Loomis stopped off at a kitchenette and grabbed a plate from the shelf. 'Do you want coffee?' she asked, opening a refrigerator and removing a carton of milk. Jaya accepted gladly. She needed her wits about her and caffeine would help. They walked on, each carrying a mug. Jaya liked Loomis even more when she took a seat on the visitor's side of the desk. Loomis offered a samosa, swallowing a bite before saying, 'Why not start by telling me how you came to meet this beggar girl in the first place.'

Jaya dove into the story. Then she mentioned hiring Aasi to run errands.

'Bad idea,' said Loomis. 'Technically it's a violation of your visa. Assuming that you're here on a tourist visa.'

Jaya admitted fault by shaking her head.

'Should that be discovered,' said Loomis, 'you'll lose the visa and be fined on top of it. But why exactly didn't you cooperate with the police? I mean, if you are innocent...'

Jaya bit her lower lip. 'I'd heard about police corruption in India. How they shake down foreigners for baksheesh. I guess I freaked.' She worried about sounding xenophobic. 'I mean most Americans are freaked out by the police, right?'

'Most African-Americans, true.'

Just then it dawned on Jaya that Loomis was African-American herself. She said weakly, 'My mother joined the protest after the four policemen who killed Amadou Diallo were acquitted. She marched down Fifth Avenue in the freezing cold. That was before I was born.'

'Uh-huh.' Loomis finished off a samosa. 'One thing I can do is prove this girl isn't your daughter.'

'How?'

Loomis stood, brushing pastry flakes from her pants. 'If she was your daughter, it would have been noted on your passport record. Any child would have their own passport, too.' She stuck out her hand. 'Tell me you didn't mess with the chip?' said Loomis, examining a burn mark on Jaya's passport cover.

'My mother did it. Edward Snowden had just blown the lid on illegal government surveillance, so she put our passports in the microwave oven as a way of protesting. She read online that ten seconds was enough to fry the chip. I tried to stop her - really I did - because at the time I was applying to join the Peace Corps and I figured they need volunteers to have the chip...for some perfectly good reason.'

Loomis did a *tut, tut* rebuke and then got to work. The only sound in the office was the clicking of a keyboard. ''bout time,' she said when the air-conditioning turned on. 'They shut it off at night. Doesn't encourage overtime, Lord have mercy.' She viewed the computer screen through reading glasses perched on the end of her nose. 'Here we go,' she said, whirling the monitor around.

'I always hated that photo,' said Jaya.

Loomis clicked away at the keyboard before delivering a verdict: 'As I suspected. No evidence of your ever having traveled with a minor child, ever having traveled abroad until this trip to India.' She returned to the visitor's side of the desk after collecting a few pages from a printer. 'Couldn't hurt to consult with an attorney. I know a good one you can retain.'

'Can I make the call from here? I'd rather not leave the premises until everything is sorted with the police.'

'Understandable, but I'll need my office back.' Loomis

placed a hand on a stack of files. 'We have a cubicle you can use with a computer hooked up to the Internet. Meanwhile, let me get you that number. He's a very good criminal lawyer.'

'Criminal?'

'He represented the Pakistani-American implicated in the Mumbai terrorist attacks. The defendant was also a drug trafficker.'

'Not that I'm a drug trafficker *or* a terrorist.' Jaya feigned a laugh. 'I don't even smoke pot. You know, clove leaves and stuff once in a blue moon. My mother tried to get me into it but—'

'Well, bless her heart,' said Loomis with an expression that meant just the opposite.

Jaya found her way to the cubbyhole, a prefab office divider covered in herringbone twill. The chair was the ergonomic kind big in the 90s: backless with a knee rest. Taped to a telephone was a note: *Local calls only, dial 9 for an outside line.* She got the lawyer's voice mail; the message sounded efficient, yet friendly.

Next, she checked various forms of social media. Several people had written condolences on her last Instagram post, a photo of her mother.

A friend wanted to know when and where the memorial would take place. A great-aunt in New York needed the address of the funeral home so that she could send flowers. A college friend offered to bring over a tray of lasagna. Jaya teared up and wiped her eye with the edge of the lungi.

She sent an email to the neighbor, asking that he continue to water the plants. Her mother had had a green thumb. Their living room was filled with plants reaching to the skylights. Then there was the greenhouse out back, crammed with terracotta pots, bags of potting soil and seedling trays. It was likely that Jaya would kill everything before long, either by over or under watering. She added a line to the email: 'Take any plant you want. I'm sure my mother would want you to have something.'

She called the airline and was told that her ticket was non-changeable and non-refundable, something she already knew. She would have to buy a new one-way ticket but the travel insurance might cover the expense.

'What else?' she said, talking to the computer screen.

Something had been bugging her for a while now. Maybe it was the copy editor in her, always on the lookout for anachronisms. Aasi's stories were set in India, and yet—

She typed the word *rattlesnake* into the browser.

Loomis signed a few forms and then laid down her pen, saying, 'What can I do for you, Jaya? We haven't heard back from my co-worker, if that's what you were wondering, but it shouldn't be much longer. Did you manage to reach that lawyer?'

Jaya took a seat and said, 'Okay, I'm probably reading too much into this, but did I tell you about Aasi's fairy tales?'

Loomis rolled her eyes, picked up a pen and continued to sign forms.

Jaya began with, 'Once upon a time...'

A few minutes later, Loomis said, 'So what if the princess has a dragon tattoo?'

'*Rattlesnake tattoo*. Aren't you listening? There's always a rattlesnake in Aasi's stories. She says her mother had a rattlesnake tattoo. Her *American* mother from Arizona.'

'She's imaginative, I'll give her that.'

'But rattlesnakes aren't indigenous to India. I Googled it: cobras, Russell-vipers, sure, but not rattlesnakes. And yet they *are* indigenous to Arizona.'

'Did you call that lawyer yet? I think that ought to be your first priority. And let me tell you something, sweetie.' She laid down the pen, making eye contact for the first time. 'People'll do anything to get to the States. We had this handsome-as-all-get-out Kashmiri man in the other day telling us 'bout how he married a American woman for *love*. Love it was. On her side anyway, bless her heart. All'd she been doing was shopping for a shawl when he began professing his undying passion. Lordy, they hadn't even finished negotiating a price before she accepted him. *Whirlwind* ain't the word.'

Jaya thought about the Taj Mahal guide. 'But something rings true about Aasi's stories,' she said, half-heartedly. 'Couldn't we look into it?'

'On the basis of what exactly - a fairy tale?'

'But the girl has no one. She's an orphan, I think.'

'This is the American Embassy, not UNICEF.'

'But what if she really is an American citizen. Couldn't we—'

'You mean *me*, not *we*.' Loomis motioned toward the stack of files. 'Look, I've got work to do. I'm not on vacation.'

'I'm not on vacation either.' Jaya crossed a leg over a knee and her arms over her chest. She let her head swagger a bit. It was as if she had inherited one of her mother's character traits but it had only now begun to show.

Loomis propelled herself forward in the chair. 'Jaya, sweetie, your naiveté is breathtaking.'

Jaya swaggered her head again, trying for even more bravado. Loomis lifted the fattest of files. Then she swiveled her chair until it faced the window.

An hour later, Jaya needed to use the ladies' room. 'Don't think I've given up,' she said.

'Shut the door on your way out, would you?'

Loomis waited a minute before consulting a phone directory. After dialing three numbers, she said, 'Neel - it's Meg Loomis. When you have a sec give me a callback.'

Chapter Twenty-Seven

A CHAIN RATTLED AGAINST THE CELL BARS. Aasi watched as the guard opened the lock. Standing behind him was Inspector Kumar. The Inspector said, 'That one,' and motioned a hand toward Aasi.

'*Zdravstvuyte*,' said Aasi to her Russian cellmate, not knowing the word for goodbye.

She followed at Inspector Kumar's heels. 'Have you come to take me to school?'

'Not yet. But there is someone here needing to speak with you.'

Aasi expected to find Jaya. But when she entered the room - the same room she had been in earlier - she realized her mistake. Sitting in a chair was a different Westerner. She wore Indian clothing with a white turban wrapped around her head and a dupatta - a long scarf - draped across her neck. A few strands of hair had escaped the turban. They were brown, Aasi saw, and her knees began trembling.

The woman stood, reaching out a hand.

This must be my mother, thought Aasi. Their hands clasped and Aasi tightened her grip, not wanting to let go.

Inspector Kumar said, 'I'll leave you two to talk,' shutting the door behind her.

'Why don't you take a seat here?' said the woman, pulling out an empty chair.

Aasi knew it was best she sit down. What does one say to a long-lost mother? she thought. The woman was older than in her memories, but that would be the case after all these years. And she was heavier, too. Aasi remembered her mother as being slim. There did seem to be a small puncture mark where a nose stud used to be.

'Call me Mrs. Singh.' The voice was American but not the name.

'You have taken a Sikh husband?' asked Aasi.

'That's right,' said the woman, playing with the turban until it was properly balanced on her head. She took a pad of paper from a briefcase and fished around for something else. 'Why can't one ever find a pen?' she said. Aasi had no answer, never having had this problem herself. The woman clicked the pen open and shut.

'Is your husband a good man?' asked Aasi, 'Will he be a good father?'

'What a funny question. Well, yes, he's a good man, and I think he's a decent father.'

'You have other children?'

'Other children?'

'Besides me.'

'Oh, I see. You've mistaken me for someone from Child Protective Services or whatever the Indian equivalent. But actually, I work for the American Embassy.' She found a badge hidden below the dupatta.

'Embassy is a good job,' said Aasi. 'Did you attend college?

Is that why you left me?' Her voice broke. She was shocked by the strength of her anger. All she wanted to do was kick her mother and shout a curse. This was nothing like the reunion she had imagined, where her emotions were infused with love and devotion.

'I think there's been a mistake,' said Mrs. Singh. 'You see, to get right to the point, I've been called in at the request of Inspector Kumar. She's the police officer who was just here. Because according to Inspector Ankita Kumar, you claim to be an American citizen.'

'Where are you from?' asked Aasi, beginning to realize her mistake. She looked closely at Mrs. Singh. The woman's right nostril was pierced, not the left. Aasi closed her eyes and brought up the memory of a stud on the left side of her mother's nose. This time the stone was bright emerald green. Besides that, Mrs. Singh's earlobes weren't right. They hung from her head at a strange angle. And another odd thing was that the hair color on her arms didn't match the color on her head. If only Aasi could get a close look at the roots. She wanted to rip the turban from Mrs. Singh's head and fling it to the ground.

Aasi calmed herself by biting the inside of her mouth.

'I'm from Minneapolis, originally,' Mrs. Singh was saying.

Aasi looked at her suspiciously. It was not a place she'd heard of.

Mrs. Singh said, 'Look, you're going to have to be candid with me. From what I understand, you've been charged with possession of drugs. A serious offence in this country. In any country, for that matter. Since you were arrested in Paharganj, I'm guessing your parents are the types that frequent that place. I'd like nothing better than to help you, but first you'll have to tell me where to find them.'

'I'm not knowing where my parents are,' said Aasi. 'I'm not know.'

Mrs. Singh clicked open the pen. 'Now, come on. Be honest with me.'

'No, I don't know.'

The pen was used like a timer: click, click, click it went. Mrs. Singh waited for Aasi to break down and give an answer. Flinging the briefcase open, she said, 'Do you want to end up rotting in prison?' Inside the briefcase she found a sucking candy and popped it into her mouth. 'Let's try another tactic,' she said.

She had a habit of licking her teeth, which made Aasi think of a hungry tiger. 'Inspector Kumar says you claim your mother is Jaya....' - she examined her notes - 'Now what was her last name again?'

'Gravy,' said Aasi.

Mrs. Singh grinned menacingly. 'That's exactly how we know that Jaya Gravely is *not* your mother. If she were, you'd know her surname. In fact, Miss Grave*ly* has been in touch with my colleague, confirming this fact.'

'Gravely, I mean Gravely.'

'It won't do any good to protect your parents,' said Mrs. Singh, shaking her head mournfully. 'It wasn't right for them to send you to buy drugs.'

'She didn't. My mother didn't send me for ganja.'

'Then who, may I ask, did?'

'A different American but I'm not telling.'

Mrs. Singh shifted through a handbag and found a cellphone.

She repositioned her chair so that it faced the wall and pressed the phone to her ear. After a pause she said, 'Well, this was a fool's errand. I seriously doubt that the girl is an American citizen, whatever she might say to the contrary.' Lowering her voice she added, 'Her accent is British with Indian inflections. What should I - okay, sure, I'll hold.' Taking the phone from her ear, Mrs. Singh spun until her eyes met Aasi's.

'I'm happy you are not my mother,' said the girl.

Mrs. Singh stuck out her tongue, rolling it into a tight circle. Immediately, her attention was back on the phone: 'Yes, I'm here,' and after a minute, 'I see your point. And the answer is no, I don't think they'll release her to me. Not until the deadbeat parents are in custody and we have proof that at least one of her parents is a citizen. Say that again...Jaya Gravely is there? Fine, call me back.'

While they waited, Mrs. Singh flipped the pages of a paperback. It was a new book, Aasi saw, one that would be perfect for trading. But Mrs. Singh had folded the ends of the pages to mark her place, something the bookseller frowned upon. He gave away bookmarks to prevent such a practice. 'Vandalism,' he called it.

'That is a filthy book,' said Aasi, as a way of getting back for the way Mrs. Singh had insulted her esteemed mother.

Mrs. Singh slammed the book shut.

'My mother would never read that book.'

'Oh, your sainted mother - who sends you to purchase drugs!'

'She never!'

The book slapped against the table. 'Then who did!?'

'Edward Rodgers!' shouted Aasi, before she could stop herself.

'He's your father?'

'No, my friend. My boss.'

Mrs. Singh sat back in her chair, licking her lips like a dog at a trash bin. 'Now we're getting somewhere. And this Edward Rodgers fellow - he's American?'

Aasi was too angry with herself to speak. Mrs. Singh leaned over the table, bridging the gap between them. She whispered, 'I have no intention of turning an American citizen over to a foreign police force, however abhorrent his actions. But don't think for a second I won't have his passport revoked and his sorry you-know-what hauled back to the States. That is, unless he tells me where your parents are.'

'He's not knowing my parents either,' said Aasi with a whimper.

'Either?'

Aasi began to cry. 'Nobody knows what happened to mother. Something bad, this I know.' When Aasi sniffled, Mrs. Singh handed over a pack of tissues.

'I think she was...sold into slavery.'

Aasi began telling her favorite story, but Mrs. Singh interrupted: 'Your mother had a snake tattooed on her leg? Are you sure about that?'

The phone vibrated on the table. Mrs. Singh answered and said, 'Listen, I'm making headway. First thing is we have to locate an American by the name of Edward Rodgers - no, he's not the girl's father, but he may have sent her to buy the heroin - yeah, I know - uh, huh. And see if there's been a missing person's case: American woman with a snake tattooed on her leg - with a child. Ask around the embassy - try Neel Ray. He's been there the longest.'

'Brown hair,' said Aasi. 'My mother had brown hair!'

Staring right at the girl, Mrs. Singh spoke into the phone: 'Yeah, I know - far-fetched.'

Inspector Kumar entered the room and invited Mrs. Singh to join her in the corridor. Aasi crept to the door so that she could listen to their conversation.

'The lab report is in,' said Inspector Kumar, lowering her voice. 'Laundry powder. Same *exact* brand I use. I ought to have known immediately by the fragrance. The minute I heard Zulfikar Ali's name I knew something wasn't quite—'

'—copasetic,' said Mrs. Singh. 'I think I get your drift.'

'Ali was already in custody, that much I've been able to confirm. And, by the way, the other bag contained dried *tulsi* leaves.'

'Basil,' said Mrs. Singh.

'The arresting officer, I happen to know, is in the process of building himself a villa in Maharashtra. Last week they began pouring concrete. It's to have a wraparound balcony with sea views. Shameful.'

Aasi tried to guess why it was they were talking about laundry detergent, tulsi leaves, and villas, but gave up. She heard Inspector Kumar say, 'Well, I'm releasing this child, Cathy. Do with her what you want.'

Mrs. Singh said, 'A night in jail probably did the girl good.'

When they returned to the room, Aasi said, 'Cell is very nasty wouldn't you agree?'

Inspector Kumar glared at Aasi, wagging her index finger. 'I've been working all night on your case without so much as a single break. I skipped dinner even. I'm absolutely starving.' Aasi didn't believe it. There were rolls of fat around Inspector Kumar's stomach and her toes bulged over the edges of beaded thong sandals. Aasi whirled her feet around hoping to impress the woman with her new slippers. Her narrow feet, she saw, fit perfectly into the pointy toes. With the exception of her big toe, which pinched something terrible. They were slippers for truly starving people.

'Stop squirming,' said Mrs. Singh, then turning to Inspector Kumar, 'I have my car. I can give you a lift home if you'd like. We'll unload the girl first.'

'Let me collect my shawl!' said Inspector Kumar.

Once she was gone, Mrs. Singh packed up the briefcase, placing the paperback under the laptop. She loosened the dupatta and said, 'How she can possibly wear a shawl in this heat is beyond me.'

'It's very cold in here, wouldn't you agree?' Aasi began to shiver, thinking about the concrete floor in the jail cell and how much she hated sleeping there.

They returned most of her few possessions. *Grimm's Fairy Tales* hadn't weathered the ordeal; the cover was completely torn off. A whole section was missing out of the middle, along with Aasi's favorite story. The lining of the bag had been ripped open and the contents of her small purse spurn around. They let her keep the wooden bowl she used when performing acrobatics. A pack of Wrigley's Spearmint gum was short two pieces.

The foreign coins were there, but anything Indian was gone.

The ankle bracelet, her most precious possession, had been returned. She was glad not to have rubbed the black tarnish from the silver.

Mrs. Singh collected her keys from a security guard and got into the driver's seat. Aasi didn't know where they were taking her and was afraid to ask. She hoped it was to the Borstal School Inspector Kumar had mentioned earlier. She pictured herself in a neat uniform, a dark blue skirt with a pale blue shirt. She envied the school children she saw walking the streets of New Delhi, carrying their books in buffalo leather backpacks. Her new slippers, she thought, would go well with the uniform.

Mrs. Singh drove herself. Aasi wondered if this was the usual practice for Americans. She sat in the back seat with Inspector Kumar.

'Are you taking me to school?' she asked in a whisper.

'No.' Inspector Kumar said no more.

If she looks the other way, I'll jump out, thought Aasi. But before she had a chance, the doors were locked automatically. In the rearview mirror she caught Mrs. Singh eyeing her.

The car picked up speed and Inspector Kumar grabbed onto Aasi's hand. In a pleading voice, she begged Mrs. Singh to drive more cautiously. Whenever Mrs. Singh slammed on the brakes, Aasi felt the Inspector's hand tighten around hers. A couple of times, her arm reached in front to prevent Aasi from flying forward. They raced past lorries and checkpoints and took traffic circles without slowing. Several times, Inspector Kumar was pinned against Aasi's side. Aasi didn't mind in the least.

They pulled through a set of gates and a soldier instructed

everyone to get out of the car. Aasi wondered if they had taken her to another prison. She saw a three-story building with bars on the windows, enclosed in a wire-topped chain-link fence. Another soldier approached, led by a dog on a leash.

Aasi had trouble swallowing.

Mrs. Singh said, 'Up and at 'em. American Embassy.'

Aasi's heart thumped when she realized where she was.

Strangely, it was no different than India. The trees were the same and so were the bushes. An Indian man swept the ground using a whisk broom. Hindi script was written below English on the signs. Where were the wide lawns and swimming pools she had heard about? Where were the cowboys and Indians, like the ones in a novel she had skimmed before trading? The *American* kind of Indian, with a feather crown and tomahawk? The building was the usual Delhi type, concrete and rectangular. The cars in the parking lot were Fords, Hondas, and Toyotas - the same brands as outside the gates.

She tried not to let her disappointment show, forcing a smile as the soldiers examined Mrs. Singh's car. They checked the engine, searched the trunk, and waved a mirror along the underside of the car.

'Is something wrong with the car?' she asked.

'They're searching for bombs,' explained Mrs. Singh.

Inspector Kumar wasn't surprised by any of this. The whole time they waited, she stood a little way off making calls on her mobile. How nice, thought Aasi, to have Inspector Kumar for a mother, one who prepares traditional Indian dishes and teaches her daughter to make chutney. Aasi had been looking forward to lunch at the prison. An American jail would serve something inedible.

A helicopter came into view, hovering above the embassy.

'The Ambassador returning from his trip to Washington,' said Mrs. Singh. 'Notice the seal?' Aasi turned her head sideways, making best use of her good eye. The helicopter had the same emblem she had seen on American passports.

The soldier said, 'All clear, ma'am.'

Mrs. Singh lowered her sunglasses. 'Back in,' she said.

Aasi asked Inspector Kumar, 'Will they ask hard questions? Make me name all fifty states? Can you tell me the capital of Arizona, please?'

Inspector Kumar whispered in her ear: 'Ever hear of waterboarding, you silly child?'

'No,' said Aasi, softly. 'Is it fun?'

'You'd better watch your step around these people, that's all I've got to say.'

They parked a few feet from the gate.

Chapter Twenty-Eight

AASI CAME BOUNDING FORWARD, causing Jaya to stagger backwards.

Jaya brushed the girl's hand away. She said, 'You're doing this to prove I'm your mother and I can't have that. Now let go of my arm.'

'Sorry, Auntie.'

'I'm not your aunt, either.'

Jaya watched as Aasi lowered her eyes to the floor. The girl seemed to have gotten smaller and even more fragile. Jaya placed a hand on one of the girl's shoulders, feeling bone under her fingers.

'You must be Jaya Gravely,' said Mrs. Singh.

Jaya was reminded of a friend of her mother's, a convert to Sikhism. Everyone in the family wore a white turban like this woman's, even the children. Jaya wasn't sure if she should reach out a hand or salaam.

'I work with Ms. Loomis in the Consular Office. Cathy Singh.'

Jaya was relieved of indecision when Mrs. Singh extended a hand.

Inspector Kumar stepped forward and introduced herself. 'Ankita Kumar, Delhi Police, Special Police Unit for Women & Children.'

Ankita Kumar was the opposite of the policemen at the Hotel Jyoti. *Ethereal* was the word Jaya landed on: Venus De Milo but with more coverage. Yet there was something alarming about the way in which the Inspector's eyes darted around Jaya's face, narrowing into slits. As if to say, 'I don't trust you, not for a second.'

Aasi turned her big eyes to Jaya's, begging to apologize. 'Sorry, lady,' she said in a whimper. 'Edward Rodgers say everything safe, no trouble.'

'Ed said what?'

'Why don't you two wait here,' said Mrs. Singh.

Before Jaya had time to protest, the two women were at the glass doors, Mrs. Singh swiping an ID badge over the scanner.

'Funny that they left you unsupervised,' said Jaya. 'How come you're not locked up?'

'This is the *extra-dish*. Means I go to jail in America. Please say you're my mother.' She wrinkled her nose, 'Jail in India is oh so nasty. Smells like sewage drains. No mats on the floor for sleeping.'

'Just stop with the mother thing, please.' Jaya pressed her temples. She found two seats together and threw a Hindi language magazine into Aasi's lap, choosing *Vogue* for herself. Flipping through the pages, she took her anger out on perfume ads. 'At this rate I'll never get to Varanasi,' she said aloud. Before long, scratch and sniff cards were scattered on the carpet. Aasi's good eye stayed fixed on Jaya the whole time.

'Read your own magazine,' said Jaya.

'Can't.'

'Why not?'

'Can't read Hindi.'

'That story about your mother being American? I doubt you'll be able to convince them. I'm easy to bamboozle, but that policewoman looks like a shrewd character. And Mrs. Singh - well, I will say no more. They hear all sorts of sob stories and they're beyond calloused.'

They sat quietly after that. The crowd, Jaya saw, was mostly Indian. Many had visa applications in hand. According to Loomis, very few stood a chance of getting one.

Aasi's good eye became glassy with tears. Jaya said, 'Here take this,' handing over a perfume card, this one for Chanel Coco Mademoiselle.

'What is it?' asked Aasi.

'A surprise. Peal it open and see - or smell, rather.'

'Smells nice.' Aasi held the card to her nose. 'Can I keep?'

'Did the police do that?' said Jaya, meaning the black eye.

Aasi spoke too quietly to be heard. 'They made me sleep in cell with thieves.'

'Well, what did you think would happen when you bought drugs?'

'I wasn't knowing. I *really, really* wasn't knowing. It is a matter of fact. Edward Rodgers was needing ganga, a little ganja for his health. He say, ask for his friend Zulfikar Ali at left-luggage shop. He promised to buy me carton of Nag Champa incense sticks, but first he needing ganja. No ganja, no Nag Champa. You believe me?'

Jaya's jaw dropped as the pieces slid into place. She said to herself, 'That self-righteous, self-centered, son of a...'

There was a hippie in the waiting area, a young woman

cradling a baby. She turned when Jaya raised her voice. They sat close enough to speak, although the hippie had to bend awkwardly to do so. Aasi crouched toward the baby. She tickled under its triple chin. Both the baby and the mother made gurgling sounds.

I'm through with hippies, thought Jaya.

The hippie said, 'Only three weeks old, I'm sure you were wondering.'

'You gave birth in India?' asked Jaya.

'At a birthing center in Goa. It's run by an Austrian midwife. Really beautiful place, kinda bohemian-chic, if you know what I mean. You give birth in a mosaic pool, under a canopy of papaya trees. So *shanti*.'

It was a word Jaya's mother used. She knew it meant peaceful.

'Super shanti...well, right up until the actual birth. The problem was a Cephalopelvic Disproportion, the baby's head was too large to fit past my pelvis. They had to call for an ambulance. I should have known because my hips are sooooo narrow.'

Jaya could see that for herself. The girl wore a floor-length, gauzy skirt and the elastic waistband hung below her jutting pelvic bones.

'Such a bummer,' the girl continued, 'that the *first* thing she saw coming into the world was an operating room with all that torture equipment.'

'You had a Caesarean?'

'It was that or die!'

The girl crossed an ankle over her knee, revealing her calf. Aasi examined the leg and then returned to the seat beside

Jaya.

Jaya wanted to change the subject. If she weren't careful, they would soon be discussing her recent bereavement. There she was, baring her soul to Edward Rodgers, and what had that gotten her?

She said, 'Are you here to get the baby a passport?'

'Eventually. My partner and I don't have plans to return to the States yet, but they make you file this form.' A multi-page form was flapped in the air. 'Consular Report of Birth Abroad. They need to see the birth certificate and my passport, make sure it's all legit. Only after that can we apply for a passport. I hate the idea of it, being coerced into registering her with *The System*. Now she'll have a name and a number.'

'Not to mention the chip they imbed in the passport,' said Jaya.

'Oh! I hadn't thought of that.' The hippie whipped her head around. 'My number's been called!' After throwing things into a hemp bag, she ran toward a digital signboard, franticly searching to see which window she had been assigned.

Aasi sat rigidly in the seat with her arms stretched out in front of her, hands in tight fists resting on her knees.

'What's gotten into you?' asked Jaya. 'Have you eaten? Maybe you're thirsty? They have coffee and water over there.' She could see that something had been triggered by this encounter. She wasn't sure what exactly it was but took a stab. 'Does she remind you of your mother?'

'What if I don't have a mother?' said Aasi.

'Everyone has a mother. It's a biological necessity. I doubt you're a test tube baby, but even those have mothers technically speaking. There's surrogate mothers and egg donors and they all count as mothers. My father was a sperm donor but technically he's still my father...whoever he is.'

Aasi looked at Jaya angrily.

'Calm down,' said Jaya. 'I'm sorry that you don't have a mother. I'm sorry you're an orphan. It's a stinking, rotten deal. I'd be upset too.' She took a deep breath. 'I used to wish I didn't have a mother.'

'Why?' Aasi said beseechingly.

Jaya had trouble breathing. 'I don't know why I said that.' She thought for a minute. 'She was controlling, for one thing. Like I was some sort of experiment to raise a politically correct, spiritually sensitive, non-consumer, compassionate human being. I never got to eat what I wanted or dress according to my own taste. She had me in tie-dye from the time I was born, these little tie-dye onesies. I had to wear amber beads around my neck until my adult teeth grew in. I wanted...I don't know...to wear skinny pants or fishnet stockings. If I wanted to buy camo pants, I got a speech about non-violence.

'We made our own soap. I was never allowed anything white - no white sugar or bread, not even white chocolate. Only 98% dark, which taste the same as instant coffee. We had to recycle everything, even the cardboard toilet paper rolls. And we had a compost toilet, a bucket and sawdust. Which is really embarrassing when you have friends over.' Jaya paused, thinking how best to sum up: 'My mother was a nut-job.'

'Do you think my mother was a nut-job, too?' asked Aasi.

'I don't know...maybe.'

'Because of the snake tattoo?'

'I mean, who but a crazy person wants a snake crawling up their leg? It's creepy, don't you think? My mother had dancing bears tattooed on her back - a Grateful Dead thing - which I have to say is normal, comparatively.'

They both laughed, little hiccupy laughs. Aasi let her head wobble, a sign of resignation. They leaned back in the seats exhausted. Jaya supposed that their situations couldn't really be compared. She had had a mother, at least. Who did this girl have? Amber beads, she remembered reading, lessened the pain of teething. Primary colors were said to stimulate a baby's brain. White sugar led to obesity. And what use was a flush toilet when human waste made for perfect fertilizer? Jaya's mother had a green thumb. It was doubtful that the garden would ever be the same now that she was gone.

Jaya bent over and picked up the magazine Aasi had rejected earlier. The girl accepted it this time, running her finger over photos of Bollywood actresses.

Jaya found a Cliff Bar in her bag and offered half to Aasi. She watched as Aasi struggled to fit her portion back into the wrapper.

'You're not hungry?' asked Jaya.

'No. I save for later and give to Kamika.'

'That's sweet.'

'I tell you a story, Jaya-ji. All the words are up here.' Aasi tapped her head.

'Go ahead, I'm listening.'

The Dhōbin

THERE ONCE WAS A WOMAN who worked as a dhōbin, which in Hindi means laundress. Her husband worked on an oil rig in Saudi Arabia and always forgot to send money. Rather than starve, his wife replaced missing buttons, mended torn garments, and altered clothing too big after bouts of amebic dysentery. With three daughters to feed, she had no choice. On days when everyone needed laundry at once, the dhōbin hired a girl named Aasi to work alongside.

In the third month of a new pregnancy, when the husband was home from the oil fields, and they performed the Punsavana, the 'male making' rite to awaken the diety who decided these things. He placed a drop of Banyan leaf extract in the dhōbin's right nostril, ensuring that the baby would be a boy. After that he flew to a new job in Kuwait.

The dhōbin went to the government hospital, hoping to learn the baby's gender, convinced that the ceremony hadn't worked. It was illegal for the doctor to disclose the gender of a fetus. Too many girl babies were aborted. Even so, the dhōbin knew the truth by the way the doctor hurried away before she had even closed her legs.

The dhōbin returned to her village, searching for a jhola wala doctor, but couldn't find one. Returning to Delhi, she drank liters of whiskey but only got drunk. She jumped from *a stupa, only to sprain an ankle. During this time, Aasi did the laundry.*

Then one day, the dhōbin saw a snake charmer, encircled by a crowd of onlookers. She began taunting the cobra, hoping to be bit. Aasi pulled her to the back of the crowd, saying, 'Maybe it's a boy. Why kill a son?'

All day, the dhōbin did puja, beseeching the gods to take the baby from her stomach. She offered rice to the temple priests, leaving nothing for her children but half-rotten bananas. Day by day her stomach grew round as a melon. During the festival of Diwali, a baby girl arrived.

The baby cried night and day. The dhōbin lost sleep and began behaving oddly. She stopped washing herself and let her hair go wild.

Then she disappeared, along with the children.

The police said she had thrown herself and the children into the Jamuna River. But only four bodies were fished from the water.

A day later, Aasi found the baby behind a dustbin.

Placing a small amount of ghee and honey on the tiny tongue and whispering the name of God into the baby's ear, the child became hers. Eleven days later, she performed the Namakarma Sanskar, the naming ceremony:

Kamika means desired.

Chapter Twenty-Nine

AS IF SHE KNEW WHAT Aasi was thinking, Jaya opened her eyes and said, 'Don't worry, that Irish nurse will take care of her.'

'Maybe best I go see,' said Aasi.

'Don't you dare run. It will only make matters worse for you.'

'Maybe you call clinic on your mobile?'

After searching for her iPhone, Jaya said, 'Oh crud' - hitting her forehead. 'I lost it, I think. That, or it was stolen. I have a vague memory of a hand reaching into my pocket. Are there pickpockets in Paharganj?'

'Pickpockets?'

'Never mind. What I'm trying to say is that we're not calling the clinic.'

'Lady lost her phone?'

'While I was running from the police.'

'Lady ran from police?'

'You're the one who told me not to trust them. You and that Ed.'

Jaya looked at Aasi nervously. 'Look, I'm not saying that the police are any worse in India than they are in America. In my country it's all over the news about police brutality. Especially when it comes to...people of color.'

'People of color?'

'People with...darker skin.'

Aasi examined her arm. 'Maybe lady buy whitening cream for me? Good prices at chemist. Cheap-cheap, nothing for you. Two-for-one sale, maybe. Your skin is too dark like mine.'

'Your skin color is nice the way it is, and so's mine. In my country people go to tanning salons to get this brown. They spend fortunes on bronzing creams. You'll find ads for them in *Vogue*.'

Jaya began fanning through the magazine, searching for bronzing cream ads. After finding nothing, she said, 'We could look for a pay phone. Do they even have pay phones anymore?'

'Yes, at markets selling SIM cards.' Aasi was happy to be able to offer this useful suggestion. 'But most Westerners use WhatsApp on mobiles.'

'Have you had lunch? I'm getting hungry. Maybe there's a commissary or something. We'll be okay so long as we stay in the building.'

They found a vending machine selling chips and cookies. Jaya let Aasi put the coins into the slot - Indian coins, Aasi noted. She picked Masala spice chips and a Limca. Jaya chose mineral water and Wheat Thins, which got stuck halfway down the chute.

Jaya noticed a glass enclosed telephone. 'Well, this is a throwback.' They pushed inside and closed the accordion door. Aasi was the one to speak to the operator. When the East Meets West Clinic answered, she handed over the phone.

A nurse explained to Jaya that the staff was busy with a medical emergency and that there wasn't anyone free to go searching for a lost child. A Canadian had what looked like

Japanese Encephalitis, she explained.

'Really? That's horrible! Will she live?' asked Jaya.

Aasi heard this and charged toward the entrance. Past the soldiers and out the blue gate, taking one backward glance.

Jaya stood between the soldiers, shaking her head. 'Oh well,' she sighed, 'maybe it's for the best. There really isn't much more I can do for the girl.'

Then she remembered something the hippie mom had said.

Consular Report of Birth Abroad.

Chapter Thirty

AASI WAS LOST IN A MAZE OF STREETS that kept looping around to the same place. While she waited for a traffic signal to change, she watched a group of beggar children storm a taxi. The occupant in the backseat - a businessman of some kind - rolled up the window and pretended not to notice them. When the signal changed, the taxi lurched forward leaving the children in a cloud of exhaust fumes. They ran to the side of the road, out of the way of speeding cars, waiting for the traffic signal to turn red again, on the lookout for a more generous target. Beside them stood a man peddling bootleg DVDs.

Across the road was a bookstore. Aasi stopped to look in the window display, at the brand-new books with clean book jackets and pages that had yet to be turned.

A security guard stopped her at the entrance and she almost turned away.

'Your bag,' he said. Behind him was a wall of cubbyholes. 'Purse and mobile keep with you.'

In exchange for her bag, Aasi received a plastic tag. The guard stuffed her bag into a cubbyhole, then turned his attention to a young woman who had just entered. She carried several shopping bags, all marked *Fabindia*. The young woman wore tight-fitting jeans and a tank top, in the Western fashion. She reached into her rhinestone-studded shoulder bag and retrieved a smartphone and a credit card, which she shoved into a back pocket. Without being told, she dumped everything else on the counter, receiving a plastic tag identical to the one Aasi held in her hand.

Aasi smiled. After all, she hadn't been singled out as a potential thief. The bookstore owners didn't trust anyone, not even this rich girl.

Aasi followed behind the rich girl, who spoke with a salesgirl, together scanning a bookcase.

'Here it is! *Life of Pi* by Yann Martel,' said the salesgirl.'

Brilliant,' said the rich girl.

They were speaking English to each other.

The salesgirl turned to Aasi. 'I'll be with you in a minute.'

'Do you trade books?' asked Aasi.

'Of course not.'

Once she'd paid for the book, the rich girl hiked the stairs to a restaurant called Café Frog. Aasi followed.

'Let me show you to your favorite table,' said the Maître d'.

Aasi took a seat at a leather bench, wanting to circle up on its buttery surface. The air-conditioning made the air frosty and she shivered. Peering into the interior space, she saw that it was full, although tables on a patio were empty with no one wanting to sit below the midday sun.

While the Maître d' showed the rich girl to a table, Aasi read a menu.

'Three hundred rupees for a salad!' she said with a gasp. Café Frog was obviously run by scam artists. Nothing on the menu was recognizable: Orange Infused Paneer Sandwich, Superfood Mixed Fruit Bowl with Flax Seeds, and a dish called

Egg Extravaganza. She overheard two women, seated at a nearby table, compare arugula to kale.

'I'm waiting for my mother,' she told the Maître d' when he returned. 'I'm choosing from the menu while I wait.'

The Maître d' pressed a palm to his cheek.

'What is Jaunty Jasmine tea?' she asked.

'It's made from a flower native to the Himalayas...'

'A special tea.' For one thing, she'd seen the price: 125 rupees a glass, twenty-five times the price of chai sold from a cart in Paharganj. She asked, 'What manner of business scheme allows patrons to afford these inflated prices?'

'Most work at embassies or in high-tech,' said the Maître d', scanning the restaurant. 'That's the assistant to the French Ambassador next to the ficus tree. Her friend designs apps. Some have *Fortune* 500 fathers.'

They listened in on a conversation taking place at the nearby table:

'I'm tired of hearing people cribbing and complaining all the time. There's no place I'd rather live, especially now that the issue of gender inequality is being addressed at the highest levels. *We've* had a woman Prime Minister. Can other developing nations make such claims?'

'I need to use the toilet,' said Aasi.

'That way.' The Maître d' turned his head to the left.

'*Arre wah!*' she cried out when she saw the chrome-plated washbasin taps, the cooper-flecked wallpaper and matching marble countertop. A stack of towels had been placed between the washbasins, hot to the touch. Naphthalene balls rolled near the drains. There was a plate for tips, but it held only a fifty paisa coin.

The toilets were Western style. Aasi stood on the seat and squatted. Afterwards, she washed her hands using soap that smelled of lavender. As she walked back to the Maître d', she pressed both hands to her nose.

'Do you know the way to the East Meets West Clinic?' she asked.

'Let me check for you. I have a tablet for reservations, one of the perks of this job.' He side-stepped to his lectern. 'Here it is...turn right from the bookshop and then the third left and right at the circle. Point six miles, within walking distance. Unless, of course, you have a driver waiting downstairs.'

Aasi returned the menu.

'I didn't think so,' he said, without explaining further.

Her search for Kamika began in the garden. As she walked in the direction of the fountain, she saw a helicopter lift from the roof. Trees bent and a coconut fell nearby. Sheltering her eyes from the sun, Aasi watched as the helicopter grew smaller and smaller. Nurse Mary-Louise stepped onto the veranda and dropped into a chair. Kamika, sat at the nurse's feet.

Aasi could see that the girl's allegiance had shifted.

'Medevacked to Tokyo,' said Nurse Mary-Louise when Aasi approached. 'An acute case of Japanese Encephalitis. We need to do something about that eye, child. Give me a wee breather and then I'll get an ice pack and some ointment.'

Dr. Patel exited the building, wiping his brow with a handkerchief. From her position at the bottom of the stairs Aasi heard him say, 'Nothing we couldn't have handled perfectly well here, but—' He sounded as if he had received an insult.

Aasi called Kamika to her, but the girl refused to come. Jumping onto the veranda, she pried Kamika's hands from the chair leg.

'Sorry, Doctor,' she said, seeing that the doctor had grown impatient.

'Quiet that child!' he said.

Kamika calmed down once they had reached the fountain. By then, Aasi was stroking the girl's hair and kissing her cheeks.

She said, 'Nurse doesn't love you. This is a matter of fact.'

As these words escape her mouth, she began shaking. She pulled Kamika to her chest and imagined Inspector Kumar saying, 'Where's that bad girl?'

Kamika said, '*Māṁ* okay?'

Chapter Thirty-One

LOOMIS WAS HANGING A SWEATER behind her door when Jaya barged into the office.

'There you are,' she said. 'I had a word with Inspector Kumar, the policewoman who stopped by with Cathy Singh. Says she's satisfied that you're not the girl's mother.'

'That's a relief,' said Jaya.

'But you need to stay in town in case they have further questions. I shouldn't worry though.'

'But I have plans to go to Varanasi.'

'They're hoping to straighten everything out by tomorrow. Turns out the girl never accused you of sending her to buy narcotics. And now that she's bolted, I can't see how they'd insist upon your sticking around. Why not visit the National Museum or something?' She slid a laptop into her briefcase. 'Have you been to the Red Fort yet?'

'It was Ed - Ed Rodgers. He was the one who sent Aasi to buy drugs. He's a heroin addict. I don't think Aasi understood what she was being asked to do. The girl...well, she's just a—'

'Mule? Isn't that what they call it?'

'Child,' said Jaya.

Loomis changed her pumps into sandals. 'Like I said, I shouldn't worry if I were you. Go back to your hotel and enjoy the evening. Go to the movies. See what's playing at the Regal on Connaught Circus, they show Hollywood films. Get a good night's sleep and then check back tomorrow. These things have a way of sorting themselves out.'

'I'm not going back to that hotel. Not when the police know I'm staying there.'

'Not my business,' said Loomis flexing her toes, a signal that the conversation was ended.

Jaya was too tired to search for a new guesthouse. And besides, Ed had taken her guidebook. She thought about Yoel then...he'd been incredibly sympathetic when she was sick, the way he brought her tea with real ginger root. 'I'll see if they have a room at my old guesthouse,' she said, knitting her fingers together this way and that. 'Would it be okay if I borrow a couple magazines from the waiting area? I promise to bring them back.'

'No,' said Loomis, deadpan.

'Government property, I get it.'

'Anything else I can do for you?' Loomis checked her wristwatch a little longer than necessary.

Jaya placed her hands on the doorframe, blocking the exit. 'Yes actually, thanks for asking. Any chance you can access *Consular Report of Birth Abroad* records on that computer of yours?'

'Not tonight, I can't,' said Loomis.

After checking into the Sujay, Jaya picked up a mixed-bag dinner from the lobby bakery: a veg pizza, cinnamon bun, apple juice, and another oversized donut. The room didn't have an air-conditioner, but she turned the fan to full speed.

On her way back from the communal bathroom, she passed a seating area and saw that someone had left behind *Dune* by Frank Herbert. Jaya looked both ways before tucking it under her arm.

She returned to the room, wishing they'd had one with an attached bathroom.

'At least the sheets are clean,' she said aloud. There were crosshatch stitches where they had been mended, but at least they weren't stained.

She lifted a hair from the pillowcase. The window was open and she dropped the hair to an alleyway below. Two floors down, a small figure walked along the narrow passage.

For a second, Jaya thought that it was Aasi.

It turned out to be a different girl, this one in oversized flip-flops. The girl stopped in front of the Yes Sir guesthouse to beg from a couple who were checking in. They carried backpacks with an assortment of cloth sacks hanging from their elbows. They looked exhausted, as if they had just come from a long bus journey. The woman sneered at the girl, dismissing her with a wave of a hand. The girl was suddenly invisible, slinking into the shadows.

Jaya ran back to the bed and retrieved the donut. She called down to the girl, who lifted her eyes expectantly. Reaching her body over the windowsill, Jaya dropped the donut into the girl's waiting hands. 'Did I really need a cinnamon bun *and* the mega-donut?' she said to herself.

She had never been into sci-fi but decided to give Frank Herbert a try. Halfway down the first page, she realized she had re-read the same paragraph twice. This always happened with fiction, especially sci-fi and fairy tales: Jaya couldn't focus. She preferred non-fiction. David McCullough was her favorite. It was sort of amazing, she thought, how she'd managed to follow any of Aasi's stories.

She considered going downstairs to the Internet café. Maybe a Facebook friend had posted another message of condolence. She drifted off and woke from a strange dream: two baby snakes, one with Aasi's face and one with Kamika's.

She shook the nightmare off while taking a shower. By the time she'd dried off she was sweaty again. Back in the room she laid spread-eagle under the fan thinking about the frozen margaritas at a taqueria in Bolinas, the one with an outdoor patio hanging over the Pacific Ocean. You could get hypothermia swimming there.

After throwing her clothes on, Jaya grabbed the room key. The door faced into an inner court nowhere near as nice as the Hotel Jyoti's. Some of the rooms had barred interior windows. From the room across the way came the sound of pulsating trance music and the pungent sweetness of marijuana. It had once been Yoel's room.

Jaya took hold of the banister.

'*Yalla!* Where are you going?' said a familiar voice.

'You're still here!' said Jaya. 'The guy at the front desk said you'd checked out.'

Yoel wasn't wearing a shirt. Only jogging shorts, the kind with two white stripes down each side.

'What, no hug for Yoel?' He cocked his head, holding out a joint stuck between two brawny fingers.

Jaya said, 'I was going to check Facebook.'

'The Internet room is closed for the night.' He squinted to avoid smoke. 'Use my laptop. I'm getting a good Wi-Fi connection for once. Almost finished downloading an episode of *Game of Thrones*. If you want, we watch together.' He gestured toward his room.

'I'm allergic to smoke,' she said, wondering if it was a good idea to accept the invitation. She was feeling very vulnerable right then.

'Come,' said Yoel, in a beckoning voice. 'You can check from my laptop.'

She woke hours later to find herself circled up on Yoel's bed. The room was dark and she pulled back the curtains, panicking when she saw that the window was barred and the door locked from the outside.

She tried to recall what had happened in the room, but her head was foggy and aching. 'I checked email...told Yoel the story of my life...watched him nod off after smoking a bong and eating multiple bags of potato chips.' At least her clothes were intact: zipper zipped, hook and eye fastened, panties in place.

It was Yoel who answered Jaya's cry for help. He apologized profusely - with Nescafé and a donut - after opening the combo lock. '*Slach li,*' he said, 'I didn't want somebody to steal my laptop.'

'You mean—' Jaya tapped her chest.

'No! You I trust, my queen.'

'A thief might have simply reached through the bars,' she pointed out. The laptop was sitting on a Formica-topped coffee table, placed under the open window.

'I ran downstairs and back *chick-chock*.'

'I don't speak Hebrew, Yoel, remember?'

'*Chick-chock* meaning super-fast.'

'You should have woken me. It's not nice to wake up and find yourself locked in a room.' She looked down at her toes. 'Nothing happened last night?'

'You are safe with Yoel!'

'It's all that pot smoking you do. It's messing with your libido.'

'I know, I must cut back. But—' He reached under the bed and pulled out a quart-sized Ziploc bag full of cannabis buds. '*Yalla!* Parvati Valley. It's growing everywhere like weeds.'

'It *is* a weed, Yoel. That's why people call it weed.'

'But I mean growing up to here.' He was tall enough that his fingers brushed the ceiling. 'And cheap-cheap. In Israel I don't smoke because Hezbollah controls the hashish trade. Plus, back home Yoel needs to stay sober to study astrophysics.'

'That's all very interesting, but I need to go. I can't be around that stuff. Not when the police suspect me of drug dealing.'

'You, Jaya?' He laughed. 'What can Yoel do to help?'

'Give me that for starters,' she said, grabbing the coffee cup.

It was lunchtime and the Sujay café was in full swing. Voices bounced off the low-hung ceiling and increased the pounding in Jaya's head. She could do with another cup of coffee but it turned out they didn't have takeaway cups. She asked for a can of Red Bull instead.

Since there were no auto rickshaws around, she hired a pedicab version. The seat was at a weird slant and she pushed up on her toes to keep from sliding forward. The rickshaw driver was emaciated. He tried to guess how much Jaya weighed; she refused to answer but decided to pay double fare. When they finally arrived at the embassy, she handed over a 500-rupee note. The poor man was so thin she could see his heart pounding in his chest.

She was greeted by two swashbuckling soldiers. After passing through the X-ray machine, she ran up the stairs and rushed full speed at the glass doors.

They were locked.

A man was approaching the door from the opposite side. A version of Willy Loman, Jaya thought: disheveled and over-worked. His feet barely left the ground and she wished he'd move faster. As his hand pushed the door open, she grabbed the handle so that it wouldn't close behind him.

He smiled and said, 'Are you new here?'

Their bodies were almost pressing. Jaya wasn't about to give up the door. 'I'm working with Loomis, Megan Loomis.' Which, to her mind, was true.

'Did you lose your security badge?' His body blocked the entrance to the Ambassador Hall of Fame. Jaya decided to admit to the truth.

His face brightened when she mentioned her name. 'Jaya Gravely? Hey, it's you!'

'Have we met?' she asked.

'I've left a hundred messages. Done everything to track you down short of calling out the Navy SEALs.' Grabbing Jaya's hand, he squeezed until her bones felt as if they would break. His palm was dry, which wasn't what she expected.

'I'm Neel Ray,' he said, showing Jaya his badge. 'We really have to talk.'

'Okay, sure.'

He looked over Jaya's shoulder, still grasping her hand.

'Isn't Aasi with you?' he asked.

Neel escorted Jaya to his office, which turned out to be on a different floor. It was decorated in mid-century modern furniture with tapestry pillows on the couch. In better hands it might have been called eclectic. On a coffee table was a plate of homemade muffins. He offered one to Jaya.

'That's okay,' she said.

He invited her to take a seat, rubbing his hands enthusiastically. 'We haven't had this much excitement around here since—' He paused to think.

'David Headley and the Mumbai attacks?' she offered.

A pained look drifted across his face but was quickly replaced by a smile. 'I was going to say the president's visit to New Delhi.'

'Really?' Jaya wondering if he'd mistaken her for someone else. Then she remembered that Neel knew her name, so that couldn't be it.

Neel darted over to his desk and found a file. He rolled a chair across the tile floor until it was inches from where she was sitting. He placed the folder on the coffee table and opened to the first page. 'Do you know what this is?' he said, tapping the top page with the rubber end of a pencil.

Jaya bent her head sideways. It was a copy of a certificate

resembling a diploma of some sort, with calligraphy that read *Death Certificate*. It was issued by the U.S. Department of State for someone named Nicole Perretti.

Jaya lifted a shoulder. 'I don't get it.'

Neel removed another page, this one was a copy of another certificate: *Certification of Birth Abroad*. It was issued for a child named Bella Perretti.

Female.

Born June 25, 2005.

Thiruvananthapuram, State of Kerala, India.

'I don't understand,' said Jaya. 'Why are you showing me this?'

'Because something you told Meg Loomis rang a bell. A snake tattoo. That's what this girl Aasi claims her mother had on her leg?'

'Yes, a rattlesnake, to be exact. Which I find interesting because—'

'—because rattlesnakes aren't indigenous to India.'

Neel and Jaya shook their heads in unison.

Jaya took both certificates in her hands. 'Are you telling me that this, this woman Nicole Peretti, had a rattlesnake tattoo?'

Neel took an intake of breath before saying. 'I remember hearing that she had tattoos all over her body. The man who ran the crematorium mentioned this to me in passing during my investigation. *Reptilian*, that's how he described them. On her arms and legs. One coiled on her abdomen - Kundalini symbol, I'm guessing. We were trying to identify the deceased. It was a long time ago, I know. But reptilian could mean snake.'

Jaya lifted the second form, 'But this child would be almost fifteen by now,' she said, 'and the Aasi I know claims to be twelve or thirteen. Besides, the name is wrong.'

'Unless you translate Aasi to Italian.'

'Aasi means pretty in Indian?'

'In Hindi it means pretty girl, and in Italian that would be Bella. Maybe I'm grasping at straws here. As for the age discrepancy, I doubt that a child made to fend for herself would know her date of birth.' He placed his feet on the chair's pedestal and began twisting left to right.

'Here's the thing. I've been with the embassy for almost twenty years now and that's why Meg called me in on this. I'm practically the only one left who'd have any memory of this case. And I wouldn't, were it not that I was personally involved.'

'How so?'

'Do you want a drink? I keep a little something in the proverbial bottom desk drawer.'

'I'd kill for a drink,' said Jaya.

Neel used a key to access a bottle of Jack Daniel's. Pouring two glasses a finger's width, he said, 'I'm the one who went looking for the child, Bella, after her mother died.'

'Wowsers,' said Jaya.

'We searched everywhere for that child. No stone unturned. Nicole was the bohemian type that frequent India. I got a good enough description from her acquaintances. Shaved head, facial piercings, the whole nine yards.'

'Did you actually see the body?'

'Like I said, she was cremated already. Not that I have anything against cremation. I'm planning for it myself. But in this case it meant there wasn't a body to identify. Only the passport she'd left behind and a few items - assorted clothes and a SLR camera - that was about it. All I had to go on were eyewitness accounts: a bunch of spaced-out devotees at the ashram where she died. They weren't exactly cooperative.'

'But can you be sure this—' Jaya looked again at the certificate '—this child of Nicole's is the Aasi that I know?

'No. I can't be. It's nothing more than a hunch. But the name, the tattoos, the fact that your girl claims to have had an American mother. And also, here's the kicker: Nicole's baby disappeared without a trace.'

'How could that happen?' Jaya asked, visibly upset.

'The mother...there's a picture somewhere in the file.'

Flipping through the file, Jaya found a snapshot. It was a school picture, probably taken for a yearbook. The girl was lovely, high cheekbones and a Roman nose, squeaky clean in a turtleneck sweater with her auburn hair tied back in a ponytail.

Jaya said, 'This, I'm guessing, was taken before her hippie days.'

'High School. Her parents provided the photo. They came to India after I contacted them with the news that their daughter had died. It's routine for the police to report a death to the appropriate embassy. Nicole's parents knew she had a kid but they were vague on the details. There had been a falling out and they weren't in touch. The father was a big-shot lawyer. The mother some kind of psychoanalyst or psychiatrist, can't remember which. Moneyed people. Nicole had been in India four years when she died.'

Neel chugged the whisky in one gulp. 'We drove to Pune in a chauffeur-driven Mercedes. I didn't even know you could hire them at the time, but apparently nothing was too hard for the Kempinski Ambience. The hotel had only recently opened and that's where they were staying. His Holiness the Dalai Lama inaugurated that hotel. I mean, to my mind the place is as far from a Buddhist monastery as you can get.' He chuckled and tried to take another sip of whiskey but found that the glass was empty.

Jaya took the liberty of pouring shots. 'Go on,' she said.

'Gene and Cynthia were the parents, but you were supposed to call her Dr. Perretti, excuse *me*. We drove to Pune in search of the baby. The police were making a botch of it. Time to flash around some cash, that's what the Perrettis were thinking. I advised them to dress down and keep their wallets in their pockets, but they weren't taking advice from a low-grade civil servant like me. Didn't matter that I'd been in India seven years at that point.'

Jaya did the math and said, '2008.'

'The baby was almost three when Nicole Perretti died.'

'Kids remember things at that age. I remember—.' Jaya stopped herself from reminiscing. Instead she said, 'A rattlesnake tattooed up her mother's leg would have been memorable.'

'I mean, who does that? Sorry, guess I should stop now.' Neel pushed the bottle toward Jaya.

She was feeling a buzz and knew that she should slow down. Whiskey and Red Bull, it turned out, didn't mix well. She suggested they take a bathroom break and Neel raised his glass in the direction of a door. Seeing that he had a private bathroom, Jaya guessed that he was no longer a low-grade civil servant. When she joined him again, she said, 'You aren't the

Ambassador, are you?'

He laughed. 'No. I'm only the Consul-General. Number two, hierarchically.'

Jaya whistled. 'Should I even be calling you Neel?' she said, sloppily.

'Neel will work.'

'Go ahead, Neel, continue with your story.'

He planted his feet on the coffee table with his hands folded on his lap. After taking a deep breath, his joviality vanished. 'Tragic. I mean the Perrettis losing their only child.' He picked up the photograph, continuing to speak. 'She joined an ashram - doesn't matter which one. The guru had a thing against families. Told his followers to ditch the kids.'

'Seriously? That's like the worse thing I ever heard.'

'He was dead by then, that one. But his devotees were still pretty fervent, everyone in purple robes. Look, I love India. My father's parents were both from Madras, our roots go deep. Wouldn't be here if I didn't love the place. But these kinds of shenanigans?

'Nicole left her child with a woman who lived near the ashram,' he continued. 'It took us days to track her down. By then Nicole had been dead two weeks.'

'How did she die?'

'Amebic dysentery.'

Jaya gulped. 'She didn't get treatment?'

Neel shook his head. 'She might have been treated, but *au contraire.* Don't get me started, worse than Christian Science. We found the caregiver eventually, if you could call her that. I mean, the place was a hovel. You should have seen the look on Dr. Perretti's face. But at least we'd come to the end of the trail, or so we thought. Because the caretaker insisted that the baby had died too.'

'Of what?'

'I can't remember. Nothing specific. Another case for the infant mortality statisticians.' As a side note, he added, 'Although they're improving, improving every day...Still, back then. I know it was only a few years ago, but in *those* conditions? None of us were surprised.'

'And you believed the woman?' Jaya wanted to shake Neel.

'There was no body or death certificate for the child. There wouldn't have been. Nicole hadn't exactly brought the child to a Montessori School. The Perrettis were satisfied. If I had my doubts, wasn't much I could do about them.'

'You did have doubts?'

'All I'll say is that anything might have happened. Without proof, we had only the caretaker's testimony to go by. She showed us a jumper and a pair of booties - green, I remember that. The child had been cremated, she told us. My guess is that she sold the child after she figured out that Nicole was dead. It happens. The gall of it is, the caretaker insisted the Perrettis fork over the money spent on the funeral. She claimed to have paid for mourners, extra hot fire, the whole shebang. I think that's what made the lie believable.'

'Did they pay up?'

'They sure did. And gave a fat donation to a local NGO, a Non-Governmental Organization, caring for orphans. Although I told them that most of the kids weren't actually orphans, but from impoverished families. The Perrettis are still probably funding that children's home.' He closed his eyes, signaling exhaustion.

The phone rang. Neel apologized and took the call.

'You'll find me at the vending machine,' said Jaya. She needed fresh air, for starters. Staggering out of his office, she tried to right herself by pressing her palms alternately between opposing walls.

Neel met up with her at the snack machine. 'Come on,' he said, at the same time pressing speed dial on his phone.

'Where are we going?'

'Paharganj, God help us.'

'That's where I'm staying!'

She said this a little too loudly. Even after two servings of vending machine coffee she still felt wobbly. Neel held onto her elbow. A soldier snapped to attention and saluted as they passed through a side entrance. Jaya was slurring her words. The rush of heat only exacerbated her drunkenness. Neel brought her to the left side of the car and she manage to say, 'Neel, should I be driving?'

'Hey Raj,' he said. 'We're headed to Paharganj. Drop us near the Main Bazaar.'

The driver opened the back door for Jaya. She needed his help getting in.

'Are we going to look for Aasi?' she asked.

'That would be the idea,' said Neel.

'Then we'd better start at the Sujay guesthouse.'

Chapter Thirty-Two

THE MAIN BAZAAR WAS TOO crowded to drive a car into. Neel and Jaya got out near the cinema. Jaya was more emotional than normal. She kept thinking, What kind of mother abandons her child? Her mother's virtues came into sharp focus. She couldn't remember a single thing she hadn't loved.

'My mother died recently,' she told Neel. 'Of breast cancer. She'd been in remission for ten years when it came raging back. I didn't even know about the first bout, she'd kept it from me.'

He gave Jaya's arm a squeeze.

'Her ashes are in my backpack. Meanwhile,' - she began sobbing - 'I'm supposed to be scattering them on the Ganges River. But instead, I go to the Taj Mahal. What kind of daughter does that?'

'We'll have you in Varanasi in no time,' he said, watching to see that she didn't trip.

They passed hippies and Jaya kept sighing. A tour guide approached, offering a package deal to Kashmir. Jaya nearly collided with a hippie who was attempting to roll a crystal ball across the back of his shoulders. 'You're so talented!' she said. Another group of travelers sat in front of the coffee shop banging on drums. 'See what I mean, Neel? They're *super* creative.'

Her head wobbled on her neck. 'I think I'm getting the hang of it,' she said, apropos of nothing. 'Why, some of them make their own clothes, Neel. I can't even thread a needle, not even using one of those needle threader thingies. I must have gotten my lack of talent from my father. I mean, what kind of loser sells his sperm? Did I tell you that my mother was a master potter? She made the dishes we ate off of. The mugs, too. They have, like, this green iridescent glaze that looks like a firefly wing.'

'Interesting,' said Neel without much enthusiasm.

'Did I tell you that my mother crocheted afghans? She made jewelry out of copper wire and wrapped it around tourmaline and moonstones. She wasn't an amateur, Neel - she'd taken classes! Did you ever hear of the Kate Wolf Music Festival? My mother was a vendor there! We got to park in the vendor parking.'

'She must have been something,' he said.

'Your suit, Neel, it's making them nervous. Maybe you should take the jacket and tie off. They don't trust the establishment and who can blame them? Did I tell you that my mother campaigned for Jill Green? The bumper sticker is still on our car.'

'That's nice.'

'But then she lost. I didn't vote, so maybe it was my fault.'

'Don't beat yourself up.'

They were approaching the Sujay.

'This is where I first met Aasi. I saw her doing backflips and decided to invite her for a meal. My mother taught me to be compassionate. Compassion is a virtue, Neel. In every single religion it's a virtue. But it wasn't until she followed me down the Main Bazaar offering recommendations to restaurants and hotels and bookshops that I finally did. I took her for a thief. I'm too suspicious.' For the first time Jaya noticed that the hotel sign hung crookedly. 'The place sort of grows on you,' she told him.

'This is where you're staying?' Neel didn't blink once.

'Not exactly. This is where I *was* staying and I stayed here last night because - oh, yeah, because I was afraid of the police.'

The waiter greeted Jaya and she shook his hand vigorously. When she asked if he'd seen Aasi, he answered, 'The two girls - one small, one big - they were here last night sweeping.' He bent and pointed under the pool table. 'They sleep there.'

'Under the *billiard table*?' Neel used his palm to stretch his forehead flat. 'When did you last see them?'

'Before many hours now. About six in the morning I give them cinnamon roll because Mr. Joe saying it's okay.'

'Any idea where they might be now?'

'Sorry, sir.'

'Maybe a Red Bull will help me,' said Jaya. 'I'll grab one from the bakery.'

As the man at the counter handed over the can, Neel stepped beside Jaya. 'I'll take a mango lassi, light on the sugar.' He reached for his wallet. 'Jaya, let's sit for a minute and talk this through.'

Chapter Thirty-Three

ON RARE OCCASIONS, MR. WADHWA hired Aasi to refold shirts and pants. He paid generously. He shared his tiffin lunch as well. It was only ever an hour or two of work, on a day when the shop assistant was home with a cold, or caring for his dying father, or taking his annual holiday.

But it was the dry season now, not a time for colds. And Aasi knew that the old man had died recently. The shop assistant used up his holiday making arrangements for the funeral. Afterwards he told Aasi how he had washed his father's body with a mixture of milk, yogurt, ghee, and honey, and how he had tied together the old man's big toes, placing the hands palm-to-palm in a position of prayer. Aasi was so moved by the story that she brought the shop assistant an orange.

In any case, Mr. Wadhwa's shop was only a few buildings from a police station. It wasn't safe. She would work the narrow alleyways and stay out of the Main Bazaar. Aasi said a blessing for the shop assistant and his grieving family. Then she waved Kamika away, but said, 'Stay close.'

She was glad for Kamika. Having the girl was better than having eyes at the back of her head. This time Kamika was keeping watch for policemen.

Maybe today Aasi would ask people for pens. There was

a stationery shop down a back alley, next to a guesthouse. All she had to do was show the fairy tales to prove that she needed one. Her pen, she would say, had run out of ink. Once she had collected enough pens she would go to the coffee shop, where travelers drank espresso while writing in their journals. She would be there when their ink ran out.

Aasi opened her bag and searched for the fairy tales. They weren't in their usual place, tucked into *Grimm's Fairy Tales.* She dumped the contents of the bag onto the ground. Her hands began shaking when she saw that the pages were gone.

A woman dressed in a red saree stopped and said, 'Have you lost your mother, child?' Aasi wobbled her head and the woman went on, 'This always happens in the market! Getting separated in this crowd, easily done. One minute you are side-by-side and the next...it's happened to me, what to do?' She sucked her lips before deciding. 'You may use my mobile to call your mother.'

Aasi explained that she didn't know the number. 'I use speed dial. I've forgotten the number.'

'This happens, I know. But you must know your address.'

'*Ji haan,*' said Aasi, inventing an address in South Delhi.

The woman emptied a change purse. 'Go directly home. Take a rickshaw instead of the bus. Your mother must be frightened to death!'

Aasi counted the coins: 220 rupees. It was enough for a rickshaw to South Delhi, but not enough for the journey she had in mind. She dropped the coins into her bag. Nothing like that had ever happened to her. Was it the new clothes and beautiful shoes that had moved the woman or was it the black eye that did it?

She thought about setting up the wooden bowl and doing an acrobatic show, but that had never earned more than a coin or two. Besides, it was too hot for backflips.

A familiar face passed in the opposite direction. Aasi hesitated before turning to follow the man. He was known to lure street children into his car after purchasing them an ice cream, then promising a visit to Appu Ghar, an amusement park that had been closed for almost ten years. The unsuspecting children, momentarily distracted by a melting ice cream pop, would then be delivered to the Joy Children's Home. The children were rarely seen again, although one boy had returned to tell the story.

After a few yards the man noticed Aasi, turned, and smiled.

More than once she had managed to get the ice cream pop in her hand before bolting. But in this heat it would be impossible to sell a pop back to the merchant. It would melt before they'd even left the shop.

She said, 'What about your promise to buy me a Snickers bar?'

'Did I?'

'Last year you promised.'

They were now face-to-face, although Aasi was half-a-head shorter and standing on her toes, ready to run if need be. The man wiped his brow with a handkerchief and then unscrewed the lid of a steel water bottle, guzzling until it was empty. 'A popsicle would be nice in this heat,' he said. 'A mango ice lollie, now doesn't that sound good?'

'Tomorrow, maybe. Today I'm thirsty. Today I'm needing water bottle.' Aasi stretched out a hand. 'No good to you empty.'

'I have a water filter back in my flat.' He scratched his head. 'I'll buy you a bottle of water if that's what you'd prefer.'

'Snickers bar,' said Aasi, in a whining voice, knowing that no one would buy a bottle of water from her, fearing that it was filled from the tap.

The man weakened and Aasi brought him to a shop. She tried to up the order, asking for a Kit-Kat bar and then adding a request for shampoo packets.

Before handing the candy bar to Aasi, the man ripped open the package so that it couldn't be resold.

When he tried to grab her hand, Aasi shook him off.

Hiding in a vestibule, she licked the chocolate, thinking about the REI water bottle she had once owned. Kamika stepped over and Aasi split the candy bar in half.

'A Banjari boy stole my water bottle and went north,' she told the girl. 'We'll go north too. It's not safe here. Keep watch for policemen, Kamika. Next time we go to the railway station, we'll board a train.' She put an arm around the girl. 'You've always wanted a train journey and now you will have one. Won't it be fun?'

'Pretty please,' said Kamika.

There were ways to sneak onto a train if only she timed it right, waiting for the conductor's back to be turned, lifting Kamika to the roof where tickets were never collected. If she waited much longer, Kamika would be too heavy.

The Banjari boy had mentioned Rishikesh. He described the Ganges headwaters. Crystal clear water, icy to the touch.

Perhaps the travel agent would have a train schedule. She would remember to ask after his son, to compliment Guru

Nanak, to mention her life-long desire to see the Golden Temple in Amritsar. The travel agent would be putty in her hands.

And it would be easy enough to enter the Sujay without being stopped. Earlier that morning Aasi overheard the hotel staff, as they rejoiced over the news that Mr. Joe's wife was home with a tummy ache.

'Stay here,' she told Kamika, placing the girl in a shady spot.

'You'll need a train to Hardwar,' said the travel agent. 'There are twenty-two trains daily.' He examined Aasi's clothes, widening his eyes. 'It seems your fortunes have changed. A girl your age...well, beware of unsavory men who take advantage. I tell my son, "Do not go with strangers." There are many unscrupulous individuals about.' He puckered his mouth as if something distasteful had landed on his tongue. 'Now, where were we? Yes, trains to Hardwar. It's a short bus ride from there to Rishikesh.'

She thanked the travel agent after admiring a photograph of his son.

Scanning the restaurant for Mrs. Joe had become second nature.

And even though Jaya's back was turned, Aasi recognized her. Jaya was talking to a man Aasi didn't recognize. He sipped mango lassi through a straw and seemed to be doing most of the talking. He reminded Aasi of the businessmen she once begged from.

She would ask him for a Kit-Kat bar.

As she approached, Aasi tried to decide on the best opening. 'Good day, friend,' was what she chose. Surely the fact that she was Jaya's friend would weigh in her favor. She might ask for two candy bars.

Before she could begin the greeting, she heard the man speak her name.

The man removed his jacket, laying it over his lap. He rolled up his shirtsleeves and said her name again 'About this girl Aasi, or Bella I should say, there's another thing I ought to have mentioned.'

Aasi stood dead still. If she didn't move, maybe they wouldn't notice her.

Jaya wiped perspiration from her neck. 'Is it my imagination or is it getting hotter every day?'

The man said, 'We're coming into the warmest time of the year, the months preceding the monsoon. Make sure you drink enough water. People die from heat exhaustion.'

Jaya pulled a half-empty plastic bottle from her bag.

The man said, 'Used to be this time of the year the whole government decamped to Shimla, back during the British Raj, but now we have air-conditioning. So, anyhow, could be another coincidence.'

'The names you mean?'

'The names and—. I thought about calling the Perrettis and asking about the camera. I think I mentioned it, the SLR we found among Nicole's possessions. A good one too, a Canon AE-1. There was film in the camera, I remember. So that's got me thinking that maybe we'd be able to get a photo taken close to the time of Nicole's death.'

'One that showed her leg? To see if she had a snake

tattooed...'

'Exactly. Although it's not likely, given that Nicole would have been the photographer. But even those old cameras had timers so that you could take self-portraits.'

'Way before selfies.'

'Yes. It crossed my mind to ask the Perrettis. But then I thought, What reason would I give for being curious all these years later? They'd flip if I suggested that their granddaughter was still alive. I mean, *years* after their daughter's death?'

'Begging in the streets of New Delhi. What a disaster.'

'Dr. Perretti, boy oh boy. But I did look for a phone number in the file.'

He reached into his pant pocket and removed a slip of paper. On it was scribbled the Perretti's contact information. Jaya took it in her hand and looked up inquisitively.

'The area code,' he said. 'I'd forgotten. The husband was a big-shot lawyer in Phoenix. Mind you, I'm hoping I'm wrong.'

'Arizona *and* rattlesnakes,' said Jaya.

'My wife and I went hiking in Saguaro National Park once. They were behind every cactus, scared the living daylights out of us. We planned on camping but got a hotel room instead. At least they warn you with the rattle, unlike copperheads.'

'It's always the part of Aasi's stories that intrigued me. I know what you're going to say - that she could have read about rattlesnakes in a book. Do you happen to know if rattlesnakes are mentioned in *Grimm's Fairy Tales*? Because she carries around a beat-up copy.'

'In German fairy tales? Doubtful.'

'Are you going to call the Perrettis?'

The man took off his glasses, rubbing the bridge of his nose. 'You don't have an aspirin, do you?' he said.

Aasi ducked behind a rack of clothing. Her new slippers, she thought, were causing her to feel unsteady. She sat on the ground cross-legged, examining the heels. The restaurant seemed to have grown noisier.

'Well, imagine this scenario,' she heard the man say, 'your daughter is dead and you're told your granddaughter is as well. Years later you get a call telling you that your granddaughter, Bella, is actually a beggar. In India. What would you make of it?'

'I'd be skeptical,' said Jaya.

'And so might I be.' The man pulled on his chin and said, 'We could suggest a DNA test. Because no way are the Perrettis taking a child into the bosom of their family without a definite match.'

'So that's why we're looking for Aasi? To get a swab of saliva?'

'If you have a better idea, let's hear it. At the very least I'd like to ask the girl a question or two. For all we know she remembers a detail that matches with the caretaker. The green jumper perhaps. Okay, I know it's a stretch. We might put a few photos in front of the girl - one being Nicole's - see if she picks the right one.'

'Like a police line-up.'

The man tilted his head backwards to receive the last drops of mango lassi. 'Time to start looking,' he said after a swallow.

'I still can't get over the idea that Nicole abandoned her baby to go into an ashram. It's a sobering thought.' Jaya looked at the empty Red Bull can. 'That helped, I think. I've been sick with dysentery and not eating much. Normally it takes a lot more to get me trashed. The Jack Daniel's went straight to my bloodstream.'

'Had I known...' said the man, letting the sentence hang in the air.

'What about Bella's father? You haven't mentioned him.'

'From what we gathered, he was from Kerela. Someone Nicole met at a yoga instructor course. By the time she died he was long out of the picture.'

'I have one more question for you,' she said.

'Fire away.'

'What about Kamika, the little girl Aasi cares for? What will happen to her should a DNA test prove that Aasi *was* the daughter of Nicole Perretti? What are the chances of the Perrettis taking Kamika too?'

'My gut tells me none whatsoever.'

'Then an orphanage?'

The man shook his head. 'At last count there were tens of thousands of kids begging on the streets of New Delhi. Meaning, there's not much chance. Although there is that children's home the Perrettis were supporting. Maybe they'd have pull there.'

Aasi dragged Kamika by the hand. 'In Rishikesh we will have mountain views,' she said.

Kamika dug her heels into the ground, her eyes fixed on a Westerner who was stepping down from the chemist. Aasi reached across the space that divided them and slapped the girl's face. 'Don't waste time,' she said. Out of habit, her eyes drifted to the woman's bare leg.

Two boys, both in rags, began to cross the street. One punched his open palm.

'Run, Kamika!' she shouted, skirting around a stout woman.

They came to the road facing the New Delhi railway station. Kamika stopped in front of a fruit seller, riveted by a stack of apples. Aasi felt around in her bag.

She heard Russian and called out, '*Zdravstvuyte!* Hello!'

'*Zdravstvuyte!*' they said in unison.

'One apple for each.' Aasi pointed back and forth between her mouth and theirs.

The two men lifted pomegranates and apples, then squeezed a melon. After weighing the fruit on a scale, the produce seller began filling a plastic sack. Aasi waited expectantly, but was disappointed when one measly apple was put into her hand.

'We save for later,' she said, seeing that Kamika was staring at the apple. 'We have a long train journey. On the roof there will be no samosa sellers. Only poor people will be on the roof with us, and they will be hungry too.'

She let the apple drop into her bag, where her fingers touched the beloved ankle bracelet. Although she wanted to believe it was her mother's, Aasi had a vague memory of having found it on the ground.

'This bracelet is no good,' she said, shaking it near her ear. 'See how the bloody clasp is broken and the bells are missing?' She shook the bracelet. 'Garbage!'

Kamika looked as if she were about to cry.

'Ahh! This is real silver, Kamika. See the mark?' She scratched at a tiny mark near the clasp. Out of the corner of her eye she spotted a jewelry shop. With a gentle push, she indicated the place she wanted Kamika to sit. 'Do not stray,' she said.

A half an hour later she returned, her bag stuffed with candy bars, chips, Oreo cookies, two sticks of deodorant, baby powder in a tin, two packages of Lifebuoy soap, a pack of double-edged razors, and a large bottle of Johnson's Baby Shampoo. She showed Kamika a fine-toothed comb, still in its plastic wrapper.

Her voice was shaky. 'After much bargaining, the shop owner gave very good price for silver. But now we must hurry or miss the train.'

Taking her first step toward the railway station, Aasi heard a bell ring. A tone that was clear and true. And even though the bracelet would have to remain hidden from Kamika, she felt sure that she had made the right choice.

Chapter Thirty-Four

LATE ONE NIGHT, JAYA RETURNED to the Jyoti Palace. 'I'm here to collect my things and settle the bill,' she said.

The hotel owner - the older of the two brothers – said, 'The police have stopped by a few times inquiring after you. Has there been trouble? Maybe your wallet was stolen? This is what we have been thinking. There are many thieves working the Main Bazaar ever since the Commonwealth Games. We are afraid it attracted a new class of criminal.' He waited for Jaya to tell her story, but finally gave up and said, 'We hope that every-thing has been to your liking, madam.'

'Oh, yes. It's been perfect.' She handed over a credit card after looking at the bill.

'We told the police that you had gone to Varanasi. My brother remembered your telling us something of your plans...'

'But my things were still in the room. I was in the hospital,' she said.

'Oh! That explains everything. But you might have phoned us. We were concerned - the bed not slept in, and then the visits from the police.' He hesitated before adding, 'They insisted on access to the room.'

'I noticed that things were moved around and not where I'd left them.'

'But nothing is missing, you can be sure. My brother insisted on escorting the police officers to your room. He watched carefully the whole time they were there.'

Jaya laid the key on the counter.

The owner drew her attention to a card, propped up on the counter: a Facebook logo with the universal symbol for 'like.'

'If you would be so kind,' he said.

'No problem.'

He handed back the credit card.

The room at the Sujay had undergone improvement. All it had taken was a bottle of disinfectant, a sponge, and elbow grease. She ate her meals in the hotel restaurant, trying every pizza on the menu and settling on one with pineapple topping. Some of the time she spent working on a copyediting assignment. The editor of the small Buddhist press was thrilled that Jaya was working from India.

Neel left baksheesh up and down the Main Bazaar, with the promise for more if someone were to find Aasi. At least thirty girls were brought to Jaya for her inspection.

Ankita Kumar saw to it that Jaya was cleared of wrong-doing. Still, whenever Jaya left the Sujay she did so with the lungi wrapped over her head and her face concealed behind sunglasses.

During their time together, Inspector Kumar vented her frustration with rampant police corruption. The police report stated that Zulfikar Ali, the dealer, had escaped with the money, but Aasi's story contradicted this. She had seen the policeman pocket the rupee notes.

'The minute I heard that name,' said Inspector Kumar, 'I became suspicious. It was his apartment, all right, but Ali was already in custody.'

Inspector Kumar was furious.

At first, Neel came by in the evenings. He and Jaya scoured back alleyways, describing the two girls to everyone they met. After a while, he began to express doubts.

'This isn't really my area of expertise,' he said. 'So maybe I jumped to conclusions. I mean, half the hippies in this neighborhood have tattoos. I see now how the girl might have invented a mother and made her out to look like one of them.

Anyway, I see that now. A case in point...'

Using a raised eyebrow, Neel directing Jaya's attention to a traveler seated nearby. She was calling out for the Wi-Fi password. Now she was standing, trying to get the waiter's attention by waving her arm franticly, an arm covered in various Celtic symbols.

'But a rattlesnake tattoo, Neel, a *rattlesnake*!' said Jaya.

Neel pushed his glasses to the bridge of his nose and Jaya knew that he had given up.

'What about the camera?' she said. 'Can't we call the Perrettis and at least ask if there was film in the camera?'

'I'm not sure I want to stir that pot, not when we can't find the girl. Do you know what it's like to lose a child, Jaya?'

'Not exactly. But I know what it's like to mourn someone you love. To miss them and wish you could have them back, even a small piece of them. If there was any chance, I'd grab for it.'

'I think you're strained, both emotionally and physically.

Losing your mother, and then the intensity of India and dysentery on top of it. None of that is easy.' He went to place his hand on Jaya's but she pulled away.

'My suggestion, for what it's worth,' he said, 'is that you go to Varanasi. Scatter your mother's ashes and get some closure. I'm pretty sure that after that you'll be more settled about this other business.'

'That's unfair,' said Jaya. 'It's like you're suggesting I made this all up.'

She threw a 100-rupee note on the table and stood abruptly.

'Call me before you leave India,' said Neel. 'Let me know you're safe and sound.'

'Yeah, right,' she said and walked away.

Early the next morning, Jaya checked out of the Sujay, carrying a jeweled box under her arm. It was carved out of sandalwood, specially made to fit the cardboard box. The sweet fragrance reached Jaya's nose. Her mother believed that sandalwood had a calming effect, and now Jaya believed it too.

At the New Delhi Railway station, she mounted the stairs that led to the ticket agents. The room was empty except for agents, taking their places at a row of desks. Jaya seated herself on the nearest chair.

'It will be a few minutes,' said an agent.

'That's okay,' said Jaya.

She pulled a guidebook from her bag. It was a brand-new *Fodor's Essential India*, unmarked and smelling of fresh ink. In the front of the guidebook was a map of India. Jaya put a finger on the place that marked Varanasi, then trailed it along a snake-like river moving east, then north.

'My wish, Jaya,' she remembered her mother saying, 'is to have my ashes scattered on the Ganges River. I could ask Stephan to do it - you know he goes every year - but it would mean more if you were to go.'

'Me?' Jaya had said. 'Please don't ask that, Mommy.'

Who was it that suggested Varanasi? Jaya wondered now. Someone at the memorial service. Stephan, probably.

Every river had a source, she thought now. A place where the water was cleanest. Jaya imagined drinking straight from the river without getting sick. She pictured herself stripping off her sweat-soaked clothes and jumping into an icy pool. She located the place nearest the headwaters of the Ganges. Turning to that section of the book, she penned a small star next to a listing for a guesthouse.

The agent said, 'Where to, madam?'

Jaya held open the guidebook, placing a finger exactly where she intended to go.

'*Accha*!' said the agent. 'You must take a train to Hardwar.'

He got to work on his computer.

'Can you check in first-class, please,' she said.

And after a minute: 'Yes! Every train is fully booked, but I have found one last seat. An upper berth - will that do?'

Jaya rocked her head side to side.

Backstory and Acknowledgments

Thank you to Gita and her band of Indian street children. Back in 1999, on my first trip to India, you touched my heart in a deep way. The character of Aasi was inspired by you, Gita. I pray that, all these years later, you are thriving.

I first learned about a certain ashram, where the guru encouraged his followers to discard their children, in an eyewitness memoir. This account was confirmed to me by friends who were at the ashram about the time my fictional Aasi's mother would have been there. My story is a work of fiction, my characters a figment of my imagination. But, as they say, truth is stranger than fiction.

> *"The light shines in the darkness,*
> *and the darkness has not overcome it."*
> – John 1:5

An author works in isolation, until a final draft is finished. (Or what the author hopes is the final draft, anyway!) Then it becomes public to a small circle, those brave enough to crush the author's ego. (Not the author's mother, in other words.)

My thanks to those who read my first – "finished" – draft. Caradoc King, my then literary agent at United Agents, London, who gently let me know that the novel needed a ton of work, and who pointed out some of its major flaws. Anne Raustol, who read an even earlier draft, and who's writer's chops did their work, resulting in a slash-and-burn edit, the death of several characters, and the creation of new ones. Victoria Fisch, who told me that my early proses were "too precious." (Ouch!)

Six years and many drafts later...

Thanks to Trisha Devenish, Julie Eargle, and Christy B. for copy-editing and fact-checking, for finding hundreds of typos, misplaced punctuation, even correcting Hindi words.

About the Author

C. M. RUANE is an American/Irish author who, for many years, lived out of a backpack, traveling the globe. Born and raised in New York, she has lived abroad, mostly in India, and now resides in Asheville, NC.

Under her pen name, Cate M. Ruane, she is the author of a mystery series set during World War II.

*Font*s

Titles and chapter headings are in ILShakeFest,
excepting the lowercase "s" which is in Goudy Old
Style. The body of the text is in Franklin Gothic
Book.

www.ingramcontent.com/pod-product-compliance
Lightning Source LLC
Chambersburg PA
CBHW020358260626
47156CB00007B/2163